THE JUNKERS

Also by Piers Paul Read

The Junkers

PIERS PAUL READ

AN ALISON PRESS BOOK
Secker & Warburg — London

Printed in Great Britain by
REDWOOD BURN LIMITED
Trowbridge & Esher

Part
One

Chapter One

I

THIS IS WHAT HAPPENED to me in Germany. I was living in Berlin in 1963, posted there as second Secretary in the office of our Political Adviser to the Commander-in-Chief to serve the interests of my country, Great Britain. I spent much of my time sitting in the cafés on the Kurfürstendamm, normally Zuntz or Kempinski, watching the pretty girls eating cake and drinking coffee. Among their long legs—brown from the ultra-violet lamps in their small rooms—and the narrow trousers of their boy-friends, there were the long skirts of their landladies and, occasionally, the wide trousers with turn-ups covering polished, laced shoes—those of Helmuth von Rummelsberg.

I noticed him not because of the wide trousers and turn-ups but because of the girl who always sat with him. Of all the girls in the Zuntz or Kempinski cafés, of all those in the Old Vienna, the Paris Bar or the Eden Saloon, she was the most beautiful and she was the one I came to love.

After only a month in Berlin I started to go up to the Kurfürstendamm for tea. I was introduced to this habit by the first friend I made while I was there, Armand Foch, my equivalent in the office of the French Political Adviser. We were both free at that time of day and liked to meet to discuss our experiences of the night before or our plans for the night to come—plans and experiences of a sort. . . . Armand did not take to my girl but he was impressed by my fidelity to this figure at another table and in time she took on an identity and worth beyond that of all the other pretty girls.

One afternoon Armand brought a miniature camera which, he said, was standard issue to those working for the French in the East. We sat at a table quite near to the man and the girl and Armand, with professional discretion, took some snaps from which I can describe what she was like then because I have them in front of me now. There are three photographs: in two of them she was looking at Helmuth von Rummelsberg and since Armand was sitting behind him she seems now to be looking at me. It seemed clear to me when I first looked at the photograph, where she is stretching and smiling at the same time, that she was in love with the man she was looking at (but now I forget that she was looking at him and imagine that she is looking at me). The glance is as relaxed as the limbs. The eyes are as confident in him as the arms in the neutral properties of the air around them; as her body in the strength of its gravity and the friction of the seat of the chair.

She is not smiling in the other two photographs—but one smile from a German girl is rare enough. The photograph in which she is looking away from him (from me) must have been taken as the waitress was bringing the cake. She obviously liked her cake, but though the eager glance is youthful, she is leaning forward in a way that makes her look pregnant or like a nursing mother. And that gives her a look of maturity.

In the third photograph, as in the first, she is looking at

me (at him) but here it is with a fixed, persistent gaze. At the time it irritated me because of the affection expressed in those eyes.

The man—the man I thought she loved: I have a photograph of him too, taken at the same time in the same café. He was old—about fifty—and seemed proprietary, sleek and self-satisfied: it was hard for me to be detached about him because I thought she loved him. He dressed in the way Continentals think an English gentleman dresses—suits with waistcoats and heavy shoes—and this gave his appearance a cosmopolitan veneer: but his features were German—sombre and straight. I recognized that he was handsome even if he was old: his hair was half-grey; his skin hung from the lines in his face. The weakening pressure of the blood had deflated his lips so that, when they closed to swallow the Russian tea, the skin above and below them met and the thin line of darker red disappeared into his mouth.

I hesitate to describe Suzi because there are sure to be some others like Armand who do not find her beautiful, who cannot understand why I took to her like that. However I can say that her hair was blonde, her nose was small and straight, her eyes were green and her ankles and wrists more delicate than any I had seen before.

I hesitate to describe myself as I was then, but it is only fair to say something and one of my chief qualities is a belief in fair play. I was that kind of Englishman. My father had been a Colonial governor—one of the last. I would probably have followed him into the Colonial Office but by the time I left university it no longer existed so I joined the Foreign Office instead. I was twenty-five. Berlin was my first post.

*

On one occasion I followed them back to their flat. (For myself I would have been quite happy just watching her every day at teatime but Armand in his French way prodded me to act.) It was not far from the Kurfürstendamm—they went down past the Jewish memorial, crossed the Kantstrasse, went on to the Steinplatz, where, at the corner of the Karmerstrasse, they entered an apartment building. I gave them a few minutes and then went to the door. There were eight white door-bells: one of them was for two people —Graf Helmuth von Rummelsberg and Gräfin Suzanne von Rummelsberg.

There is a small café in the Steinplatz next to a cinema—I went there and drank a glass of schnapps. It seemed quite probable now that they were man and wife, as I had suspected. If that conclusion saddened me, the sadness was too deep inside me to bother my conscious mind. On the contrary, my reaction was what you might expect in a young man living in times as free as they are, in a city which was still, as Armand once described it, amazingly licentious, obsessed with eroticism. The young wife of an old husband was the perfect candidate for a liaison. It also occurred to me that she might be his daughter or his niece: but didn't her expression when she looked at him suggest more than that? Would a girl of eighteen or so go to tea on the Kurfürstendamm every afternoon with her father? Or her uncle? Not if she was like the girls I knew. Anyway, for the purposes of an affair during my time in Berlin, it would be more suitable and more amusing if she were married to him. 'After all,' Armand said to me, 'it is quite possible. Fifty, for a man, is not so old . . . and he is handsome . . . and a count.'

In November they went away for three weeks—at least

10

they did not appear on the Kurfürstendamm. Then, one Tuesday at midday, I saw them in his white Mercedes-Benz going past the Opera. They must have crossed the Zone that morning. I followed them to see him take out two pigskin cases—one larger than the other. He carried them into the building: she was not his nurse.

In December, a few days before Christmas, I went to meet Armand for lunch at the Steinplatz hotel. He stood at the bar smiling.

'Do you know who is sitting in there?'

It was Suzi in a light-brown suit I had never seen on her before. She was talking to the head waiter, Aimé. Aimé, I knew, could hardly speak a word of German (he was employed at this hotel to add style—he had once worked in Maxim's or the Ritz in Paris) and Suzi, evidently, could not speak French; so she was forced to gesticulate and talk loudly, which embarrassed her. Even when Aimé took her order to one of the under-waiters she looked ill at ease—as if she would prefer to be eating a toasted sandwich at the Paris Bar or black bread and sausage in her room.

Armand wanted to be quite brazen, to approach her, a risk he would never have taken in an affair of his own. I felt I had too much to lose—that I would prefer to watch Suzi in cafés and restaurants for the rest of my life than ever chance losing her: but that, at that time, was an expression of cowardice, not passion, because I was quite keen to get things going. However we had lunch at a table across the room from her and since I was a trained diplomat I was able to watch her and the green tablecloth without being noticed.

My love for Suzi at this stage was, therefore, the passion of a voyeur. After three months of watching I had not spoken to her, yet continued to be faithful to her with my eyes. I never missed an afternoon on the Kurfürstendamm. On the other hand I had other interests which might come within the general category of love, the activities of an evening, a night, the things Armand and I talked about at teatime (we rarely talked about politics or diplomacy). There was, for a few weeks in November, the young wife of an officer of the British garrison. We met whenever he was on duty at the Zone or Sector border—at night or on Sunday afternoons at the Schloss Grünewald, where it was very cold and sunny. There was no one there so we could, well, hold hands. But she had an extraordinarily thick neck which put me off.

In January there was a German girl who designed textiles. Armand took me to a party of that kind of person—intellectuals—who were drinking a lot. I was given a German brand of whisky, tried to catch up and became drunk. I went back with the girl to her wretched little flat—and went there again the next day to tell her that I did not really want an affair with her—but on that occasion and once or twice afterwards I made use of her until the day came when I did not feel like even that. We went for a walk in the Tiergarten. She wore high-heeled shoes: her feet got very wet—as if they were not ugly enough. It was already half-past four so I told her quite quickly that I did not love her, that it was squalid without love (a woman's argument). We walked back to her flat. I left her at the entrance to the block and went to Zuntz.

Events, grand historical and coincidental events, forced me to discover something about Helmuth von Rummelsberg. A certain Klaus von Rummelsberg, a political leader of the refugees from eastern Germany, was decorated for his services to these refugees by the Federal government. There were protests from some quarters because he had been a member of the SS. The Federal government insisted that a denazification court had found him innocent—substantially innocent. That was good enough for us but not for some others and our Foreign Office wanted to check the court's decision for the sake of opinion in Britain. Many of the cases brought up after 1947 were known to be worthless and Klaus's case had been heard as late as 1949. The Embassy in Bonn passed the case on to us and the Political Adviser, Perkins, passed it on to me since, as he said, I had nothing else to do. So I opened a file on Klaus von Rummelsberg, born in Pomerania in 1905, eldest of three brothers: thus, in a sense, I had an official file on Helmuth, one of the brothers, and Suzi.

The records showed that Klaus von Rummelsberg had been attached to Strepper's SS battalion, which was a bad mark against him. I asked Bonn through the bag if we knew what had happened to Strepper. The answer was inadequate —no more than the popular rumour that he had escaped to South America. The Israelis were still looking for him. We no longer cared, as we no longer cared about Klaus except as a political nuisance—it was considered unnecessary to worry about what Germans had done if you were concerned with what they did now. That, at any rate, was the policy and I did not care if it was right or wrong. I never knew my uncles who died in the war. The most I remember of those days was the red glow over London and sweet-rationing which hit me hard. The Italian husband of my mother's Italian cook had been a volunteer on the fascist side in Spain—but I still let him clean my shoes and press my suits when I was at home. Of course I did not much care for Germany or the Germans—few Englishmen do—but that had as much to do with the First War and with their *Lederhosen* as with the Second, with their concentration camps. In practical terms this distaste for the Germans only meant that I tried to avoid German food, German beer-houses and German conversation: it did not prevent me from becoming, in a sense, a German expert. I had studied German history at university: I knew a lot about the economic policies of the Federal Republic, trade with the Zone and Allied Rights. I was quite competent to deal with the case of Klaus von Rummelsberg.

His background was unusual for a Nazi, and as far as we knew neither of his brothers had joined the Party. I began to piece together their background—first that they came from Pomerania, lesser nobility, landed gentry—what used to be called Junkers. I did not take my investigations to Pomerania where it all started—the course of their lives which now began to encircle mine—because Pomerania is not there. The Germany of today—Munich, say, or Cologne —is as far from Pomerania as Rome is from Sofia or Tripoli, as Amsterdam is from the Orkney Islands, as Beirut is from Bagdad, as Alexandria is from Istanbul. This other Germany of the von Rummelsberg ancestors no longer exists and hardly existed while Suzi or I were alive. It is not just eradicated from the modern maps of post-war Europe. Its inhabitants are gone. There are no longer Pomeranian houses, rivers, mudflats, marshes, pine-trees, beeches or cornfields. There is no Pomerania. True, there is Pomerce in Poland, province on the Baltic coast inhabited by Slavs from the Ukraine—a different kind of place from the old Pomerania: but then there was a war, atrocities of all sorts and a clean

14

sweep of Prussia, Pomerania, Silesia—a clean sweep off the map and out of history. The smaller places—Glatz, Cranz, Oels, Jares—went too: Hundsfelt became Psie Pole and Guttentag, Dobrodzien.

As an Englishman I cared very little about the disappearance of Pomerania. Neither Suzi nor I fought in that war, nor did we suffer materially from it except for sweet-rationing. Others did but they have had their say. If I have anything to say about that war, that Second World War, it is that Suzi and I do suffer from it in our minds because for those throughout Europe who were involved, it was the penultimate act of their lifetime, the final act being to talk about it, to judge everything for us as well as for themselves in the light of it. They reminisce with a delighted nostalgia—they live in the present world as in some continuing instalment, some sequel tagged on by a Dumas or a Conan Doyle to a work that was all too successful. But a sequel is always a mistake if it tries to describe the years of happiness that follow the last page of a fairy tale, a fairy tale in which a nation of monsters slaughtered the Jews (a nation of heroes fought for their lives), imprisoned good English airmen (impounded war criminals but were vanquished . . .). Bored children listen while their fathers tell what they did during the war. A generation is trapped by millions of ancient mariners, soldiers, fliers, and when they grow up they are constrained by the pattern of prejudice formed through the gaffes of these same story-tellers; they are pulled up short by the dozen place-names—Munich, Auschwitz, Pearl Harbor, Dresden, Hiroshima—which should have become the names of railway stations for any kind of real immortality.

My knowledge of Pomerania, therefore, amounts to this: first, I have had, since my student days, and have still, an overcoat with a Pomeranian collar which remains my favourite overcoat; secondly, an aunt of mine had a Pomeranian dog; and finally, without taking into consideration the expatriate Pomeranian Suzi, I am as likely to like Pomeranian girls as Bavarian girls or Jewish girls (and, of course, Jewish and Bavarian girls as much as Pomeranians). I like light blue eyes as much as dark brown eyes; cold eyes as much as warm eyes; long limbs as much as short ones. Moreover I was an Englishman with a sense of fair play and for that alone, as well as for Suzi's sake, I would not prejudge Klaus von Rummelsberg.

I met Suzi, as I knew I would, because coincidences are very common and I have always relied on them. The Senate of West Berlin gave a reception at the Academy of Arts and I was sent to represent the Political Adviser. It was the usual provincial fling—white wine, red wine and black bread sandwiches at eight in the evening—neither cocktails nor dinner nor anything after dinner. (The French and the English were always put in a bad temper by these parties—we could never decide whether or not to go out and have a decent dinner afterwards.)

I had been there for ten minutes and was talking to a man from the festival office—a plump, shiny man—when I caught Suzi's profile on the outer range of my retina as she came into the room. The reflex of my eye must have been sensitive to my emotion for normally I would not have noticed anything so much to my side.

Helmuth came in behind her: he overtook her and crossed the room to talk to the Senator for Culture and Education. She came up to the man I was talking to and we were introduced. It was as confusing as it is to meet a television news-

16

caster—a face one knows so well that shows no recognition. She shook hands with me. At once I could not remember what her hands felt like. So close, her face was different— muscle and bone, the skeleton of her beauty, the tendons of her expression.

I have never used my knowledge of German less than in Berlin. Suzi, like all the others, spoke to me in English when she learnt who I was.

'You know,' she said, 'you should go riding in Berlin. The Grünewald is the best place. I can tell you the name of the stables I go to by the Glienicke bridge.'

'Well, we have stables for our cavalry in Charlottenburg,' I replied.

'Oh, yes, of course. The parade on the Mayfield for the Queen's birthday. But there is nowhere so nice to ride around there.'

There was a flickered look of melancholy or something. Who can tell what the glances of women mean? Then she crossed to Helmuth von Rummelsberg and stood at his side.

'Who is she?' I asked the man who had introduced us.

'Suzanne von Rummelsberg. A very charming girl, don't you think?'

'And who is the man?'

'Helmuth von Rummelsberg.'

'Is he her father . . . or . . .'

The man smiled and said, 'No. Not her father. He's not a man to waste his time on a daughter.'

'His niece then . . .'

'You could call her that . . . yes . . . I'm sure *he* does.' He smiled again. I did not want to ask any other questions.

✿

17

It was now more difficult to watch Suzi because she knew me. I had either to sit far across the café at Kempinski's or at Zuntz sit downstairs and only see her walking in and out. The latter was perhaps the best solution because I came closer to her and saw her moving body. The advantage of that was not just the excitement; as in a horror film, I had to close my eyes when the hem of her skirt swayed anywhere above her knees or the cotton of her blouse tightened over her bosom. It was rather that, dispassionately, I could tell something of her personality from her limbs—not as much as from her face but enough to corroborate what I had already learnt.

Her ankles were the finest part of her body and the hallmark of her personality. No one with a crude or dull mind could have ankles like that. Such delicacies could not support a head with an indelicate mind. Her calf, too, was fine but a little more solid—she could not be whimsical as she might have been if the exquisite ankle had been equalled in the calf. Her knees were like her calves—lovely but the knees of a dependable girl. Her hips, that is her thighs, so far as I could see as she came down the slate steps, were plump—too plump for perfection but not too plump for me. If it meant that she liked her cake and cream as much as any other girl, I liked the thought that she was no snob; if it meant that she was sometimes lazy, by nature a little lethargic, I would not want a restless woman. Her waist again was perfect and her bosom was a decent size— neither meagre nor obese; that is to say, she had the proper instincts of love for a husband, say, or her children—but not so much as to slobber over them. Her neck, like her ankles, would be a prize piece for a collector and her long blonde hair was soft; and her eyelashes were long. Where

18

the body was fine, hers was the finest. So would it be with her mind. This I divined from my extended phrenology, a study of bumps overall, behind a newspaper, stirring hot chocolate.

Once or twice she recognized me and nodded as she passed.

In March I went back to England for three weeks' leave. I spent half the time with my sister in London and half of it with my parents in Suffolk.

How I loved England—London and the country. London, after Berlin, seemed a light city because people used so much paint. (In Berlin the private houses were large and dark—as if made of Bismarck's pig-iron and black blood.) The rooms of my sister's house were elegantly proportioned and delicately furnished. My brother-in-law was an architect and my sister did some interior decoration as an extra service for their friends whose houses he built or, rather, converted and renovated. However, she found time to come round the galleries with me and her three-year-old boy. One of the galleries had just opened—the director was a friend of hers—and I bought a Braque lithograph for her and her husband. She bought a lithograph by a younger painter for me. I chose it because it was like a target and reminded me of Suzi's moderate bosom: seen from above—taking that she was lying on her back—one of her breasts must look like a target or, perhaps, a bomber's sights—blue veins like rivers below.

My sister asked me if I had any girl friends in Berlin.

'Perhaps,' I said, 'the beginnings ...'

'Well, I hope you don't marry a German girl.'

'They're said to make very good wives.'

19

'Aunt Jane had one *au pair* who never did a stroke of work and never had a bath.'

My parents' home in Suffolk was an old rectory built of brick in the late eighteenth century. I was even happier there than in London. I was left largely to myself: I did some rough shooting and went for walks but most of the time I spent reading and thinking. The library faced east and I would sit there looking out of the large windows, out over the lawn, thinking to myself that if the earth was flat and the atmosphere quite clear I would have an unimpeded view over the North Sea, over Holland and the Friesian Islands, over Holstein and the lakes of Mecklenburg, to the pine-covered hills of Pomerania.

Did this idea come from thinking about my work or from nostalgia for Suzi in the Kurfürstendamm cafés? I thought that if it had been the latter I would rather be dreaming of her toes as they veered her ankles forward or her wrists at the cuff-links holding the sleeves of the blouse.

I knew that the Baltic sea was tideless and now I visualized the straight beaches, the woods running in from the shore, fields that stretched for fifty miles inland and then the pines in sandy ground which rose around lakes to hills, hills I might have seen from England, hills which are imperceptible when you are there until, through two tree-trunks, you see them rippling away far to the east and west. Either the clouds are where you stand and there is sun in the distance, changing the light far away, or that distance is where you stand and the dead and living twigs, plants and trees are illuminated around you while shadow sweeps across the horizon.

There is what we know and what we suppose. Narrow

roads running through the forests. Villages with children under seven in the street. The cottages tall and made with dark brick; the doors and window-frames covered with old green paint.

Now, of course, the men are all together in one field of the communal farm—several standing around watching three men load manure into a trailer. A gate with a wrought-iron star above it. A community centre set back from the road, veiled by shrubs and bushes—pre-war pillars in front of the door and Slav labourers playing billiards on a large table where the mahogany is unpolished and the green felt long since worn through to the black rubber cushioning.

One wing is still gutted—the roof blown off and a gap in the wall, approximating to the window but round, not rectangular, blown by a tank's shell or mortar bomb. Over the rest of the house the pittings of the bullets have been filled in with a mortar that already crumbles. Although it must exist like this, the rural social club in Kaszewo, Pomerce, Poland, it is no easier to imagine than a country house, a castle, in Kassow, Pomerania, Germany, so now I started to imagine what it had been like for the family who had lived there before. I began to lead their lives in my mind with facts and fantasy as I led my own on the ground with arm and legs, mouth and eyes. As my life may be invented in the imagination of others—as imperialist to an African, as capitalist to a Russian—the history of the von Rummelsbergs developed in mine.

II

Von Rummelsberg: 1526–1914

There were the ancestors of Klaus and Helmuth von Rummelsberg, the Teutonic knights who risked their lives for God and Christianity east of the Elbe. They provided large estates for themselves, we know, and, we suppose, salvation for the Slavs. A particular knight, Traugott von Rummelsberg, was provincial governor in Neustettin when the Order was secularized and the Master changed his name to Duke of Brandenburg and King of Prussia. Protesting with the deeds as well as the words of Luther, Traugott unscrewed his steel cod-piece and saddled his horse. After two days' riding he reached Danzig, where fifty years of martial chastity ended in a corn-merchant's daughter. She bore him a son, Klaus, who in his time married and then made a tall girl with hammer toes who bore him a son, Traugott, who made and then married a pastor's daughter with eyes that hardly blinked, who bore a son Klaus who died at once. But there was a second son, Helmuth, who married and many years later impregnated (after a ball in Stettin) his wife, a widow whose husband had been killed at the tail end of the Religious Wars. At the age of fifty, she bore a son, Traugott, who when he was twelve was found in the loft playing grown-up games with a neighbour's grown-up daughter. His mother died but he married the girl with the special permission of the Grand Duke. After this astute move at an early age, which added the neighbour's land to the Rummelsberg estate, and produced a son, Helmuth, he went into the army and never put haunch to haunch

22

with a woman again. The young Helmuth married the daughter of a second cousin of his mother who came back from East Prussia. On the journey back to Pomerania he told her that she smelt like a cow. She cried, but that night, as she washed herself down in a tin bowl, before the fire, he broke open the door with the cry of a hussar and back in Pomerania she bore a son, called Edward after her father. He was killed at the battle of Minden but there were eight others. The second, Klaus, married the daughter of a friend of his father with estates between Körlin and Kolberg. This feeble, neurotic woman did not conceive until, caught in Kolberg during the siege by the French, making love for something to do, phlegmatic in doing so on the meagre ration of food, a stray bullet flew through the window and entered the base of the man's spine. For ten minutes he thrashed around in his death agony; she, caught beneath him, soon thrashed around as much and could not bring herself to call for help; as he stiffened above, she softened below and both lay equally still, she as dead, he dead. The result of this was another Klaus named after his dead father, and people had it that he was either half French or half burger though he turned out as tall and blond and fine as any Pomeranian Junker.

His wife was the daughter of a minister of the crown and they lived most of their life in Berlin. True to the tradition of Frederick the Great, he liked his wife standing at the fireplace (on a Sunday afternoon when the servants were out or late at night when they were in bed), her head on her hands, her hands on the mantelpiece. She, well, she was obedient to her husband as he was obedient to the king and hardly knew what else to expect; and every now and then he was a little haphazard which was how she bore three children. The eldest, Helmuth, grew up in Berlin and, when the duties of an officer cadet allowed, liked to go to balls in the Grünewald. He married a daughter of a Huguenot French family that had fled from the Revocation of the Edict of Nantes six generations before. They were fashionable and gay and known, among their friends, to be the first Germans to copulate in the sleeping compartment of a railway train. Later in life, as relations with France worsened, this Helmuth felt embarrassed at the thought that his wife's maiden name was von Fumé and retired with her to Pomerania where his youngest son, Klaus, conceived in the train, was brought up to be a German, a Pomeranian, a Junker.

This Klaus's brothers were all killed by the French, which upset the father less than their mother's maiden name. Klaus did not like the family home and spent much of his leave in the Silesian home of a friend in the officer corps. This friend had, among other members of his family, a mother who was a pietist and a daughter who hated kneeling. So, to escape praying, she set out to win the heart and the balls of Klaus. But the young men liked to talk together, smoking, boots up by the fire: there was hardly a chink in their armour: unlike his forefather, the first Traugott von Rummelsberg, Klaus's cod-piece was firmly in place. One day, when they assembled to pray to God and Luther, she saw a trace of irritation in his eye as he knelt. He too disliked kneeling and she guessed why. When they rose she stopped him and humbly wiped the smudged toe of his boot with her skirts. She understood. A Prussian officer with a mother with a French maiden name could not get away with smudged toe caps. He thanked her, did not speak to her for three weeks, then proposed marriage. After their

24

wedding, they knelt together in their night clothes—not praying—and later than that she bore a son and citizen of the German Empire, Traugott von Rummelsberg. This Traugott had a particularly conventional upbringing, was a firm Christian and did well as an officer cadet. His wife, Mächtild, who came from similar stock in Mecklenburg (her home near Malden looked out over the Plauer See), bore him three sons—Klaus in 1905, Helmuth in 1909 and Edward in 1912. Two years after the birth of her youngest son, Mächtild von Rummelsberg's husband left to play his eternal part in the Schlieffen plan.

Von Rummelsberg / von Treblitz: 1914–1920

Kassow was the home of Klaus, Helmuth and Edward. The house, the grounds and the estate were well ordered and tidy. There was hardly any garden but well shorn grass ran up on either side of the gravel drive; there was a courtyard and a vegetable garden at the back. Everything was tidy and in order.

From the age of eight the boys were dressed in uniform—at first a cadet's uniform without insignia, then, when they went to the cadet school, their school rank and badge. The servants, too, wore old battle-dress. Nevertheless, though the children wore uniforms and their life was always strict, there were picnics in dog carts, and pony-rides. There was, after all, their mother; and even if they had no sister, there was a neighbour's daughter—Katerina von Treblitz, who lived five miles away on the other side of the Western plantation. She came to tea at Kassow—later to dinner—and the three von Rummelsberg boys, or two, or one of them must have gone over to see the von Treblitz family.

There were, in Pomerania, between the wars, nine hundred and ninety-seven estates of twelve hundred and fifty acres or over, comprising three-sevenths of the land. The von Rummelsberg estate was within this group; but the von Treblitz estate was not, being only of four hundred acres. The von Rummelsbergs, through their great-grandparents' connections in Berlin, also owned industrial stocks, above all shares in the railways and coal. The von Treblitz family did not, and while not qualifying for *Osthilfe* (government aid for agriculture in the east), they can be counted among the many impoverished Junkers living in considerable modesty on small estates.

He, Helmuth, was allowed to hold the child (Katerina) in his arms. He watched her mouth sucking, her fingers clutching—the instincts working on air. At the age of three he loved babies and Katerina, when he first met her, was a baby. His mother hovered, afraid he would drop her, his little . . . . He watched the baby being bathed, the nursemaid's finger coated in soap washing the gigantic cleft between her small, bent legs as methodically, as systematically, as the whole palm covered the baby's back, encircled her limbs. The toes were ridiculous crumbs of flesh, the fingernails like toys, the head and torso unformed cocoons but the part of the body between the legs was enormous— like a single hieroglyph, a clear and final statement. The eyes of Helmuth's mother flickered from the son to the baby's mother and she saw in the mother's eyes what one might well expect to see in the eyes of a Pomeranian mother —hardness and perplexity at the male-child's interest in the baby.

Klaus, on the other hand, was examining a broken sashcord and drew his mother's attention to it with a slight frown. His mother felt more at ease. If Klaus was then aged five, Helmuth was three and both Edward and Katerina babies of a few months.

In the autumn (aged eight) Helmuth took the train to the cadet school with Klaus—Klaus who was already in the uniform of the emperor. The train left from Stolp station and stopped at Lauenberg, Wejkerowo, Gdynia and Danzig. There they changed onto the express from Berlin which did not stop until Königsberg. This was during the war, when rows of field-guns lay in the sidings. When the war was over the train went non-stop from Lauenberg to Danzig. The older cadets, who smoked in the German corridor of the German train, spat out their stubs onto the Polish workers on the Polish line through the Polish corridor.

'There wouldn't be a railway here if we hadn't built it,' they said each time. And after 1921 and the words of Lloyd George: 'It's like giving a clock to a monkey.'

In 1921 the cadet schools no longer existed, following the terms of the Treaty of Versailles. The boys did not wear their uniforms in the train and instead of going to the cadet school in Königsberg, they travelled to a castle near Tilsit. To Klaus and Helmuth these changes seemed insignificant: the discipline, the training, were the same. The beds, the benches, the desks were similar: the food was worse. They still saw and saluted the fortress at Marienburg from the train. The red-brick ramparts meant the same to them all —German honour, German glory.

Helmuth, at first, did not like the cadet school. The discipline was strict: he was bullied: he was used to playing with girls. However Klaus, who was by then in a position of some authority, protected his brother. Klaus was popular with the masters because he was able and clever: he was liked and feared by the other boys. Soon they all knew that if they touched Helmuth, they would have to answer for it to Klaus. The two brothers were fond of each other.

The von Rummelsberg and von Treblitz families spent two months of each summer in Swinemünde, a resort on the Baltic at the mouth of the Stettiner Haff. Because the Baltic is tideless, the beaches are unchanging in breadth and length; there is no strong drag of current to draw away the soil. There are no cliffs to cut into the wind and so no turf overhanging them where the soil is blown away. The sand is more white than brown or yellow, and the woods, often beech or oak as well as pine, come down to where this whitish sand begins and runs, a strip of it, sometimes in dunes, to the sea.

To reach Swinemünde, the two families would take the Danzig–Stettin train at Stolp, which would then halt at Koslin, Kolberg, Greifenberg and finally Plathe where they would change, after waiting for two hours on the same platform, onto a local train that ran from Wangerin by Schwivelbein and Plathe to Swinemünde.

Swinemünde was (I say was because, of course, it no longer exists) a well-laid-out holiday town. Both families stayed in the same hotel, a good one in the first row of buildings nearest the beach.

Each morning the two mothers, and three of the children, Helmuth, Edward and Katerina, went to the beach. Klaus, from the earliest age, preferred to go back past the four further rows of buildings, each row separated from the other by a block of public gardens and row of plane trees, through the old town, to the port where he could watch the smaller boats load and unload and the larger ones, on their way to Stettin, wait for the customs official to come out from the customs house. Also there was the ferry crossing the mouth of the Stettiner Haff which cost nothing: the ferry-boat captain's son, Egon, was his seasonal friend.

Edward would build sand castles, always a little too near to the waves so that the ramparts he built against them were inevitably broken down.

Helmuth and Katerina would bury each other in sand; or swim together, the boy feeling bound to swim out further than the girl; or hunt each other in the dunes; or throw at each other the small black crabs that were found on the beach. Or they would play with other children, bullying them whether they were Poles from Poznan, Jews from Berlin or the daughters of Oscar von Hindenburg. Helmuth and Katerina discovered that these three girls would all cry, the eldest first, if Helmuth and Katerina pulled off the legs of a black crab, and so whenever the girls were seen they were cornered between dunes and made to watch the dismemberment. When the youngest grand-daughter of the Reichspresident complained to her nursemaid, she was told not to snivel like a Pole, that the dismemberment of a crab by the von Rummelsberg boy was nothing compared to the dismemberment of Germany by the Western powers.

One summer there was a little Jewish boy called Jacob Goldberg. Helmuth and Katerina would take him to the woods and tell him that if he really wanted to be a German he must undergo some tests. With a smile Jacob would say he would certainly like to be a real German and Helmuth and Katerina would fill his mouth with twigs or take down his trousers and beat his shins with sticks. Jacob Goldberg kept grinning and each time he met them asked if he was German yet. A bit more but not quite. They tried it with one of the President's grand-daughters but she said she did not want to be more German and ran away.

Some older Polish boys once caught both Helmuth and Katerina in the woods. Their hands were held behind their backs; one youth put his face, covered in spots, close to Helmuth's, then to Katerina's and jeered 'blondy milk-sop' and pulled out some of Katerina's hair, tying it round Helmuth's nose. It smelt of cake.

The same gang of Poles were taken away by the police later that summer after what they did to Jacob Goldberg.

Jacob Goldberg, who survived the beatings of the Polish delinquents, did not survive the war. Nor did the Polish delinquents. Nor did Swinemünde.

Chapter Two

I

Now THAT I WAS ACQUAINTED with Suzi, I could not sit watching her in the cafés every day so I went riding in the Grünewald from the stables she had suggested, and hoped to come across her there.

I knew the Glienicke bridge quite well. When we went over to our Military Mission in Potsdam, it was over this bridge. The staff cars—large Opels and Mercedes which had even their chromium-plated parts painted over with matt khaki paint—were the only traffic over the bridge. The road must, at one time, have been the main road running out of the capital: but now it was deserted at both ends —at the Potsdammer Platz cut in two by the Sector boundary and again at the bridge by the border with the Zone. In between, in Schöneberg or Zehlendorf, the street was as busy as any other and it was difficult to believe that it was sealed off at both ends. In summer many West Berliners drove out on this Potsdammer Chausee to go for a walk or to have a picnic in the Grünewald or to visit the Glienicke palace and its park. No one bathed in the river just there because it was said to be mined by the East Germans; but people liked to stand staring across at Potsdam.

The place where you could hire horses was in the old stables of the palace on the left-hand side of the Chausee. These were set back from the road in a peculiar pocket of West Berlin's territory. The boundary ran down the left-hand side of the Chausee for half a mile before it reached the Glienicke bridge; then, a hundred yards before the bridge, it went back from the road, followed the track to the stables, shifted behind the stables, and ran down the middle of an inlet of the river which passed behind the stables and parallel to the road. The stables, then, were closely surrounded on three sides by East German territory.

Beside the stables there was a large block of what must have been servants' quarters. Before the temperature sank below freezing in the winter, they had been rebuilding part of this as a youth hostel—ignoring its proximity to the fortified boundary. Otherwise the area was deserted except for the children who sometimes played in the field between the buildings and the river.

The first time I went riding there was in February. I was accompanied by Armand and a German friend of his called Kurt. Armand, who normally wore rather shaggy clothes, always dressed very correctly when riding—soft leather boots and proper breeches which pleased the woman, Frau Stefan, who ran the stables. I wore only an old pair of trousers: Kurt wore boots and had a crop, both of which he said were heirlooms—accoutrements of his father's position in the Gestapo.

There was this woman and an old man and a girl who prepared the stables.

'I believe the countess von Rummelsberg comes here to ride,' I said to Frau Stefan.

'Suzi, do you mean? Yes. But she hasn't been near us for

a few weeks now. Too cold for her, I should think.' She was very German, this woman—glum but not unfriendly.

My feet have never been so cold as they were on that first day, when there must have been several degrees of frost. We rode on top of five inches of snow, walking out of the stables and down to the main road. The windows of one house on the other side were open and a bolster was airing on the sill. The sky was clear except for a haze on the horizon over Berlin. Two young East German border guards stood on the terrace in front of an elegant villa with pillars and covered in apricot-coloured plaster, their hands on their hips, watching us. The villa was empty.

We turned into the main road and away from the bridge. The border was right at our side—a wire fence about six feet high, then tangled barbed-wire and another fence. The side wall of the villa replaced this fence at one point: the window looking onto the road was boarded up. The guards were now as close as across a room. Their uniforms were open at the throat and they continued to stare at us un-flinchingly, humourlessly. Kurt ignored them: Armand and I, slightly confused, watched them but with less tenacity than theirs. Then we trotted through the wood beside the border, the white frost lining both the wire and the turret of the tower on stilts. (On this tower in summer, two guards, equally young, lounged on the roof in the sun, their calves dangling, their machine-pistols across their supine waists.) At an old café in the woods, closed now but in summer certainly open for barley beer with fruit juice as it must have been in the Kaiser's day, we crossed the road and were away from the border and into the forest.

There were special tracks for horses which led over to the Havel. The woods were wild and empty. The only building was the tall communications tower which stood quite deserted sending messages across the Zone from western city to western state. I saw deer in the wood but never Suzi nor anyone else except one day several hundred American soldiers on manoeuvres—black faces in the undergrowth under helmets and camouflage nets. I thought blank gunfire would frighten the horse but they never fired a shot —merely sat there quietly, smoking, looking bored, their jeeps and field pieces static as if stuck.

I had gone riding because I had thought I might meet Suzi, but I enjoyed the sport for itself. There were three horses—a small, stubborn one which might as well have been a mule; a large fierce animal ready to bolt as soon as the reins were relaxed; and a charming, gentle mare, best at cantering but quite prepared to gallop if that was what I wanted, and careful to slow down at corners and crossings. I avoided the small horse and asked for the mare unless I felt in a mood for danger: then I rode the big one. Kurt rode him on the first day and I rode the mare. I liked Kurt even less than the small horse and subsequently I went riding alone.

One day in April, as I rode back into the stables, she was waiting there for a horse. I might merely have nodded but I remembered that Frau Stefan must have thought we were friends, since I had mentioned her, so I said: 'Do you remember me? We met at the Academy. You told me to come riding here.'

'Oh yes,' she said, 'you are the Englishman.' She had green eyes and they looked at me. I knew her so well: I loved her more than anyone else but did not know why. It was not just her beauty or the animal attraction. I felt as if I was compelled to love her, that there was some significance

34

in my loving her which I could not understand. Yet she looked at me and spoke to me in the indifferent way of people with odd acquaintances, those they may or may never meet again.

'Is that really the East over there?' I asked, though I knew quite well.

'Yes,' she said. 'If we went for a swim beyond that notice, you see, in the middle there, we would be shot at. There are soldiers in the trees—look, at the bottom, sitting there. I can see them.' She pointed to where there were indeed some border police.

'How dreadful,' I said, not because I thought so but because most Germans like to hear it and it was, I thought, her ankles, not her mind, which were exceptional.

'Oh, do you think so?' she said smiling. 'Don't you think it's no more than we deserve? Most visitors think it is rather interesting, this partition of Germany.'

'I am not a visitor. I am a member of the Military Mission.'

She did not seem to understand quite what that meant but nodded.

'Then you can go into the East. I can too, you know. I'm not a West Berliner.' She said this as a slight, girlish boast, as if to be a West Berliner was to be a poor relation.

'Have you any family over there?' I asked.

'My mother used to be but now she lives in Bonn.' Suzi had a simple, almost abrupt way of talking.

'Tell me,' I said quickly, abrupt now myself because I knew that her horse would be led from the stables at any moment, 'were you married recently?' Then I added with an ironic smile: 'Of course you are a countess, I know, and in England you have to be married to be a countess but

that isn't so here, is it? And it's nice to know whether someone is Miss or Mrs. I had heard . . .'

She jerked her head up. She had been looking at me
before, or in my direction, but she jerked her head to look
more specifically at my expression, at my eyes. 'Another
name? You see, I ride under my maiden name. I am a professional rider—that is to say, I used to be.'

'I see. Your maiden name. Then you are married, are
you? My congratulations . . . even if they are a year or two
late.'

The horse was led out of the stables.

'Englishmen are very indiscreet,' she said in a coy, almost genteel, way. She rode off, walking the horse, so that
I did not know if she could hear or expected to hear a reply.
I gave a laugh and watched the strange chimney among
the trees on the other side of the water. It must have been
for burning the dead leaves.

I did not believe that she was married—not just because I
did not want to but because the stable-woman told Kurt
(who told Armand who told me) as she bivouacked with
him in a stall after one of his rides that at fourteen Suzi had
finished a clear round with a broken maidenhead. That,
according to Frau Stefan, was the nearest Suzi had got to
that sort of thing and she knew because she had known the
child since she was born.

It is hard to tell from photographs of old men what they
were like when young.

Helmuth: sleek, a bland expanse between the eye and
eyebrow. A permanent expression of irony and amusement
in the brow, in the mouth, now, which cannot have been
there before. Then—his hair was further forward and thicker.

His nose straight and rather large, as it is, but sleeker, less sunken in itself. A decent ear, pinker than it is now, less parched and folded. And there must always have been an un-German roundness to the back of his head. His lips were average, again always smiling now where they might have been straight in his serious youth. In the young man there would not have been the same silted-up expression but specifically, materially, he can only have lacked the lines and the faint dehydration to his skin.

Klaus: I have a photograph of him too, in the file. The same sheen but his hair has receded further back; he is almost bald—and his brows come further over his eyes. The hair would make the main difference in him as a young man. He has a more military face than Helmuth's but probably has the same kind eyes. Between kindness and stupidity. If Helmuth's are now mocking, Klaus's eyes, their expression, that is, taken with the lines in his face, look rather noble. He too has, had, a straight nose, average ears. His lips were slightly thicker and now are sunken.

Edward: there is no photograph of Edward because he disappeared on the Eastern front, but he is in the group of all of them, Katerina too, on a picnic or at a camp—all eager, fresh. If the leather breeches, the Teutonic eyes, her long skirt, would turn the stomach of my sister, and my mother and father too, I see no reason why I should not say they all look heroic. All of them. They were intelligent, able, loyal; tall, handsome; just, in their own way; Christian; proud, honourable, cultured, well-educated and certainly brave.

Helmuth von Rummelsberg / Katerina von Treblitz: 1928

The bailiff's son asked her to play croquet. She hit him so hard that he was knocked over into the rose bed. He ran to Katerina's mother who said nothing but looked at Katerina. Katerina who had been clipping off the dead rose heads now began to cut off the whole plant at the root. The boy ran to her father in the fold yard where he was prodding the shrunken testicle of his best bull. 'Katerina's in her mood,' the boy shouted from the gate, 'she's doing the roses.' The count stood up, walked through the gate into the garden, ran onto the lawn and down to the rose beds where Katerina had now destroyed seven plants. He hit her shoulders with his stick so that she fell over; then he kicked her, his boots, leaving mud and a rent in her pink dress. She got up quickly and ran across the lawn into the pine wood. 'Bitch,' her father shouted after her, 'damned bad-tempered, mean little shitting pig.'

He walked up to the house, scratching his whiskers. His face was still red. 'What set her off this time?' he asked his wife.

'Maria burnt the red dress when she was ironing it.'

'Well I wish she'd settle with Maria and not with my roses.'

'Maria's face was scratched very badly; we had to send her home so there will be no one to serve tonight.'

When Katerina was a mile from the house she saw Helmuth, who had fallen off his horse and sprained his ankle.

'Damned fool,' she said, kicking his ankle.

Helmuth fainted. She dropped damp oak leaves onto his face and he regained consciousness.

'Here, lean on me, you poor old boy,' she said. He hobbled through the wood leaning on her shoulder. Katerina led the horse. Helmuth could smell soap from her hair and feel her bosom, which could hardly be seen, against his ribs.

'You seem to have had a fall too,' he said, pointing to her torn dress and the mud where her father had kicked her.

'Shut up about that,' she said. She scowled again and then her features returned to their normal unsmiling state.

They reached her home. She took him into the pantry, leaving the horse loose in the yard. She pulled off his boot and tore the leg of his breeches. The ankle was swollen.

'Maria,' she called.

'She's been sent home,' someone shouted from the kitchen.

'Tell her that if she doesn't come here now she need never come again.'

There were mutterings in the kitchen and a boy ran out. Katerina fetched a bowl of water and some cloth which she dipped in the water and wrapped around Helmuth's ankle.

'Is it broken, do you think, or just sprained?' she asked him.

'Oh, only sprained. It's nothing. I'm sorry to be such a nuisance.'

Katerina said nothing. She held the cloth to his ankle, then, when it was warm from the heat of his skin, dipped it into the water again and reapplied it to the swelling.

A glum-looking girl in a long brown dress appeared at the door; three scratches, black now from the blood that had dried on them, ran across her left cheek. Her eyes were red, blotched with tears. She stood in the doorway and said nothing.

'You're too late now,' Katerina said to her. 'I've done it myself.'

The girl started to cry.

'Well, go and get some more water then,' Katerina said.

The snivelling girl took the bowl and went out.

'Oh, what a stupid girl,' Katerina said to Helmuth. 'All the peasants are so stupid and clumsy. The German ones are as bad as the Poles. Did you know she burnt a dress of mine? Oh, I don't mind about the dress, you know. I have quite a few. But it happened to be one I liked in particular ... even if it did come from Stolp. I don't often get to Danzig or Berlin so a decent dress from Stolp is quite a rarity ... and she had to burn it.'

Maria came back with a bowl of water and spilt it as she put it down.

'You clumsy bitch,' Katerina said, jutting her knee forward to hit the crouching girl in the chest. 'You see what I mean? I'd give this wretch some of my old dresses if she didn't burn my new ones. Then she wouldn't smell so much. She's been wearing that old brown one for months. It stinks, do you understand, Maria, it stinks and you're splitting it with that monstrous bosom of yours. It's quite indecent to be dressed like that in front of a gentleman.'

Maria blushed and snivelled and ran out of the pantry.

'You must admit,' Katerina said to Helmuth, 'that I have to put up with a lot—a maid who's not only stupid but has a bosom that gets in the way of everything she does?'

Katerina von Treblitz and Helmuth von Rummelsberg: 1929

One day in winter there was a treasure hunt on horses. (The dark brown of the leafless trees, the dark green of the perennial pines; the snow and sky.)

There were twenty-eight young people on horses and they were paired; girls with boys; the older with the younger. There were three sons of von Rummelsberg who died in the Great War; the eldest rode with Dodie von Stuck; the youngest was with Harriet von Baldenberg and the middle one with . . .

He, Helmuth, the middle one, had a contraction of the nerves in his stomach because he was afraid that she would be paired with someone else but she was always put with him because her aunt, the Gräfin, the organizer of the treasure hunt, knew that . . . between Helmuth and Katerina . . . and, like everybody else, smirked.

The first clue of the treasure hunt led to the von Stucks' dovecot; the second to the stable steps; the third to the bridge over the Weser. There was a mile between the stable and the dovecot. Helmuth and Katerina were ahead, were first at the bridge and rode on to the forest hut, three miles down the side of the plantation. There they were caught out by the aunt's cunning. There were no clues . . . and before they got there, half-way down the side of the plantation, snow slipped off the branch of a pine. The sun caught and melted an underpinning wad of snow; the lot slid off; the horse shied and Katerina fell off. She was unhurt but she fell in a puddle, that is, a rut full of mud and melting snow. It was melting a little. Enough to shift some snow, make a puddle.

Now Katerina rode side-saddle and wore a beige suit—a beige tailored jacket and a long beige skirt; a white lace blouse, a cravat, a pin. Her hair was up with other pins. Thick brown stockings, dark brown boots.

Now Helmuth, of course, saw her knees, well, the inner sides to her knees and helped her on. Poof, both were nothing in those days, in the world, in Germany, the nineteen-thirties, but in Pomerania . . . not much, perhaps, but something.

There were no clues at the forest hut (which they used for picnics in the summer) but a Polish forester by the fire.

'You could go,' Katerina said to him. He left.

'There are no clues here,' said Helmuth.

'Shit,' said Katerina. 'They must have meant the hut on the Kassow plantation.' She read the piece of paper she held in her hand: 'Could be used for a so-called treaty if it had wheels. The initial is wrong but its sound is right and the letter is correctly addressed. The letter, of course. K.C. Compiègne. Why did we think it was here?'

'The Western plantation. France is West.'

'They'll be ten miles away by now.' Katerina stood with her back to the fire, raising and lowering herself on the balls of her feet. She was tall as an American, tall as a Zulu. Helmuth was taller still. If she was six foot tall, he was six foot two and Klaus taller still, tall even for a Pomeranian, or an American or a Zulu, in fact as tall as men ever are. (The youngest Edward was the smallest, as if lesser years diminished size, as if men shrink from heroic proportion and live further from heaven as they are born nearer to the present.) His (Helmuth's) nose was straight, his eyes were blue, his hair light brown. Her eyes were blue, her hair was blonde streaked with brown and her nose turned up so that while

42

his nostrils were shaped like squat pears and were visible only to those much smaller (children, Jews) or to those who saw him lying down, hers leant forward at an angle of forty-five degrees, pulled up by the turn in her nose, and could be seen by anyone about her size and were considered (by her aunt and others) to be her one flaw: who wants to look up a girl's nose? Helmuth, taller than she was, saw much less of these little slits (Klaus saw none of them, Edward all of them) and Katerina took good care not to look up into his or anyone else's eyes.

'Anyway,' Katerina said, 'I can't go back to lunch like this.'

'You could.'

'I won't.'

Her beige riding suit was still well splashed by the puddle mud, in streaks, but less like the streaks in her hair and more like the marks of watery excrement, spurted from between dilated buttocks, forced from fear.

'They should have made it clearer, where we were meant to go,' she said. 'I'm much nearer home now. If you're hungry we can eat that Pole's black bread—look, there it is on the bench. There's some sausage too. Go on, eat it, unless you're afraid of getting some foul Polish disease.'

Helmuth wrinkled up his nose. 'Eat it yourself.'

She screwed up her nose too. Helmuth sat down, she sat down too, faced the fire, put her feet on a stool (stools, a table, shelves, logs drying) and pulled her beige skirt up to her knees. She sighed. Her feet were at an angle to each other.

'I don't see why we shouldn't go home,' she said, looking down at the spattered mud. 'Let this dry a bit first.' She brushed the mud with the side of her hand and then wiped it off again on a clean part of her skirt.

43

She was six foot, six miles from home and three times six years old. If she was not the Beast to Helmuth then at least she was a beast with breath that condensed in the cold air, legs with brown stockings instead of fur, but a head of natural brown-streaked blond hair and (to him beautiful) deepset eyes and a (to him pretty) turned-up nose and, twenty-one, six foot two, fourteen miles from home, he was young enough, tall enough, near enough to home, not to realize what she wanted.

Katerina, on the other hand, Helmuth's childhood friend, though unconscious of it, knew exactly what she wanted. Then, there, in the hut. Her father was bankrupt and the Kaiser had abdicated so why not? And she got it, then, there, in the hut, on the floor, taking it, not liking it, for the first time, not the last, and making as much of a mess of her beige skirt as had the mud from the puddle.

Chapter Three

I

JUST AS I CAME TO DEPEND upon the beauty of Suzi, I became addicted to the ugliness of the city we lived in. I came to wonder if I could ever return to England, where they preferred the ruins of Greece and Rome (as once they did in Berlin) to the gutted blocks beyond the Tiergarten. The prize pieces of spectacular destruction were, of course, in the East around the Akademieplatz. There stood the huge classical constructions of the nineteenth century, untouched since the incendiary bombs had burnt them out. Twenty years later, viewed by a conscious adult who never knew this infamous Second World War, the ribs of the roof are still charred, the pillars black, the upper stones near to toppling. There they stand, classical re-statements, waiting to be stated for a third time by the masons of the Communist Republic—barbarians careful to preserve them so that, with Rome rebuilt, they may be acknowledged as the true emperors.

It was these real ruins that I came to love—not those like the Kaiser William Memorial Church at the foot of the Kurfürstendamm, patched up as a sleek sight, but the simple blank sides, empty cubes of wall dashed with hoarding or backing a shack selling sausages and beer. My mind took its revenge on the crammed capital cities of the West by delighting in the streets broken off and the desert stretches, grey with rubble, concrete, corrugated iron, running back to an elevated railway or a single extant building. There was here a proper shattering of vanity in the creamy cornices pitted with bullet holes, the Doric columns patched up with rusty, hammered tins, the streets of the old city—empty, ending under a bridge, round a corner, ending, deserted.

The railway lines, too, were deserted. Huge junctions which once must have clanked with wagons full of coal, steel, corn, political prisoners, were now green with the weeds that had grown in the ash and open as huge vistas—valleys between the grey cakes of rubble, steel, oil, sand and cement.

And there was the wall. Was it because I loved Suzi that I loved Berlin and its wall, for if Berlin was anything, it was the wall. Even when sitting in Zuntz or Kempinski I was never away from it—it girdled me and all of them as clearly as a steel band around a cracked skull. There were so many streets which came to an end because of this wall—there were many ways you could not go. If it was not a wall, it was several strips of wire-fencing or a ditch or a belt of raked ground, floodlit and overseen by those stilted huts and utility machine-guns. It became an obsessive hobby. How did the wall look in Moabit? How did it compare there with Kreuzberg? Where was it most dramatic? The Bernauerstrasse where the windows of whole blocks of flats were bricked-in, or Lichterfelde where a simple fence ran in front of fields of soil that were fertilized, ploughed, sown, harvested? Then again it ran through lakes and rivers and changed its nature to underwater mines; or through woods where at night the floodlights shone through the pines as if a night shift was working on a huge and important construction. By the Brandenburg Gate it was like a golf course, the grass clipped short; a rise in the ground which marked the entrance to the Chancelry bunker was now a machine-gun post: and dogs were tied to wires parallel to the wall lest they maul the guards as well as the escaper.

I knew it was a way to die. I knew that if I crossed through to the other side at the checkpoint, drove my car to the left or right, to any point along the line, then walked, climbed, crawled in the dead grass and dust, past broken bricks and under the wire, someone would shoot me dead: someone felt something about me or about what I did, felt strongly enough to shoot me at their wall, their fence, their ditch, their boarded window. Otherwise, anywhere else but up against this wall, Europe was a tolerant, liberal zero. Here, in Berlin, was where the line was drawn and the line was tangible. Here a principle, heinous or just, would end my life (here my life would end if no principle made it begin).

Suzi, however, was not part of this love nor this love part of Suzi. She seemed to me at the time to be too luscious to have anything to do with Berlin. A Berlin girl is like a wet rat, critically undernourished in her first years in spite of the Tiergarten potatoes—brought up in the dark barrack slums of Kreuzberg. Suzi was more the West German visitor —the luxury product trotting in the Hilton arcade. Yet like so many West Germans, she was no Rhinelander, no Bavarian, Saxon, Swabian, Westphalian, Holsteiner, Württemberger, or Hamburger . . . she came from elsewhere.

One day, now in June, a warm evening, I sat in the lower part of Zuntz, waiting for them to go past me to that upper part. The old Polish writer and his coterie who came as usual five minutes before Helmuth and Suzi, passed by, but the two did not appear. This had happened before and it always upset me. I was worried that, hidden discreetly in a corner, I had missed them or that they had left Berlin. After a quarter of an hour they still had not come, so rather than sit there I paid my bill and rose to go, thinking of searching some other cafés—though it seemed unlikely that Helmuth had broken his routine. But at the entrance I was upon her because she was sitting alone at a table on the pavement in the sun. I was confused both that she should be sitting out there and that she should be alone (of course the one resulted from the other—Helmuth would never have sat outside). Whether I would have gone up to her on my own or not I do not know, but she saw me and nodded.

'I always seem to meet you in Zuntz,' I said.

'Yes. You see we come here every other day—but we usually sit upstairs.'

'You and the count.'

'Yes.'

'Your husband?'

'Aha.' She laughed. I sat down beside her, without asking her permission because she was certainly modern.

'I wish you would tell me; I don't know where I am,' I said.

She laughed again, in a good mood it seemed. I felt . . . well, I felt that we could get along on this line.

'And where do you want to be?' she asked.

'With *Fräulein* von Rummelsberg and . . . a friend.'

'A friend? *Sie wollen mein Freund sein? Ich habe nie einen ausländischen Freund gehabt.*'

She broke into German to say this and I give it in German

48

because of the ambiguity of German word *Freund* which, like the French *ami,* can mean 'friend' or 'boy-friend'. Thus: 'A friend? You want to be my (boy?) friend? I have never had a foreign (boy?) friend.'

'Then please let me be your first foreign . . . friend.'

'Well, I don't know . . .'

'The count wouldn't like it?'

She smiled but not at me.

'Where is the count today?' I asked.

'Can't you guess?'

'In the East?'

'Yes. He goes over there to see relations of his.'

'They are caught over there, are they?'

'Caught? Yes, caught, if you like.'

'Don't you go over?'

'To the theatre, or the Comic Opera. But I have no relations. My mother was there, you know . . .'

'Weren't you with her?'

'Yes, of course. I was there until I was eight years old. Tell me, do you like Brecht? You should see a Brecht play before you leave. They are very well acted.'

'Yes, I should like to.'

'The Threepenny Opera? That is very good. You should see that.'

'I would certainly go if . . . if you would take me.'

She bit her lower lip. 'Yes,' she said, 'we could go.' She hesitated. 'Next week would be a good time. I will get the tickets if you like. Then we can go through together on the S-Bahn.'

'Where shall we meet? Shall I fetch you?'

'No. We could meet here and then go on to the Zoo station.'

'Yes.'

'It will have to be early. At about this time.'

'Very well.'

'And now I must go.' She looked at her man's watch, bit her lower lip and tried to attract the attention of the waiter.

'Never mind,' I said, 'I'll pay your bill.'

'No. Why should you?'

'You can pay me back next week.'

'Well, I am late. Thank you.'

She rose and walked off, looking back, smiling vaguely, coldly—bumped into a pedestrian, and went on.

I did not follow her but ordered a Steinhaeger, opened *The Times* and read the law reports.

Surely a young man like myself, who has just arranged the first assignment with a girl he purports to admire, should be charged, happy, excited? I became irritable, as I always become irritable when there is some action to be taken, when my private thoughts are forced into public performance.

I was irritated too because I knew this was not a simple assignation at a street corner between a boy and a girl of their own kind, bound only to their jobs and their stoves and their lavatories across the yard. Suzi, I knew, I sensed, was loaded—involved with something unwholesome, with people spewing out a trail backwards to the days of sweet-rationing and beyond. I wanted to carry her away but then I knew she had a mother and suspected something further. The two, sleek von Rummelsbergs—Klaus and Helmuth. I hated Suzi's connection with them and the historical atrocities. How could a beautiful, innocent child like that have anything to do with Germany, the historical Germany? And

Helmuth with whom she lived: was he her decrepit lover?
At Zuntz she had surely flirted with me in a gawky fashion
—the business of friend and boy-friend. So what? Was she
bored with Helmuth? Was he flagging? I was well acquainted with the lechery of young girls (Milan, 1960).

I met her at Zuntz in the following week, as arranged, but
we did not cross to the East on the S-Bahn. As a member of
the military government I could not recognize any East
German officials and was therefore obliged to cross over in
a staff car dressed in full uniform—the only way in which
one could be admitted by the Russians. In the evening it
had to be dress uniform so when I fetched her at Zuntz, I
was wearing a scarlet monkey jacket, wing collar, black
bow-tie, tight-fitting breeches with gold stripes, high boots
and spurs. She, of course, wore a black dress (young, simple,
provincial).

'You aren't meant to cross with me in a staff car,' I
said, irritated because she looked embarrassed at my uniform.

'I could cross by myself.'

'No, no. You see, we have unofficial concessions from the
Russians. If you come out as well as in, then they don't
mind.'

We drove through the checkpoint without stopping. Our
driver was a Cockney whom I found it difficult to understand but he knew his way to the Theater am Schiffbaudamm.

Once there she became less embarrassed than I had expected. The audience ignored us—they had probably seen
allied officers in dress uniform before. Half of them were
young conscripts also in uniform but their tunics were open
at the neck. The rest were a dowdy lot.

In the interval we went to the bar and bought some acorn coffee. Suzi was very polite. I felt old.

'Did you come here when you were young?' I asked.

'Oh yes—once—to a children's thing. That was when Brecht was still alive.'

'It must be boring for you to see The Threepenny Opera again.'

'Oh no. I love it. I have seen it seven or eight times. I went to My Fair Lady five times, too.'

'I must give you the money for the tickets.'

'No, no. I'll pay for them.'

'Of course not.'

'You paid for my drink at Zuntz. Don't you remember?'

'I am sure the tickets cost more than your drink.'

'Well . . .' she grinned, 'they didn't because I smuggled in some black-market money.' She looked furtively around, her gaze stopped over my left shoulder and her face stiffened. I quickly turned round too. There were two men, one a high-ranking People's Army officer, the other in a plain grey suit. Both were middle-aged and the civilian had a long nose. They both looked our way. Suzi looked at me. The bell rang for the second act.

'Who were they?' I asked.

'No one. I didn't know them.'

'It seemed as if you knew them.'

'I just thought he was a policeman, the one in uniform. I thought he might have heard about the money.'

She lied, of course, in the blithe, pure way that women and girls lie to anyone, their mothers, husbands, lovers. With ruthlessness they sacrifice the lesser truth of words and reality to the greater truth of their hormone-cells of intuition. I knew she lied because, as we left the theatre, the two men

52

stood beside us for a moment as we waited at the entrance. They both ignored me but the civilian looked at Suzi and said with a smile:

'*Dein Ami, selbstverständlich.*' Suzi drew in her breath and blushed. They went out in front of us.

'*Dein Ami, selbstverständlich*'—'your (boy?) friend, of course.' But why did he use the French word *ami* instead of the German word *Freund*? Was it, I wondered, that by the word *ami* he did not mean '(boy?) friend' but was using the German slang expression for an American soldier, a GI lover?

I wanted to change out of my ridiculous uniform before having dinner, so we were driven back to my house in the West. It was a government house, too big for me, but because of the peculiar status of Berlin I was classified as a major (I who had never done a day's drill in my life, who did not know how to fire a rifle), and most majors have wives and children. We dismissed the driver. Suzi waited downstairs while I changed.

'It is very nice here,' she said, when I came down.

'I don't like it.'

'Why not?' I did not like it because the windows were double-glazed and the heating was too hot; the furniture was comfortable and dull—in fact it was typical, and that was probably why she liked it.

'Because it is too big,' I said. 'It makes me feel I should have a wife and children.'

'And why not?'

'Why not? I'm only twenty-five and I prefer sleeping alone in a single bed. Up there I swim about in a double one.'

She laughed. 'You are not too young to get married, I should say.'

'Don't you prefer to sleep alone?'

'I . . . don't know,' she said—simply, cleverly.

I had booked a table at a French restaurant on the Tegler-see in the French sector. I drove by the city motor-way and we were there in twenty minutes. The sun had set: it was almost dark. We sat out on the terrace.

'You know,' she said, my Suzi said, 'I like French food but I would not like to have it all the time. Would you? It's too rich.'

'Have you been to France?'

'I've been to Strassburg, riding. But that hardly counts as France.'

'With the count?'

'No, of course not. It was with my mother and Frau Stefan—you know, the woman from the stables.'

Later: I looked straight at her and said: 'You must have known the two men at the theatre. They wouldn't have spoken to you if they hadn't known you.'

'How could I know them? I haven't been to the East since I was eight.'

'You said you went to the theatre.'

'Yes, once or twice. But only to the theatre. I never talked to anyone. Anyway, it's none of your business.'

Later: 'Is your name von Rummelsberg?'

'Why not?'

'I refuse to believe you are married. What is your maiden name?'

'Aha!'

'What is your mother's name?'

She laughed. 'She is von Rummelsberg too.'

'Then you are his niece.'

'No. I am no blood-relation at all.' Her eyes were bright

with the game but she never meant to lose it. Not with wine, nor with riddles, did I find out about her relationship with Helmuth von Rummelsberg.

Otherwise she told me that she studied physiotherapy. That was all. But she was gay and exciting—flirtatious in a young, sultry, German way. And there were her candle-lit green eyes.

I took her back to the Steinplatz.

'Sometimes,' she asked, 'would you come to have supper with me? I would like to pay you back; I am sure it was expensive.'

'Oh, you mustn't worry. I am very well paid. But I would like to come. Would it be with the count?'

She tittered. 'No, better when he is away again. I will ring you up.'

So what? I had had some hours with her. I knew that she was studying physiotherapy, that the count was jealous too and she lived with him. That was all.

II

Helmuth von Rummelsberg / Katerina von Treblitz: 1930

The final year in the Military Academy in Tilsit for Helmuth. (Klaus by then must have been in the regular army.) Instead, however, of military strategy, Helmuth was preoccupied with the strategy of seduction.

How clever he had been to persuade a girl, a thoroughbred girl like Katerina, to do it. How completely he had won the final fight, the culmination of all the fights of their childhood. She had lain on her back, supine—and without

55

even twisting her arm, she had given in. At last his strength had told and he had squashed her for good and all on the floor of the forester's hut.

He had not seen much . . . but he had tugged at her underclothes and stuffed about under her petticoats and rutted until she had shown him in (some elastic of hers had cut into his skin). But once the fight was finished, that was that.

Back at the cadet school, then, and his imagination spoiled for another fight of that kind, his images were as ideal as . . . my image of Suzi . . . the statues in the Bode museum. (One thing he knew now. He liked neither to bugger nor to be buggered and, a cadet-officer, could make his feelings plain.) What a shock it was, then, when the following summer, in an attic at Kassow, he saw that her breasts were no larger than drop scones; her thighs were tubular; there were spots on her back and, more intimately, the hair that grew on her body was neither blonde like the hair on her head, nor brown like the streaks in it, but orange (not orange like the citrus fruit but a whitened orange as celery or chicory would be if they were orange instead of green).

The uncovered straw mattress was brown: the leather buttons that held the cloth to the horse-hair were a darker brown. There were cobwebs and dust, streaked dust, on the windows. The sun shone in. It was not warm and he had pulled his trousers up again, but she lay, looking at him, unsmiling (lovingly), open, her orange hair like a fly trap.

The hieroglyph itself was hidden by this hair and even so seemed much smaller than it had been in the baby; but the statement now came out of her eyes . . . and so . . . though he was shocked, disgusted at her physical defects—he was profoundly caught in love by her eyes. Her yellow hair hung back by the black enamelled bars of the bed: the skin

56

between the yellow flow and orange clump was as if covered in sand—a desert, her eyes, always, the drawing mirage, her mouth the water hole he was making for, the hieroglyph the water hole he had left. His hand was a spider or a camel, the spots were cactuses, the nipples, hardly larger than his own, the ant-hills, her breasts the dunes, her cheekbones the horizon, etc.

So high-flown, romantic, is a septic imagination clamped with love onto a carcass.

'If they knew . . .' she said and hiccupped.

They met every day and Helmuth felt there was not enough strength left in his legs to grip the sides of his horse.

She was gay. They planned the improvements he would make with his money to her home when her parents died.

'Oh, they would make it over to us now, if we were married.'

They planned a career for him. He had no wish to stay in the army: and, having passed the examinations at the cadet-school, was to start in the Foreign Office in Berlin that autumn. When he had finished his first year they would be married and she would join him.

Gradually this was understood by everyone.

'It's lucky,' said her aunt, 'that he's taller than she is. He can't see those nostrils. Nor her gums.'

'Good,' Klaus said to Katerina, 'I always wanted you in the family.'

Even the young Edward, who alone of the three prayed on his knees each night, was pleased; and smiled about the attic assignments. He saw to it that their mother kept out of the way.

(In midsummer Katerina went to the dentist in Stolp.)

If Helmuth thought he had won a final fight, he was wrong. Often he would know what she wanted by a tackle in the woods or he would tumble her; and she was rougher now than she had been when she was thirteen, grabbing him where she could, where she wanted. Helmuth protested.

'Pfui,' she puffed, taking leaves out of her hair.

'How would you like it if I kicked you there?' he asked.

She blushed. Helmuth imagined it was because she was still only eighteen.

Katerina von Treblitz / Dr Strepper: 1929 (i)

Katerina, I imagine, had not only spots on her back, but bad teeth too. Therefore she went to the dentist in Stolp.

The dentist, Dr Strepper, had consulting rooms in a street off the market. Katerina always went at eleven in the morning when the sun shone in the front room where she waited, reading magazines. The surgery was at the back, overlooking a small garden. Dr Strepper's was the first town house she had ever entered and she was fascinated by its perpendicularity and gloom.

Dr Strepper was thin with a pointed beard. He was benign but his eyes rolled and when his face came down close to her face she smelt the antiseptic, the laundered coat, pipe tobacco and his body. He was known to be the best dentist in Stolp (the von Rummelsbergs went to him) but he talked casually, incidentally, about her teeth and most of all about history and other dentists.

'Do you know, countess, that there are Germans who go to Polish and Jewish dentists? It is difficult to imagine, isn't it, but it is true. Don't think I mind for professional reasons:

58

I have a full list of patients. But do they know, I wonder, the risks they run? The Poles are incompetent. To give modern dental equipment to the Poles is . . . ha ha . . . like giving a clock to a monkey. Not that they use the equipment. Their only idea of treatment is to pull the tooth out with nut-crackers. The Jews—their only idea is to keep the tooth in and stuff it with gold. They say it is the only form of savings neither the government nor inflation can get at but it is also the only form of savings that sabotages the German economy. Had you thought of that, countess? Perhaps not, but I think that is just what they have in mind. I tell you if all the gold in Jewish teeth was melted down and put in our national reserves we would have no balance of payments problem. As it is we pay prohibitive taxes, the economy is depressed and we all suffer except the Jews. It is high time a clean sweep was made of these traitors and the Polish bunglers too, don't you think, countess? We had put up with them long enough.

'I suppose you eat chocolate, countess. That is what makes the holes in your teeth. Of course chocolate is difficult for a young girl to resist but have you ever thought, countess, who makes the chocolate? The Quakers. And who are the Quakers, countess? They are pacifists. They are those who use their money to prevent Germany rearming but do not hesitate to make it out of rotting German teeth. I never touch chocolate, countess, and I would heartily advise you to summon up the strength to resist it yourself. You may think I exaggerate, countess, but bad teeth are passed on to children and children with bad teeth eat soft foods. What does that mean? It means they are deficient in the brittle, scouring substances that build strong bodies. I am not saying these Quakers are conscious of it but it is for them a convenient coincidence that their chocolates will debilitate the German race over three or four generations.'

Katerina tried not to laugh. 'But if we didn't eat chocolate, Dr Strepper, you would have no work to do.'

'My dear countess, I would gladly, gladly starve if there were no rotten German teeth. But I would take to another profession, the army perhaps . . . if we had an army to talk of.'

'But you are such a good dentist.'

'Countess Katerina, my best customer is my son who has never had a bad tooth in his life. Why not? He never eats a sweet or a piece of chocolate. I would never allow it and quite soon he saw the wisdom of it. Günter is a good boy.'

Dr Strepper gesticulated with the drill. 'And he has no need to be a dentist. He is in politics, you know.'

Sometimes Katerina would stay to lunch. This embarrassed her but they knew which train she took back so she could not always refuse. Then she climbed the dark stairs to the second floor where the sun came into the parlour and the dining-room looked over the garden.

Mrs Strepper was placid and irritated her husband. When he had another patient to see, Katerina would try to talk to Mrs Strepper but she never said much; she was fearless and contented and seemed (to Katerina) not to notice that she irritated her husband—nor did he seem to notice that he was irritated by her.

At twelve Dr Strepper would come up and, soon after, his son Günter, breathless in his brown uniform. Günter was always teasing and rowdy with Katerina—treating her like a little girl of ten. He was thickset (I know) like his mother and like her in every other characteristic except his eyes which came from his father. Katerina's attitude towards him was polite but reticent—first because she thought him (and his parents) rather common and then because the von Rummelsberg boys said they did not like him and she knew why.

Klaus, Helmuth, Edward von Rummelsberg / Günter Strepper: 1928

Klaus, Helmuth and Edward attended Dr Strepper. Afterwards Günter went with them to the station and the four sat in a coffee-house waiting for the train.

'That is a smashing girl,' said Helmuth, nodding at a dark girl sitting across the room with a private soldier.

'Ugh. Not her, she's Jewish,' said Günter Strepper. 'That soldier is mad.'

'Is she Jewish?' asked Klaus. 'How do you know? I've never seen a Jew . . . I don't think.'

'Of course you have,' said Günter. 'Look at that black greasy hair. And if she turns round again you'll see her hooked nose and shifty little eyes.'

'I wouldn't marry a Jew,' said Helmuth, 'but I don't see why a soldier shouldn't have a bang-up with her when he's on leave.'

'She looks to me like a student,' said Edward.

'You don't know much, you lot, do you?' said Strepper. 'If you get your thing into a Jewish girl, you've had it. You know the stuff the girl leaks out . . . the stuff to help it slide in? Well, Jewish girls are as juicy as niggers only with Jewish girls it's acid. It'll burn the skin off your tail, quick as anything. That's why Jewish men are circumcised. And I'll tell you another thing. Jewish girls have black hairs growing out of their tits.'

If Katerina's jaw was stiff she would have lentil purée. The Streppers got their good teeth into pig-knuckles and cabbage.

As soon as they had finished lunch Strepper would rush out again. After all, there was an election campaign and his party had to make up for the losses of 1928. Katerina was not interested in politics. She thought Günter Strepper's brown uniform ridiculous and, though her father was an old Knappist, she thought, like the von Rummelsbergs, that the National Socialists were a disreputable rabble. What (to her) was appalling about Günter Strepper was that his hair was cropped, frizzy and greasy and the mouth covering his perfect teeth was so proper that it could never kiss. Yet she knew he thought he was fine-looking—his head tilted upwards not because he was smaller than she, but, with or without her, it was the visionary stance. Then there were sometimes wet patches under his arms—doubtless some of the alkaline juices that were wrung out of him (dripping everywhere) by the conflict between revolutionary sentiments and respectable instincts.

Klaus von Rummelsberg: 1930

At that time Klaus was stationed at B. with the Third Pomeranian regiment. He served as adjutant to the divisional commander.

The commander said: 'You've come at the right time, von Rummelsberg. No more marking time, if you ask me. And you won't see one of these men as private soldiers in a few months' time. We've trained them all as NCOs. Once the word is given, they'll take on ten rusty civilians apiece and make them into the privates. It won't be long now.'

'The treaty, sir . . .'

'No one cares about the treaty now, von Rummelsberg.'

Klaus worked on the contingency plans, and thought such thoughts as: 'If only the Americans would cancel the Allied war debts—then they would cancel the reparations.'

In the mess in the evening he would drink with his friends from the cadet-school days and once a week dine with the general, his wife, his daughter (Waltraut). His friends and the general were all good imperialists whose hearts beat faster when they heard that the Crown Prince's son was to be on the autumn manoeuvres. There was another clique of officers who had not been to the cadet-school—mostly seconded from voluntary cadet corps to prepare for the expansion of the army. They sat apart and talked quietly together. They were considered a dull lot (by Klaus and his friends) and were thought to be up to no good because their standards of turn-out were perfunctory; their boots were not as polished, their tunics not as well pressed (as those of Klaus and his friends). Klaus, however, was as kind and courteous to them as he was to the general's daughter. He escorted her to the regimental ball. He was charming and polite even though (to him) all women had a nasty smell. The middle-class officers might smell, too, but he often talked to them.

'I can't think why you bother, Rummels,' his friends would say, hacking at the orderly's shins with their boots, 'they're such a common lot.'

'Well, they are German officers, aren't they?'

'Seconded.'

'Officers all the same.'

63

Seconded and despised though they were, the small group of officers did not seem pleased (to Klaus) when Klaus sauntered over. Occasionally, however, and then time after time, they would revert to their normal talk about the trial (of National Socialist army officers) in his presence. Klaus would even join in.

'It's ridiculous trying to keep politics out of the army. If a man's a soldier, he's bound to take his duties as a citizen just as seriously. After all the president is a soldier,' he said.

Those around him made wry faces.

'The president may have been a soldier,' said one of them, 'but you'd hardly think so now.'

'How do you mean?' said Klaus.

'He won't appoint the one person who would do something for the army and for Germany.'

'Schleicher?'

'Hitler.'

'Oh, Hitler,' said Klaus. 'He may be for rearmament but isn't he for a few other things too?'

'Social justice.'

'Well, perhaps you're right.'

Gradually Klaus spent more time with his new friends and less with his old ones.

'I don't know how you stand those guttersnipes,' the latter said of the former.

'Aren't you rather bored by those swashbucklers?' the former said of the latter.

Klaus did become bored by his old friends who only talked of the Tilsit days and the great war. He was more interested in the future and in social ideas. The military way of life was not an end in itself. His ancestors the Teutonic knights had put their military skill to a religious and social purpose. So too did the group of officers, who later confessed to him that they were in touch with the National Socialist Party.

Anton A., the most fluent, the tank expert, would talk for several hours after dinner in a low, persistent voice.

'What is the point of an army? To defend Germany? To defend what kind of Germany? A lot of swindlers and sheep? To police money-grubbing at home and abroad? You know, Rummelsberg, as well as I do, that the destiny of Germany amounts to more than that—and to more than the fancy-dress parades of your friends over there. Either Germany has a noble mission or it is nothing. We should stand for order, archetypal order: but what is Germany known for these days? Its night spots. Its prostitutes. Its gambling casinos. Its strikes. Its balance of payments problems. Vice and weak government. We've reached a stage of helplessness when even the shoddy bands of gypsies to the east and west of us can laugh their heads off with impunity. You know a Pole, Rummelsberg. His smell's his only strong point—yet he's laughing. And the French. Laughing through their petticoats. We could smash them in a stroke and teach them a lesson, God's lesson, if only we had a leader.'

Or again: 'The country is falling apart, Rummelsberg, you can see it. The workers are just out for more wages and the businessmen for profits. Neither side cares about the nation. You'd think the workers would be grateful enough that they aren't starving but no, they want more money. And this question of profits! My father is a businessman so I know something about it. He's rolling in money but all the same he sweats it out over profits. The company, the mills, are all private, so there's no need to attract investment. No, it's just that he wouldn't dare show his face in his club if his puff-fish profits weren't a little bigger each year. And as you know there have been mill closures—so the money has to come out of the workers' wages and they don't like that. If we had a leader, a purpose, a mission, my father would forget his profits like that.' He snapped his fingers. 'He never worried as much before the war. We need someone to tell my father and the workers to get on with it, instead of everybody asking everybody else what they want every five minutes. Keep asking and they'll come up with one answer—Bolshevism'—at the enunciation of that word the whole room went still —'and Bolshevism, you know, we all know, is the cancer, the anti-Christ, the poison of conscience, the negation of all values . . .'

Anton A. never needed to continue beyond this point: everyone there knew what Bolshevism meant.

Klaus came to agree with Anton's whole diagnosis of the situation. He was (it seems) the nicest (to all) if (to some) the simplest of the von Rummelsberg brothers. Being decent he was uneasy and had always been uneasy about, say, his spanking motor-car, his horses, his stock in Pomeranian railways and Silesian brown coal and the way it contrasted with the von Treblitzes' battered Mercedes painted up with household paint, their one good horse (Katerina's) and their uneasiness at harvest time.

He was the eldest son of an ancient Pomeranian family—his arm was moulded to protect the weak, the unfortunate (Katerina)—not to creak new leather or lean on table-tops. Show him another Barbarossa, another Frederick the Great, and he would follow his country, his people, his cause. He had no greater love than Germany, no sweeter vision than grateful children playing in the barns of the settled land behind the fortress (his arm), their hair as gold as the corn, their eyes as blue as the sky. What was the body, if not an encasement of love, whirling within love, of his mother, his brothers, the groom, Peter, the women who worked in the house; Katerina, her father, the old Knappist, her mother with the tattered skirts and soft voice; did it (this love) not radiate from the room through the walls to the Kassow plantations—over the fields, down the road to Stolp, even to the shop-keepers, and east to Danzig, the merchants (their daughters, his ancestor, Traugott's bride)? Or West, did it not reach the Oder, Stettin; down over the lakes to Berlin— even to the grey-faced workers and the fallen frumps on the Friedrichstrasse? His family stretched to the Rhine and like an animal he loved and would fight for his family first and for the faith of his family, the order of his family, and its way in the world. So while his friends grew drunker, he joined the new knights and they brought him in touch with their contact in the National Socialist Party—Günter Strepper.

Klaus von Rummelsberg / Günter Strepper: 1930

Klaus had not met Günter Strepper since the incident in the station coffee-house two years before, which he remembered quite clearly. Initially his distaste for Strepper remained.

Strepper was extremely glad to have enrolled Klaus, and persuaded him to leave the old army for the new. Klaus became the first of the Pomeranian gentry to join the National Socialist Party and what (to Strepper) was Strepper's position if it was not set against a back-cloth of Junker estates?

Now Strepper was not (for Klaus) as persuasive as

67

Anton A. but Klaus was already convinced and had accepted from Anton that Strepper—like Hitler, Goebbels and Himmler—was the best kind of man to lead the party. He was a man in the middle. Those like Klaus and Anton, Anton pointed out, were unconvincing revolutionaries. They must accept that. The new order of knights required humility. Klaus saw that he was right. The bakery and brewery men who were members of the party obeyed and adulated Strepper but mimicked Klaus's high-German accent.

Strepper was able. The organization of the party in Stolp was superb. In the election campaign no other party could put itself in the field. Posters were torn down as soon as they were put up; meetings were invariably broken up. Strepper gave commands and they were obeyed; he made the kind of coarse joke that shocked Klaus but amused the bakery and brewery men.

Strepper knew the streets of Stolp. He knew what the people at one end thought of the people at the other: just as Egon had known all about the ferry and the fishing-boats at Swinemünde. If the shop-keepers and artisans of Stolp were not the masses, they were at least Germans of whom Klaus knew nothing.

Strepper knew the German people because he was of the German people. He was (for Klaus) the link between Klaus and Klaus's duty—his historical, hereditary duty. He was the knight's squire, the officer's NCO—the one with the common touch who brought the plight of the miserable to the eye of his master. If it was apparently the other way round in this case—if Klaus was always a rank below Strepper in the Party—this was the result of the times they lived in, a last tribute to the democratic consensus. Strepper

68

could have the rank if it pleased the people that one of their kind should have it. Klaus would ride a temporal mule if his spirit was on the charger. That he never doubted. Strepper could not do without him—why else did he always keep him at his side? Strepper had his own half-baked ideas but Klaus had the cohesive vision. Strepper could communicate his ideas to the people—Klaus evolve his in communion with God. The miserable collation of prejudice that made up the National Socialist philosophy in the minds of many of its adherents would fuse in Klaus's vision with the historic destiny of Germany as it fused in the mind of Hitler himself. Klaus deferred to Hitler because he, he alone, combined the qualities of both Klaus and Strepper; he was man of the people, man of action and yet visionary and philosopher. Destiny, working as it so often did, through a gigantic paradox, had chosen this Viennese decorator to be leader of the German People as it had chosen a carpenter's son to be the Son of God.

Edward von Rummelsberg: 1930

Meanwhile Edward von Rummelsberg prayed on his knees: 'Oh God, save Germany. Save us from our quarrels, dissensions; the prejudice, hatred, violence. Teach me how to overcome my own prejudices, my own instinctive selfishness. Teach me to see the right path for Germany, for Germany entire and alone. I am your centurion, oh God. I shall live by the sword and die by it but I pray to you to have me in heaven nonetheless. Teach me true charity to my fellow men—to the Poles, the Jews and other Germans; teach me the meaning of true charity in our age.'

Chapter Four

I

WHAT WAS THE SITUATION? I was in love with a stranger who persistently remained a stranger, who would not tell me her real name, who hid her background from me. She lived with an old man—aging, rather—not old enough for me to be sure that he was not her occasional lover. This man was the brother of an older man, a sleek West German, Christian Democrat, ex-SS, whom I was professionally assigned to investigate for my country, Great Britain—for my people, the British.

Happy coincidence, one might think, this link between private and public life: but it was nothing of the sort. Knowledge of Klaus meant indirect knowledge of Helmuth, Suzi's sugar-daddy, and knowledge of him meant indirect knowledge of her: thus the presence of a girl who was hardly interested in me and whom I might otherwise have forgotten was forced on me by my professional duties.

The poor devil Edward was presumed deep frozen under the Ukraine, rotting only in the summer months: but that was only supposition. I had the historical facts on other matters—elections, movements of population, mobilization orders—and some annals of the family—diaries, albums, registrations, certifications—and it was not hard to imagine the rest (the cherry-blossom that year, the silt at the bottom of the stream). The result of it all—a steady progress in my investigation, the satisfaction of my superiors that I was doing something, and more love for Suzi.

If I had known she was completely uninterested in me (that the old man was enough because that, I was sure, was the question), I would have been contented as a voyeur. I might have taken a room in the Steinplatz hotel and watched her in their flat with Zeiss binoculars. But I could not be certain: after all, she had come to the theatre with me and to dinner afterwards. She had said she would ring me up.

All this time my colleagues were leading the lives of men of action—becoming involved with the nuances of our precious Allied Rights, West German intrusions into them, East German manoeuvres around them, Russian inscrutability and American stupidity, while I was preoccupied with rather inactive love.

I tried, now and then, to put her out of my mind, but it was not easy. If one accepts Stendhal on the subject of love, the process of decrystallization is as necessary to falling out of love as the process of crystallization is to falling in love. The latter had happened without my noticing it and from a distance—the distance across the café Zuntz. I might have counted on proximity to disillusion me—it always had done before—but this time it failed. She (Suzi) was physically flawless: there was no boil on her neck or smell of sweat from her arms on which to concentrate. I told myself that she was vulgar, trite, boring—a typical little physiotherapist —but there was always this air of mystery about her which persistently suggested that she was something more.

Just when I thought I had convinced myself that she was

71

common—it is easy enough for German girls to seem so to Englishmen—my mind leapt back to her physical flawlessness. I could not escape one fact about myself—I was a fastidious person, for all my escapades. Adultery and fornication left me disgusted—I never persisted in them. Up till then I had never had an affair that had lasted more than a week—and these were only possible through a forced schizophrenia induced by alcohol, whereby my voluptuous imaginings attempted realization. It only happened when I was drunk: when I was sober the two—the imaginings and the reality—would not meet and the affair came to an end. This had been the case with the officer's wife, and the girl who designed textiles.

Suzi had been around now for six months. I had talked to her several times—I had taken her out to dinner—and she remained a person with whom I would gladly have performed all the obscenities of love—whose body I would gladly have fused with my own, at any point, with incessant hugs and hookings, sucks and swings. Whatever German shopgirlishness I may have seen in her manner, these were strong, self-evident factors about the situation.

My mother and sister would not have appreciated this line of justification—they would have thought Suzi very common, title or not; and even Armand thought it a negative basis for love. 'You don't think she is wonderful—you think all the other women in the world are revolting.' Perhaps that was true. Perhaps that was what love meant to Englishmen. Perhaps the start of it was as negative as that—but it was growing at that time into something more formidable (and even when I thought it was a considerable passion, I had no idea of how great that love, or any love, could and would be).

It did grow; it had grown without my noticing it. To start

with she had been just a pretty girl—a Zuntz or Kempinski girl—a possible pick-up or easy lay; then she became the pretty girl who was always with the old man; then the wife, daughter, niece or mistress of Count Helmuth von Rummelsberg; then the young countess involved with Nazism and Pomerania. Suzi's prettiness now eases over into the shades of beauty—her name is surely not just Suzi but Jolande or Mechtild. She is an aristocrat with the blood of the Teutonic knights. She is a princess in modern, urban disguise—as well as a creature whose limbs I would gladly wear as a scarf around my neck; whose porous, leaking, folded skin I would squeeze in my mouth as happily as a halved orange.

If these two reasons—her beauty, her mystery—are not enough, then look to me for the explanation of why I loved her. She was my type: she had my sense of humour (whether this was English or Prussian, I do not know). Or, if you like, I loved her because she looked like the girl wearing fish-net stockings and bending a riding-crop in a pornographic photograph I had seen at sixteen; or because she had the same eyelashes as a fourteen-year-old boy at school; or because she was good-natured; or because she was German and I was tired of English girls; or because she smiled sadly; or because her bosom had the same proportions as my mother's when she nursed me; or because, quite simply . . .

She asked me to dinner.

I was an hour late. Germans eat at half-past six. I had forgotten and arrived at half-past seven. She had lit two candles which had melted half-way down. I first saw the Karmerstrasse flat by candlelight—though daylight still shone in through the drawn curtains.

I could see at once, even by candlelight, that the decoration and furnishing of the room was unusual. Helmuth had either been able to salvage many of his family possessions or had bought pieces of eighteenth-century furniture since the war. There were several of them in the first room—black lacquered chinoiserie—a large cupboard, a table and six chairs, a sideboard and a sofa. It was not a large room. The walls were lined in grey silk and on them were hung three paintings by Delvaux—dark classical landscapes, naked women with prominent mounds of pubic hair and faces like Suzi's (the faces)—simple and round with large eyes.

'Would you sit there?' she asked me, pulling out one of the chairs. 'If you wait a minute . . .' she left the room.

There were five plates, four with a different kind of sliced sausage—liver sausage, garlic sausage, a larger sausage with small chunks of white fat, and Italian salami. On the fifth plate there was sliced, smoked cheese. There was butter in small, wrapped pats, black bread already curling at the edges (it must have been laid out for more than an hour). The knives and spoons were of Scandinavian design; there were plain white plates, cups and saucers.

I was left a few minutes alone. Then Suzi came back with a tray carrying baked eggs and a tea pot. I felt a pleasant suffusion in some system of nerves deep in my body: it is her unselfconscious assumption of domestic duties, I thought, that is a German girl's most charming characteristic.

'I made some tea because you are English,' she said.

She sat down and we started. Only the salt and pepper were in cut-crystal containers. In this tent of his luxury and elegance, the pots and pans were hers.

'This is very fine,' I said, waggling my fingers at the walls.

'Oh, do you think so?' she answered—pointing, smiling, blushing.

'Did you decorate the flat?'

'I helped.'

'Do you like Delvaux?'

A blush of a different kind. 'No, those are Helmuth's. I think they are . . . rude.'

She quickly started talking about other painters—then about films, plays and novels. She was up to date. I asked her if she had read anything by Céline.

'Is he French? No. I don't speak French at all. Helmuth has some French books through there.'

The tea was weak but the eggs, bubbling in their small crenellated white bowls, had been cooked in sour cream and tasted very good.

'Who taught you to cook eggs this way?'

'Oh, my mother. She loves them like this—with chives. Only I couldn't find any chives today. It is easy to do, you see.'

Her lazy thighs.

After that we went through to another, larger room lined with books—not old editions of Thomas Mann and Hermann Hesse, nor the collected works of Stefan George and Jean Paul in Gothic script, but a very complete library of international pornography. There were paintings in this room (a Renoir) and sculpture (a Maillol) on the one wall where the shelves were waist-high.

One end of the room was taken up by a fitted sofa—it seemed like a step up to the wall—in button leather that went back parallel to the floor, then gradually inclined. At one end there was a pile of grey silk cushions. To the side of them there was a leather chair and beside it (between it and the sofa) a small table and lamp. This, I thought, was where he sat to read. The whole room stank of him, but of a different man to the one I had supposed.

There was nothing nostalgic or pathetic about the apartment—it was a fine, opulent, cosmopolitan place. The only thing that did not fit in it was Suzi and her pathetic cups and saucers.

'Do you have a room of your own?' I asked.

'I have a . . . yes . . . a little one down there.'

'What sort of room?'

'If my girl-friends come to see me, we go in there.'

'You have girl-friends?'

'Of course I have.'

'When do you see them?'

'At the hospital, but sometimes they come and have coffee in my room.'

'Shouldn't we be there?'

'No. Why? I use the whole apartment when Helmuth isn't here.'

'Where is he?'

'In West Germany.'

'Does he know I am here?'

'I don't have to tell him everything, do I? I don't have to tell you, either.'

Suzi may not have liked being asked questions but she saw that such a form of conversation interested me and so—perhaps like other girls—would rather put up with the interrogation than lose my attention.

'Would you like to listen to the gramophone?' She put on some chamber music.

'Who is this by?' I asked.

'Oh, I don't know. It's one of Helmuth's records.'

I lay back on the sofa and crossed my legs. Suzi remained standing, then sat down on a chair—not the leather chair but another.

76

'Do you have a girl-friend in England?' she asked.

'No.'

'You should have.'

'Why?'

'Well, you are quite old. You are twenty-five years old, aren't you?'

'Yes.'

'Well, soon you will be too old. No one will marry you. But just now it should not be too difficult. You are not so ugly.'

'No, but love . . . you cannot just decide to love. It has to happen.'

'Poof. You are more sentimental than I am. Do you really believe in great passion?' she laughed. 'And now you look quite sad.'

'Don't you believe in love?'

'In love? I don't know, look at Elizabeth Taylor. All the film stars are always in love with someone, marrying them, then falling in love with someone else. I want to lead a very ordinary life. Have children. One husband. See him off to his work, then the children off to school. You know. Perhaps that is dull. Perhaps I am a dull person.'

'I should not have thought so.'

'Thank you for saying so but I am afraid you are wrong.'

'You have very beautiful ankles.' Her ears went red. 'Ankles,' I repeated.

'Does that mean I am not dull?'

'Yes.'

'Oh. I wonder.'

'Stand up so that I can see your ankles,' I said. She did. She wore a plain red woollen dress that came down to her knees. Inelegant. Her ears, half hidden by her hair, were red again.

'This is not a beauty contest,' she said.

'Then come and sit here.'

'Why?'

'Or show me your room.'

'No.' She sat on the sofa three feet from me. I could not sense what she wanted or expected me to do. She was probably embarrassed and would have liked me to go. I took her hand. She let me drag it slowly towards me, two loose fingers falling into the dips made by the buttons in the leather upholstery.

'Could I have a drink?' I asked.

'Of course,' she leapt up. 'What would you like? Some beer or schnapps?'

'Perhaps some schnapps.' She fetched a bottle and some glasses from a cupboard and put them on the table by the leather chair on which she sat down. She poured me a glass, I fetched it, sat on the sofa again, and drank it down.

'Won't you sit here again?' I asked her.

She looked at me sternly, yet at the same time as if she would cry. Without a word she stood up and came across to where I was sitting.

I helped myself to another glass of schnapps. We said nothing. I took her hand again. It was as cold as before and dragged as lifelessly.

'Your hand is cold,' I said. She looked at me again, sternly, quivering. I pulled her towards me and kissed her on the lips which were as cold as her fingers. Her lips: they were as lifeless as her hands. They neither opened nor shut. My lips: they opened and mouthed around, conventionally; they moved, by their impression, all that was to be moved of the soft skin covering her gums.

I looked up. Her nose: straight. Her eyes: faint sternness —otherwise nothing.

But: the lower half of her body remained where she had sat on the sofa—three feet from the lower half of my body. Her trunk therefore leaned towards me: her neck was strained round. Hence her immobility was not lifelessness. Every muscle was strained for her mouth to be where it was. Only the mouth was still.

'I am very fond of you,' I said.

The same empty face.

I kissed her again, put my hand over her ears, leant back and pulled her with me. Our teeth bumped together. I smiled. She did not. I raised myself on my elbow: she now lay on her back—without expression. I kissed her again and put my face on her shoulder—stroking her neck with my fingers, etc.

'Don't you like me?' I asked her.

'Yes, I do,' she said quickly. No smile.

'Then . . . has no one kissed you before?'

She did not answer but took my tie in her left hand and pulled it, sliding her hand down it and squeezing it, over and over again, as a hand squeezes milk from a cow's udder.

I kissed her again. The record stopped. I pulled her chin down so that it came down onto her chest. Then, with my thumb on her chin, I pushed up beneath her nose with the side of my index finger. Her mouth opened. I kissed her again, my mouth open too.

If now my helicine arteries dilated and the flow of blood increased, it was not from any stimulation at the spinal centre. Her hands lay limply on the leather—mine clutched her shoulders, then one pressed her waist. What, then, passed down the pelvic para-sympathetic nerves from the

79

brain? Which senses gave the orders to the arteries? I saw a cheap red dress—a small string of pearls which may have been real or false, a neck, nose, lips, mouth, eyes—all stern and static. Only the fair hair was fluid. I smelt a cheap scent, leather and, when I exhaled, schnapps. I touched the skin of her neck, her hair, her squashy lips, the wool of her dress—then nylon, more skin, more nylon—there—and the blood pumped, no more, no less, through the helicine arteries. Was it the natural fibres or the artificial ones? An unreal question because the flow of the blood had come before the touch of the hand. The message that was sent from the brain down these parasympathetic nerves was not from sight, smell or touch. There were the higher centres and it was from them. The arteries opened not for the hair, the lips, the skin or the stockings but for a creature, a soul—Suzi, Suzi von Rummelsberg.

As I had thought, Suzi was no pushover. Each time my fingers, twisted in elastic, came near to what was sought by the higher regions of my brain, she lurched. She was deferential but the message from the higher centres of her brain led not to her glands but to the strong muscles of her thighs and a lurch.

When I left she was still quivering and my blood still flowed, if in a more desultory way.

Then I came upon the final personage (the Jew). He too came through the file on Klaus von Rummelsberg.

Next day. I was happy to have bungled the seduction of Suzi. I was still free of her. I returned to work—sat warm, alone, in my office. Other business was soon over and I was back at the file, looking at the inescapable fact which was also the missing clue: when Klaus returned to Germany after the war, he must have been vetted by the American authorities.

Gerry Stone—the American Political Adviser. We knew he was the most powerful American official in Germany. The others, with higher ranks—the general, the Ambassador in Bonn—were decorations. Stone was the most intelligent. Since his position was related to mine, he did not refuse to see me, though I knew that his black telephone was the one linked to Washington and Western Germany. (If I had snatched it and blown hard, it might have been into THE PRESIDENT's ear. But Gerry was always modest—as if the telephone only led to the switch-board.)

Gerry Stone and his secretary: he was small, broad-shouldered and had a large head. He had black hair and a large nose. He was one of those people who made me feel guilty, arrogant and embarrassed because I was taller than he was and my body had grown more in conformity with the Hellenic ideal.

His secretary, Miss Baedler: she spoke excellent English, was taller than her employer. She wore dark blue suits, like an air-hostess, which were well pressed. The skirt uphols-tered her thighs like the seat of an aeroplane. She had mouse-brown hair, a modulated face, pig eyes.

Gerry Stone (I thought) came from New York—he was said to have a Brooklyn accent but to me it was just American. He was cheerful and open, in the American man-ner. When I went to see him, as always he opened his hand, also large, also covered in black hair, and stretched it out to shake mine.

'I hope Mary's all right,' I said (his wife).

'Fine, fine.'

81

'And the girls?'

'The girls are fine, fine. Now what can I do for you?'

'Do you know this Klaus von Rummelsberg?'

'Yeah. Yeah. There was this trouble . . .'

'Exactly. Well, we wanted to check.'

'I don't think you have to worry about him.'

'No, but check. There is British public opinion.'

'Yeah. Well, what would you like to know?'

'What you know about him. You must have vetted him after the war.'

'Yes, well . . . Miss Baedler . . . if my British friend made eyes at you, would you perhaps bring him a cup of coffee?'

'Certainly, Mr Stone.'

Miss Baedler left the room (unit built with her skirt on).

'I'll have to be quick,' Stone went on. 'We don't like discussing West German affairs in front of our German staff. Von Rummelsberg . . . we dealt with him when he reappeared after the war. As far as we are concerned, he is a political innocent—taken in by Strepper. You know that he acted as Strepper's aide? The only thing we could have pinned on von Rummelsberg was his complicity with Strepper's war crimes but what was the point? He told us what he knew about Strepper, lay low, wrote his memoirs or something, and now is in the Bundestag.'

'That's all?'

'Yeah, that's it. There was some family connection with Strepper, I think. Both came from Pomerania, you know. I think . . . I'd guess that von Rummelsberg's position in Bonn is based on the refugee organizations. They're tough as hell to deal with but he's a tough old lion if a stuffed one and more or less has them in hand.'

'How were Strepper and von Rummelsberg related, do you know?'

'No, I don't think they were related, quite ... perhaps just friends or neighbours.'

'Is there anything on the other brothers?'

'The other von Rummelsberg brothers? No. One, I think, is dead. The other, Helmuth, lives here in West Berlin.'

'Yes, do you know him?'

'Not now. He was a diplomat, but these days he's in the theatre, or something like that.'

'When did you know him?'

'I came across him here in Berlin both before the war and after. You see, I was born a Berliner. I didn't leave until 1930.'

'I never knew that. I always thought you were ... American born. Why did you leave?'

'I'm a Jew.'

So it seemed. Miss Baedler, who was certainly listening to our conversation or was summoned by a secret bell, came in with two cups of coffee.

'I hope your daughters still like Berlin,' I said.

'They like it even better now, thank you. You must come and see us sometime.'

There was me and there was Suzi: with Suzi there was Helmuth and with Helmuth his brother Klaus, Katerina and now this Gerry Stone or Gerhard Stein as he was called in those days. Now, with an Anglicized name, the German Jew has become an American Jew—but from whatever community, he is the Jew in this story: and there is the Jew's persecutor, Günter Strepper, who himself had negroid hair. He chased out the Jew. Strepper with Stein and Strepper with Klaus.

83

II

Helmuth von Rummelsberg / Gerhard Stein: 1930

Helmuth went to the Foreign Office in Berlin, known in the Cadet School as the madhouse (*Idiotenhaus*), in the autumn of 1930. This was one month before the elections. He stayed in the house of a second cousin near the Grünewald. Gerhard Stein also started that year. Helmuth was urged by his friends to ignore the Jew but, like Klaus, he considered himself above the prejudices held by the middle classes and so they became friends. Of that generation of diplomats, Stein and von Rummelsberg were the most brilliant—Stein more brilliant but von Rummelsberg more suitable. Stein was squat and a Jew. Only someone as tall and well-connected as von Rummelsberg could get away with keeping the company of 'pebble' Stein.

Gerhard Stein asked Helmuth von Rummelsberg to visit him in his parents' home, which was not, to Helmuth's relief, in the Grenadierstrasse but in the Tiergarten. Helmuth hesitated but finally went one afternoon.

The Jewish apartment in pre-war Berlin: the walls, the floorboards, laden with hangings, cloths, papers, pictures, cupboards, cushions, varnished lion's-paw legs: bell-ropes and faded photographs in oval gilt frames.

It was the first time that Helmuth had been in an apartment like this—the first time he had been in an apartment at all. The atmosphere was gentle, comfortable. Gerhard's mother brought in coffee and astonishing cakes made with different coloured cream. The mother was small and warm; she hung onto Helmuth's hand with her own warm hand.

He drew it away, then, since she still held it, he took hers again, then again drew it away, then again pumped it up and down. She just held it and smiled into his eyes.

Old Dr Stein was something like the Rabbi in one of the photographs; he had a hooked nose like a stage Shylock and might well have worn robes over his suit. He addressed Helmuth as 'my young sir'. 'These are bad times, my young sir, but we are very honoured. Gerhard has told us so much about you.'

Helmuth sat down. The father and son started to argue.

'Nonsense, father. The times are much better than they were. The Communists and Social Democrats can expect a good beating at the next elections.'

'You won't be so optimistic when the Nazis start beating you, my boy.'

'Being a Jew doesn't stop me from being a patriotic German, father. I think Hitler is just misinformed about us. There are many of us young ones who would go along with him all the way . . . except on that.'

'Oh, no. Oh no, no. You are *wrong*, Gerhard.'

'No, father, I am right. Germany needs strong revolutionary, nationalistic government.'

'Be quiet for a moment, will you?' Mrs Stein said as Rosika came in behind her. 'Hasn't the count anything to say about it all? You don't give him a chance to speak.'

The girl had come in so quietly that only Helmuth had seen her. Should he introduce himself or answer his hostess? He pretended he had not seen her.

'We're rather out of touch in the east, you know, Mrs Stein. But I do think all this business of Hitler's about . . . about you, well, your people . . . is quite stupid.'

'Thank you, thank you.' The old man nodded his head.

85

The girl stepped forward and stood behind a large arm-chair, so loose and plush that it seemed a pile of cushions.

'This is my daughter, Rosika,' said Mrs Stein.

'Yes, old boy,' said Gerhard, waddling forward. 'You must meet our Rosika. She's a bit shy but she'll get used to you.'

Rosika was as small as her brother but while his torso was thick and his head large, her form and limbs were delicate and exact, her features were fine: everything was in exact proportion. She had the gentle manners of her mother and the wise air of her father. She had flickering dark brown eyes.

She said nothing throughout the afternoon. Helmuth thought that she was quite probably no more than fourteen years old, but Gerhard told him later that she was twenty.

'Gerhard,' Gerhard said, 'is not a Jewish name. It was my uncle who insisted I should have a German name. My father would have liked to call me Jacob or something like that, but my uncle insisted. Then he was killed in the war. He was a great believer in the integration of Jews.'

'It is a pity,' Mrs Stein said, 'not to have some respect for tradition . . . your traditions, Gerhard, are Jewish as well as German.'

Helmuth was less interested in the discussion than in the place. His surroundings made him feel that he was in a foreign country yet he had only crossed the Tiergarten to get there. The objects around him certainly had something German about them, yet they were not German, not, any-way, like the furnishings of Kassow. The objects—photo-graphs, paperweights, lamps, pictures, ashtrays—were arranged, as in other houses, to converge on one object of religious veneration. Here it was not a crucifix nor an icon but a candlestick with seven branches surmounted by a strange pagan insignia—a metal geometric sign making a star out of two triangles. It had a disquieting effect upon him.

Helmuth von Rummelsberg / Gerhard Stein / Rosika Stein: 1930

From then on, whenever Helmuth and Gerhard went out together, Gerhard would bring Rosika with him. At first it did not seem that she wanted to come. Gradually, however, she became more talkative and when they visited cafés or nightclubs she would loosen up. Helmuth preferred her company to that of his cousins or their friends. His friendship with Gerhard had been one of benign, gracious condescension ('so this is a Jew') and curiosity in the different species (that a Jew could despise the Poles in just the same way as a German). Rosika, however, was more pleasant and reminded him of Katerina because the two girls so contrasted with each other.

This was the first time that Helmuth had been in Berlin. This was also the first time he had led an independent life: for example he now dealt with money; in Pomerania everything had been bought on account and these accounts were settled by their agent. And now he was a civilian. No longer responsible for the honour of the army, he could observe or enjoy the world of street-fights, suicides, bankruptcies, sexual scandals, clubs, cabarets, restaurants—a stew of titillations he had never tasted before. He learnt his way around; he discovered that the cheap whores were to be found on the Ackerstrasse, the under-age girls Unter den Linden, those with big bosoms on the Dorotheastrasse and those wearing boots on the Tarientienerstrasse: and that the Schlesischer Bahnhof was not only the terminal for trains from the east but the place where the male prostitutes met their girl-friends in secret when their work was over. He saw it all with horrified fascination—Pomerania was still the setting for his eye, still the skull for his brain which registered and judged. Those like the Steins, to whom the city life was a matter of total involvement, were, to him, poor devils.

He only gradually realized that they too thought they were poor devils not because they were city-dwellers but because they were Jews. He only gradually realized that his was the last straw at which they clutched with their daughter's (sister's) . . .

Helmuth, Gerhard and Rosika were looking round a book-shop near the Alexanderplatz.

'There is a lot of degenerate trash published these days,' said Gerhard.

Helmuth and Rosika went by the shelves of religious books. On a stand facing them was a pyramid of a new popular edition of the Bible. Rosika picked up a copy from the top of the pile and said: 'It is funny. Most of this book is sacred to us too, but as a Christian Bible it seems quite strange.'

As she picked it up, as she touched it with her small delicate fingers, Helmuth would have snatched it immediately out of her hands but he checked himself. It was a cheap edition of the Bible. For one of the very few times in his life the side of his face contracted of its own accord. His skin dappled.

As Rosika turned towards him with a (soft) interrogatory glance, his hand was in mid-air without purpose. The interrogatory glance intensified when she saw him. But Helmuth was no epileptic. His correctness, his graciousness, returned. He even smiled as he walked past her—not touching her— towards travel books. Rosika's face went russet brown and she put the Bible back on its pyramid.

The Ninety-Nine Bar. The bar ran off the Friedrichstrasse, stainless steel down the side of a long, narrow room. At the end was a curtain and behind the curtain the cabaret-room —large, dark, tables forming a crescent around clear sections of the floor. On this the customers danced or the performers did their tricks.

Helmuth, Rosika, Gerhard and Annaliese (a girl studying medicine at the Technical University). They came at half-past ten having eaten at the Savoury Sow (the speciality, pork in white wine sauce). They ordered schnapps, they danced and they laughed, couple to couple, at the cold draughts around their ankles (in spite of the curtain). At eleven the club filled up. The draught was sucked into sodden lungs and wheezed out, a gaseous ash. At eleven-twenty, the floor show.

Two men, one wearing military uniform, the other dressed in a nightshirt and wearing a spike-topped soldier's helmet. The second stands stock still, saluting and at attention throughout the act... The first stands at his side, groping at the nightshirt of the other man in the region of his genitals. A piano plays slow, mournful jazz. The active partner holds out a fold of the nightdress in a point. He turns to the audience, wiggles his eyebrows and, quickly turning his back to his partner, juts his buttocks towards the point. He rolls his eyes. (Rosika lets out a puff or a sigh. The audience laughs loudly.) The uniformed soldier's face falls—he turns to the saluting one in the nightshirt who remains immobile, staring straight ahead. He runs his hand down the night-shirt close to the stomach and legs. There is no point in the linen. Again he begins to grope. There was applause. Helmuth was flabbergasted. 'It is meant to insult the army,' he said to Gerhard.

'Yes, yes, of course. For goodness' sake, don't look so serious. Have a laugh for once.'

Gerhard was still laughing. Tears of laughter streamed down the face of Annaliese. Rosika smiled—kindly, quizzically—at Helmuth.

The second scene: a middle-aged woman—stern, masculine, her hair in a bun—comes on with a young girl in school uniform. The older woman wears a brown suit and carries a rolled-up diploma—two red seals hanging down from its end. The piano plays heavy chords as the woman nods her finger at the girl: then it resumes the mournful jazz. (The room is full of smoke. Helmuth's eyes water.) The older woman crouches, watching the schoolgirl; the schoolgirl takes off a shoe. The woman stands; the girl takes off a second shoe. The woman crouches; the girl takes off a stocking. The woman stands; the girl takes off a second stocking. The woman crouches—slowly. The girl slowly removes her underpants. The woman slowly rises and comes towards the girl: the girl turns away from the woman and bends over a few degrees. The woman slowly lifts the girl's tunic to the waist and raises the diploma: there she hesitates, then quickly hitches up her own skirt, holds the diploma to her groin, swings the girl to face her and seemingly impregnates the girl with the diploma.

The audience burst out laughing, louder even than before. Helmuth pretended to laugh. Gerhard leant across the table and said: 'This really is the best place in Berlin.'

Helmuth looked at Rosika. She smiled. He poured out the schnapps. The waiter brought a bowl of savoury biscuits. Helmuth felt . . . (a weight in his stomach).

'You know,' said Gerhard, 'this is the only place where they don't shave the girls.'

The final act: a girl dressed in country fashion, the Bavarian National Dress. She has fair hair and an innocent expression. To the same music as before she takes off her bonnet. Then, demurely, innocently, she takes off her dress. Underneath she wears nothing above the waist. Her bosom is free. Beneath the waist, however, she wears a clumsy metal contraption that surrounds her thighs and passes a strip of steel beneath her legs. In the middle, above the navel, is a large padlock. The girl lies down and pats her bosom, making them quiver as a child does a jelly. A priest (the same actor who played the saluting soldier) comes in. He watches her, kneels beside her, kisses her sweetly. Then he stands up, pulls her up too. She stands abashed, her hands over her breasts. He kneels again, takes a piece of wire from his cassock, and picks the padlock. It comes undone. He removes the chastity belt. The girl, naked, puts her hands on his shoulder, kisses him lightly, slowly, on both cheeks, then turns her back on him and the audience. She leans forward. Both hands are in front of her at the level of her buttocks: one elbow jerks rhythmically back and forth.

The priest turns to the audience and shrugs his shoulders.

After the Ninety-Nine they split up. Gerhard went off with Annaliese in a taxi. Helmuth said he would take Rosika home in his car.

'I hope you weren't shocked,' Rosika said to him.

91

'No. Of course not. Why should I be shocked?' Helmuth replied.

They drove in silence. Then Rosika (she had . . . perhaps . . . perhaps . . . perhaps . . . drunk too much) laid her hand on his forearm, his right forearm. 'Helmuth,' she said.

What did she mean by this 'Helmuth'? (I wonder.)

Obviously a wealth (a wealth of meaning) because her voice was—rich, low, murmuring, musical. And the hand on the forearm . . . his hands were on the steering wheel.

Now Helmuth missed Katerina and above all he missed her . . . . Rosika was not Katerina, in fact she was quite the opposite—but opposites sometimes meet and in this case they met at the . . . . Rosika certainly had one (she knew it). What else did she know that she might have put into that 'Helmuth'? That the seam of German Jewry was about to split at the seat of the pants? That Helmuth was a Pomeranian aristocrat with a decent streak? A man with a straw to be clutched? Was this forearm the straw? Was her hand clutching it?

Helmuth stopped the car. Not, certainly not at his cousins' place. Where? A hotel?

'Where . . . I mean . . . Rosika. It would be nice to be alone—not just in the car.'

'Yes,' she said. Then a silence. Then: 'If we were quiet, you could come to my room at home.'

He drove round the Potsdammer Platz and up by the Brandenburg Gate. They climbed the stairs. They opened the door quietly and crept down the corridor (where he had never been before) to her room.

It was small: there was only a bed to sit on. The bed had a bright cover. On a table was a child's collection of glass animals—translucent elephants with coloured ears; pigs with red eyes. The floor was covered with a Turkish carpet. Helmut felt as if he was behind a shop in the casbah. The weight in his stomach sank heavier on its bed of nerves; now was surely the time for an operation to remove it.

She sat on the bed. He took her hand, her coat off, her hand again. He kissed her. She puffed as she had done in the Ninety-Nine. Her arms coiled round him. Her heels were raised off the floor. He looked at her face; her brown eyes were drowsy and direct. Her lips smiled. He heaved himself on the bed, kissed her throat, put his left hand on her hip, then in the same place but under her skirt. She heaved very slightly and puffed involuntarily. She took his head and kissed him. His left hand went down to the top and inside of her leg: then, tearing at any impediment, his fingers groped at her innards.

'The light,' she said, her voice constrained as if she too could feel the weight of the stone in his stomach. His right hand (his left hand stayed where it was), as it made towards the bedside table, unbuttoned the front of her dress. He kissed the top of her doll's bosom, then leant towards the light switch. Then . . .

He saw the Hebrew lettering and geometric star on her prayer book beside the lamp. His right hand . . . and the stone . . . dropped. He felt the acid mucus bite into the fingers of his left hand. The hand whipped out. He jerked his head up lest the wire-black hairs should stray out of her bodice and scratch down his cheek.

'What is it?' she said.

He sat up. 'I'm afraid this is impossible. I am engaged to be married.'

'I know. Never mind. I don't mind.'

'No. I must go,' he stood up.

'Please don't go.'

He did not look at her but left the room, walked down the corridor and shut the door of the flat, all of which made a certain amount of noise but did not wake the Steins because ... they were awake.

Klaus, Helmuth von Rummelsberg / Katerina von Treblitz / Günter Strepper: 1930

On 14 September elections were held for the Reichstag. About thirty-five million people voted. Helmuth von Rummelsberg voted for the Conservative People's Party, which lost most of its seats. The Social Democratic Party, though it remained the largest party in the Reichstag, lost many seats. The Communist Party increased its vote to four and a half millions and its representation from fifty-four deputies to seventy-seven. Klaus von Rummelsberg and Günter Strepper were among six and a half million Germans who voted for the National Socialist Party, which increased its representation from twelve deputies to one hundred and seven, thereby becoming the second largest party in the Reichstag.

After this election, which she followed closely and anxiously, Katerina von Treblitz's menstrual period, which usually occurred regularly every three and a half weeks (twenty-four days), came five weeks late and then with such unprecedented bleeding that she remained in bed for four days. The doctor maintained that such irregularity could only be caused by emotional disorders but Katerina denied that she was under any stress. Everyone who knew that this was not influenza assumed it was Helmuth's absence in Berlin that had caused the emotional upset which in

94

its turn caused the irregularity and excessive flow of blood.

Katerina might have written to Helmuth about this disorder (she was frank) as a proof of her love but she did not. She was a bad letter-writer and so wrote only to retail local Pomeranian gossip, and these letters, though Helmuth did not notice it, became less frequent (for the first months of the three he was away she wrote to him twice a week; then once a week; and in the last month he received only two letters).

On 16 October Brüning, the Chancellor, brought before the Reichstag his financial programme, which included the five-year *Osthilfe* scheme laid before the previous Reichstag but not yet effective because of the dissolution. It became quite clear from his proposals that the von Treblitz estates would not qualify for any relief from their debts. Katerina's father, the old Knappist, wanted to shoot himself. Katerina and her mother told him that it would be cowardly to do so and that dissuaded him. Katerina, highly agitated, told Klaus of this state of affairs: Klaus arranged for a limited loan for her father but the von Rummelsbergs' industrial resources had been hit by the recession and their agriculture had suffered from the fall in food prices that year. Katerina understood that the von Rummelsberg estate could not afford to lend more.

Since Klaus regarded her as his sister, he felt the ruin of her family acutely: if her problems were to be Helmuth's, then they were his—but the only solution, he thought, was a political one for the plight of the whole country. Towards that he was playing his part; and Katerina inevitably met that other person, also playing his part, Günter Strepper.

The swing to the National Socialists in Stolp was greater

95

than the national average, as great as anywhere else in Germany. Günter had convinced the landless peasantry that Hitler not only meant to deal with Poland once and for all, settling up the supposed atrocities perpetrated against the German minorities in Poland, but would also break up the large estates. However Klaus's presence persuaded the landowners that their interests would be safeguarded if they too used their influence in favour of the National Socialists.

Helmuth had told Katerina that he had voted for the Conservative People's Party, that Treviranus was the ablest patriotic leader, and for a while Katerina supported this point of view with Klaus and his colleague Günter Strepper, but she was upset by this party's failure at the election. Strepper teased her as he had always done, called her the 'Treviranus-child'; Klaus smiled and said, 'You're just like Helmuth—hopelessly romantic.' Klaus explained to her that National Socialism was the only practical alternative to Communism, and though she laughed at him when he dressed up in his brown uniform for Party rallies on Sunday afternoon, the election result seemed to prove him right.

Katerina could not, at first, understand Klaus's deference to Günter Strepper. She once asked him why he was so humble before their dentist's son.

'You see, Katty,' Klaus said, 'I know that Günter is rather coarse, and rough, but times are changing. We're hopelessly out of touch here on our estates. Günter is one of the new men.'

Strepper, he explained, was a Barbarian fighting his way into the decadent Roman empire and revitalizing it. The National Socialist seizure of power would be the Barbarian invasion; having conquered the old Germany they would adopt its better, civilizing values as the Goths and Huns had become Christian and created the medieval civilization —the first and second Reichs.

Katerina did not understand why Helmuth did not think in this way; and she hated being thought romantic.

Katerina von Treblitz / Günter Strepper: 1930

There were three occasions on which Katerina found herself alone with Günter Strepper before Helmuth's return from Berlin.

On the first, Günter said, boisterously, teasingly, 'That Helmuth's a lucky lad.' Klaus was out of the room, decanting a second bottle of wine. 'After all . . .'

Katerina, her eyes still on the farthest edge of the dining-room table, raised the brows of her eyes.

'Seriously, if you weren't engaged, I would be courting you, too.'

'I am not engaged,' she said. Günter sat to her left. She moved her glance to his chest, then back to the edge of the table which lay in line with the edge of the carpet on the polished floor. The iris, the table, the carpet.

'I thought you were,' said Strepper. 'Not officially, but I thought it was understood.'

'It was an idea,' she said, 'but it isn't fixed.'

'Then you wouldn't take it amiss . . .'

'I wouldn't take anything amiss, Günter. This is still a free country.' She pronounced the word 'amiss' firmly, without irony, and swallowed.

Klaus came back into the room with the decanted claret.

'Günter's a good fellow,' Klaus said to Katerina after Strepper had left, 'but he sweats a bit, and for all his racial purity he has frizzy hair like a nigger.'

97

Katerina wrinkled her nose, voluntarily; her vaginal muscles contracted, involuntarily. (Yet—it must be said because it must have been so—she did not miss in Helmuth the involuntary actions of *his* body. She did not miss him physically, in that sense, in the particular zones of her body. As with other women, the memory of the specific pleasure faded soon after: the nostalgia was more for the person.)

The second occasion: when Günter Strepper drove her home from Kassow. She sat beside him in his Party car. 'Countess,' he said, 'I realize that traditionally I would be considered an inferior match but I would assure you that in the New Order which I believe to be imminent my position would not be inconsiderable. In fact I have reason to believe that I shall be called to the weapon-carrying Security Guard of our Party, which in itself is a proof to you, countess, that my family is untainted by alien blood.' Strepper had dropped his bantering way with her. His head was always inclined. Katerina looked at the back of the chauffeur's head (like the swelling joint of a tree), then at Strepper's Party belt, then back at the chauffeur's neck (the trunk). Strepper smelt rancid: her nose twitched and . . .

'I am sure you are racially immaculate,' she said firmly. 'I hope I am too.'

'I am sure, certainly, I am sure you are. I have looked into it. Your family have only ever married the Pomeranian gentry for fifteen generations.'

'Oh good. I am glad you checked it' (firmly). 'And I congratulate you on your appointment to the SS.'

'Yes, the SS. Klaus will get an appointment too, I think. I recommended him . . . and he has all the qualifications. Himmler would like to have a descendant of a real Teutonic knight. I think I can swing it even though he is a recent recruit.'

'I am sure you can.'

Günter took her hand in his and held it until they arrived at Katerina's home.

The third. Late November. Katerina had a hole to be filled so she went to Strepper, that is to say, Dr Strepper the family dentist in Stolp.

'Well, young countess,' said the dentist, who had oiled his beard, 'what is this we hear about you and my son, Günter. He's quite a boy, now, you know.'

'What is it they tell you, Dr Strepper?'

'Ha ha. Never mind. Let life take its course. You can't help it if it's hard on some. All's fair. All's fair.'

'Perhaps.'

'And are you keeping off chocolates?'

'I never eat them now, Doctor.'

'Then let us hope that this is your last filling.'

Katerina stayed to lunch. Günter was told she was there and joined them. After lunch he offered her his car to drive her home. She insisted on taking the train, but until it was time for this train she accepted his offer to be shown round the Party headquarters. The brown-shirted Storm Troopers stood up respectfully while their leader took her past them into his office. She sat on a leather chair, her eyes fixed on a portrait of Hitler. The frame was gilt. The walls of the room were cream-coloured. The windows had a metal frame. A storm trooper brought in a pot of coffee, two cups (cream, sugar) and left again.

'This,' said Günter Strepper, slapping his hand on the desk, 'this is where I work.'

'What do you work at?' she asked.

'Why . . . you must know what I do. I organize.'

'I see.'

'And this,' he went on, flicking the top of the chair at his desk, 'is where I think about you.'

She said nothing.

'Countess,' (although she was sitting on a lower level than him, his head tilted upwards, his glance not at, but at the level of, the portrait of Hitler) 'I should like to say, respectfully, that I love you—and that . . . if you harboured feelings even remotely akin, I should like to ask you to be my wife in the New Order.'

She was silent.

He looked at her; then his head tilted a degree higher, still facing the wall.

She moved her glance to his boots, then back to the frame of the portrait.

'Günter . . . my feelings are . . . I do harbour such feelings . . . akin, you should know, and if you asked me . . . I should accept.'

'I do ask you, Katerina.'

'I do accept, Günter.'

Klaus von Rummelsberg / Günter Strepper: 1930

The Security Guard of the National Socialist Party was founded in 1928 as the Party élite to counter the influence of the Storm Troopers. It came under the leadership of Heinrich Himmler. The SS troops modelled themselves on the Teutonic knights—their ideals were loyalty, honour and obedience.

Günter Strepper and (on his recommendation, backed by that of the Pomeranian Gauleiter) Klaus von Rummelsberg both went to Berlin on 4 December 1930 to receive their appointments to the SS.

Helmuth von Rummelsberg / Katerina von Treblitz: 1930

When Helmuth returned from Berlin on 4 December, Edward was at Kassow, on Christmas leave from the cadet-school at Tilsit. No one told Helmuth that Katerina's engagement to Günter Strepper had been announced the week before. They assumed that she had told him about it in a letter.

At eleven on the morning of 5 December Helmuth drove over to see Katerina. He was shown into the morning-room —a small faded room at the corner of the house that was rarely used.

Katerina came into that room from the drawing-room where she had been sitting with her mother.

'Hello, Helmuth,' she said.

He adjusted his image of her to the person, marginally different, in front of him.

'Katty,' he said, taking her hand and looking at her face. She looked straight ahead of her—that is at his chin—concealing her nostrils; then, for a moment, up at his eyes.

'Helmuth, I am not feeling very well.'

His eyes contracted. 'Are you ill?'

'No, it's nothing abnormal, you know.' She smiled.

'May I kiss you?'

'Yes.' She did not move her lips, nor did they move involuntarily.

'You don't seem well,' he said. 'I'll come back tomorrow.' She seemed to him dull—not just for that moment—but as a person he had remembered and imagined.

'Helmuth, do you think I have changed?' she asked.

'I don't suppose so.'

'I think I have.'

'I hope not.'

'Haven't you?'

'No.'

She said nothing.

'Well, we'll see about it later on,' he said. He kissed her again and left.

At lunch he said to Edward: 'Katty seemed a bit odd.'

'I should say so. I can't understand her marrying Strepper's son,' Edward replied. 'I hope you weren't too cut up about it.'

'What?'

'I can't see what she sees in Günter Strepper. Did you chuck her? Some girl in Berlin ... or something?'

'Is she marrying him?'

'Yes, isn't she? It was in the paper ... but she hasn't been over here so I haven't asked her. I should have thought you'd know.'

'No, I don't.'

'What did she say today?'

'Nothing.'

'Well, it was in the paper and Klaus says it's true enough and he's as thick as thieves with Strepper's son these days. They've both gone off to get a change of uniform.'

After lunch Helmuth drove back to the von Treblitz home. Katerina came down from her bedroom to the same morning-room where he stood, twisting his gloves.

'Is it true that you are going to marry Strepper? Günter Strepper?' he asked.

'Yes.'

'You might have told me. I thought you were going to marry me.'

'I know. So did I.'

'When did this happen?'

'About three weeks ago.'

'I must admit I don't understand you. I always thought Günter Strepper a dirty rat.'

'Please, don't,' said Katerina, not ironically, but with a firm whine. 'Ask Klaus, he understands.'

'Well, I don't and I never will. I'd better go. I'd better say good-bye. We won't see much of each other.'

Helmuth von Rummelsberg left the house, as near to tears as a Pomeranian junker is ever likely to be.

When Klaus returned in his black uniform Helmuth said to him: 'What on earth got into Katerina?'

'Marrying Strepper? I don't know. I hear she didn't even let you know. I suppose she just changed her mind.'

'But why Strepper? He's such an oaf.'

'Yes, he is a bit of an oaf, isn't he? I must admit, I don't understand it.'

Part
Two

Chapter Five

I

In the end, I got in. In Suzi. It was an event in my life, a development in the plot, just as Hitler's appointment as Chancellor or the annexation of Austria were events in their lives—and developments in the plot.

It was easy enough to make a story out of their lives—out of history—but difficult to see the direction in my own. Theirs was fast, mine was slow. What significance would there be in the seduction of a German physiotherapist by a junior diplomat? Was it random and gratuitous? Or did it symbolize a new British interest in the Continent? Was my small act to have its corollary in grand treaties and negotiations? Though this may have been the case, to me at the time it was the exigencies of nature, not of plot, that continued the story. I was ready to give up Suzi any day but gristle, nerves, blood and brain cells had me in hand. There is a strong instinct to finish off what one has begun—even Suzi—but it is difficult to know what to do on the day after a botched seduction. It was especially tricky for me because Helmuth was certainly back in his flat . . . and possibly back in Suzi.

There was Zuntz and I was there two days later with

Armand, the two of us sitting at a conspicuous table in the middle of the upstairs room. They came in, the two of them. Suzi saw us, did not know what to do, ignored us as they crossed the room, but since he, Helmuth, led her to the empty table next to ours, she came up to us.

'Good evening. How are you?'

Armand and I stood up.

'Have you met Count Helmuth von Rummelsberg? May I introduce you?' she asked. Then she turned to Helmuth: 'This is the secretary from the British Mission, Helmuth. The one I met at the Akademie.'

'Good evening. Good evening. Do sit at our table,' etc. They did sit down at our table. At first Helmuth seemed irritated, looking away from us at others in the room; then he looked happier and finally became effusive.

'I was a diplomat myself, you know. But I resigned from the service after the war. The good days of diplomacy have gone, I am afraid, with the development of the telephone— the hot lines that run from one president's desk to the other.'

Armand and I agreed that there was nothing to do.

'Nothing at all. Nothing at all,' Helmuth repeated. 'Now I run a night-club. A change. But, I can tell you, it's more interesting. It is rather an old-fashioned night-club but, you know, it is very good of its kind. You and your friend must come there. Why not come tonight? Suzi here will take you, won't you, Suzi?'

'Yes,' she said, 'that would be very nice.'

It was as easy as that, but then the illicit lover can expect that kind of co-operation from the possessing rival: they want things to go on under their nose; they believe in seizing the nettle. We went, Armand and I, that night. Helmuth von Rummelsberg's club was conventional: there was nothing of raffish pre-war Berlin about it. There were clubs like this in Duisberg or Cologne. The walls were red silk (the same kind as the grey silk on the walls of his dining-room). The chairs, the pillars, were gilt; the tables the same style as the furniture in his flat but this was fake. At one end of the club was a stage: the curtains, when we came in, were closed. The lights were always low and the place full of what seemed to be West German businessmen with their Berliner mistresses.

'Do these girls work for the club?' I asked Suzi.

'Oh yes. Some of them do,' she replied.

'It is kind of the count to provide us with his best hostess.'

'Oh no,' she said, her expression unchanged, 'I am not a hostess here.'

Armand laughed; I imagine because she did not.

Helmuth himself joined us at times: he even put his hand on my shoulder but most of the time he left us alone.

'You know,' said Suzi, 'he directs the floor show himself.'

We drank German champagne. I danced with Suzi.

'I am glad we met at Zuntz. I did not think I should ring you up.'

'No. But I think you can now.'

'Won't Helmuth mind?'

'Helmuth. You call him Helmuth now! No. He won't mind if we are just friends.'

'Then we could meet alone?'

'Yes, of course. Why not? Last night—that was just a bit of silliness, wasn't it?'

'Yes.'

Then there was the floor show which was the best of its kind outside Las Vegas. Twelve dancing girls in plain costumes kicking and wheeling with perfect precision. The best troupe outside Las Vegas.

'He has trained them himself,' she said. 'They have had offers to go all over the world—to Paris, to Argentina, to Tokyo. Even to Las Vegas.'

'Did they go?'

'No. Helmuth won't leave Germany except to go to his villa in Tezzin. And he won't let them go without him.'

I danced again with Suzi (did she share the villa in Tezzin?). She danced very well—independently, in perfect time. When the music was slower and we danced with my arms around her waist and her hands on my shoulder, I said: 'When can we meet?'

'That is up to you. We could meet for lunch.'

Nothing happened at lunch that time but we arranged to go to the cinema the week after; then there was another film we both said we wanted to see and after that we went back to my house. We drank whisky with ice: I took her hand in the same way as before; kissed her in the same way as before and she kissed back as innocently. She looked stern but less stern and sweeter. And though she tensed herself at the same gestures as before, she did not lurch away.

'I think we should go upstairs,' she said.

So we went upstairs and sat on the edge of my double bed. There was a pair of old socks on the chair. They were clean enough but darned and I had been trying to decide whether or not to throw them out. She must have thought they were dirty.

'Come,' she murmured, at the sight of the socks (or not) and we got down to it. She cried but there was none of the difficulty I had expected. So had she done it before? I asked her. She said she had not. She said she had . . . it was show jumping. I wondered. Why should she not deceive me as easily as she was deceiving Helmuth von Rummelsberg?

I could not complain. I was in. I had waited some time but now, quickly and quite easily, I was in. And it may well be called making love: the persistent, repeated sessions coagulate the emotion: it hardens, it takes shape. Pleasant and easy it may be in construction but once it is there it is hard to lose or destroy. Love is not a cake you eat slice by slice until it is finished: it is much more like a tapeworm which lies in your entrails or is purged in a painful and disagreeable way.

Love can be called a tapeworm or a cake or a statue but it is, of course, something all on its own.

The disadvantages of love and making love:

(1) I was so busy getting in that I could not remember what it was like. I might well have been one of the schoolboys grabbing for a pancake on Shrove Tuesday. I was so taken up with the seduction of Suzi that I cannot remember the details of gesture, movement, feeling.

(2) It was very awkward to have what one wanted, there, naked even as one had imagined it (her) and not want it at that moment (again). As much as possible, of course. A child with a new toy. But not as much as one would like.

(3) I wondered if she compared me with. . . . There could be something about Helmuth von Rummelsberg. . . . Or if she was as untouched as she made out, would have me believe and spread abroad (by way of Frau Stefan)—perhaps she was comparing me with what she expected, what she imagined . . . which was worse.

The advantages of love and making love:

(1) There I had a girl who would do these things I had always wanted to do. The thought of it was exciting, even as I walked along the street—the thought, the thought alone, that this creature, this creature with her fine ankles,

111

would be beside me undressed; that this perfect child whose chest rises into two soft bosoms would let me prod them at will; would let me play with tin soldiers on her stomach; would let me lay my head on her bare lap. I kept steady on my feet then for the reality of it; for her eyes looking down over her nose, her chin, the fold in her neck, between her breasts—at whatever game I was playing.

(2) It was wrong. Helmuth would have thought so; her mother too (so she says) and the world, the ordinary others, they all would have thought it a poor way to behave, not on, a fine way to thank the community for the free milk coupons, free education, student grants. The Foreign Office, the Political Adviser, my mother, my sister, would all have disapproved (of making love with a German girl). Good.

(3) There was nothing they could do about it. It was not against the law and they did not know, so . . . fine.

Neither an advantage nor a disadvantage—the truth that I had not been mistaken in her wrists and ankles. She was flawless. Any plumpness made her look better without clothes than she did with them. The parts and the whole had the same quality as her green eyes.

II

Edward von Rummelsberg: 1939–1940

The war. Of the three von Rummelsbergs, Edward was the only one in the army, the only one fighting—a tank commander with the Panzer Corps in Poland. Two weeks before this they had left Pomerania, driven over the borders of Germany. Now they had reached Wagrowiec. Polish resis-

112

tance had been insignificant. The mad slapdash cavalry charges against German tanks were particularly irritating to the younger German officers who wanted proper combat experience.

There was little destruction. The few burnt-out buildings or derelict lorries were hidden by the leaves, the branches of the trees. Fresh grass already encroached on what was singed. At every village where there were Germans they came out and waved: the daughters smiled out of prettiness; the older men and women—a blander more satisfied smile. The young men saluted with great solemnity, the fingers of their hands warped by the fervour with which they jutted and stretched out their arms.

There were only a few of them. This was Poland. In villages that must have had one hundred or one hundred and fifty inhabitants, twenty or twenty-four only came out onto the streets. The others, the Poles, skulked behind the cottages, or, if they watched the tanks, their faces had no expression; their hands only shaded the sun from their eyes.

Edward sat at the turret of his tank. At one time he had thought a Pole might throw a pitchfork in his back but now he did not even expect that. The country had been like Pomerania—the same except that for the past twenty years it had been called Poland. Pine trees, lakes, hills, running down to Silesia, up to the Baltic.

Then, as they came down onto the plain of the Vistula, the land became flat. His squadron took a forward position and sped over the dry marshes. There was the smell of the long grass—no longer the dung and dried mud of the villages; then, when the tank stopped, the smell of oil, oil fumes, uniform and sometimes that of a dead cow, shot out of frustration.

In this long grass they were attacked by Polish cavalry. It was a broken troupe of ten or twelve. The noise of the motor was so great that Edward did not hear the horses and the first he knew of the attack was the click and fleck of a bullet in the metal of the turret beneath his elbow. He turned and saw behind him the horsemen riding away now but wheeling. He sank into the turret and ordered the driver, Breb, to turn and chase. He looked through the periscope and saw the horsemen facing them. Two had some kind of recoilless rifle, probably from the first war, strung up between them; one held the barrel on his shoulder, the other held the butt and trigger.

They could not set their sites on the tank because their horses were backing away. The other horsemen watched. Edward ordered the gunner, Hensman, to fire a round of shrapnel at the two cavalrymen with the rifle. He looked back and saw that the front horse had bolted, its haunches scissored at its terror. The barrel of the rifle trailed on the ground.

The turret swayed as the shell was fired. The hind-quarters of the bolting horse skidded under it; its joints were blown out and the rider too must have had something in the back of his neck because his hand went up beneath his helmet before he toppled off.

Blood came out from under the saddle of the other horse before it fell; and the rider's boot fell to the ground full of his leg beneath the knee, cut clean by the same shell.

Hensman had switched to the machine-gun but the other horseman rode off behind a rise in the ground into the long grass. Edward ordered Breb to return to formation.

Later, on scout patrol near Plock, Edward came across three of the few Polish tanks. He was expected to report their presence over short-wave radio but already Breb had changed gear for attack. Hensman knocked out the first with a single armour-piercing shell before the Poles realized that it was a German, not a Polish tank. The two others separated; one came towards Edward, the other reversed to give covering fire from a wood by the road. Breb swerved the tank off the road through a hedge into a field: he was then in dead ground to the tank by the wood. The tank chasing them came into the field but as it broke through the hedge a shot from Hensman hit its right track and it stuck. This Pole still fired a few shells at the German tank but they burst yards to the side and the fragments were deflected by the armour. Breb finished the turn, then zigzagged forward until Edward felt they were near enough to be sure to finish the Pole stuck in the hedge, though not yet within the field of fire of the Pole by the wood. But this latter tank now backed from its position behind the wood and came down into the field. As it rounded the wood, Hensman put an incendiary through the driver's window. The tank swung to the left, crossed the road and exploded on the other side.

The Polish tank crews now climbed out of the first and second tanks with their hands held above their heads. The officers in both had been killed. The drivers and gunners were taken prisoner.

For this Edward was awarded the Iron Cross.

Nevertheless there were few such opportunities and Edward, like his brother officers, wanted to get to the Western Front, even though it puzzled him that the governments of Britain and France should have declared war over Poland when they had allowed Hitler to march into Czechoslovakia. Poland was not a democratic state—in fact its government was more unwholesome than any other in

Europe. And it seemed natural and proper (to Edward) that the Germans should rule Poland, as it seemed natural and proper (to Carson) that the English should rule Ireland or (to Curzon) India. That the strong should rule the weak, the capable the incompetent, seemed (to Edward) self-evidently true and pragmatically proper. What, if not this philosophy, lay behind the French and British empires? What, if not hatred of the Germans, made these two nations prevent their neighbour from following their example? And, more relevant and interesting (to Edward), what were their tank tactics?

Each night he prayed, kneeling by the tank track: 'Oh God, accept the souls of those we have killed. Protect my mother, my brothers and Katerina. Help us win the war: but whatever happens, thy will be done.'

Klaus von Rummelsberg / Katerina von Treblitz / Günter Strepper: 1939–1940

If God was watching over Edward's brothers and Katerina, as he was asked to do, what would he have seen? A reception at the Chancelry. Adolf Hitler smiling, a little ill at ease. Goering at one side, Ribbentrop at the other. Klaus von Rummelsberg in the middle distance. Katerina Strepper between him and her husband. Her husband, Günter Strepper, hovering on the movements of the party leaders. His function, he knew, was to interpret Sepp Dietrich to Goering and Ribbentrop who seemed (to Himmler) to hate him. The function of Klaus—to discuss genealogies with Ribbentrop. The function of Katerina—to smile at the Party leaders, but from a distance, lest she over-shadow them with her height: if caught in conversation, to sit and slide low in her chair; to intermingle aristocratic and National Socialist sentiments.

The official position of Günter Strepper—colonel in Hitler's bodyguard. The official position of Klaus von Rummelsberg—adjutant to Günter Strepper.

These were the happy days. There was a sense of urgency, not of crisis. The news from the front was good. Günter and Klaus planned adjoining estates in the liberated Ukraine. The black collars and black boots of the SS uniform hushed a restaurant when they entered; they produced an interested, respectful manner in other men who deferred; and in women there was a pleasantness.

If Katerina and Klaus had felt privileged and pre-eminent before, it had only been within Pomerania—as far, perhaps, as Stettin or in the aristocratic colony in Berlin. Now they were superior in the cities. When Katerina went shopping with her husband, other women stood aside. Of course she was expected to wear dowdy clothes which she did not like. Brown skirts and brown jerseys. Brown combinations, even brown silk slips. Her shoes were flat and plain. She wore a party pin in her brown blouse. But then the other Party wives wore the same.

These were the happy days. Katerina ate potatoes and cake but remained tall and thin. Because of this Günter would seem (to Katerina) angry but it was a pattern of behaviour—running smooth after ten years.

'You are as thin as before,' Günter would shout from the bathroom. She, in her brown slip, leaning over her dressing-table, the tops of her legs like soft-wood planks. 'There's nothing to get a grip on,' he shouted (always).

'I know, darling, I'm sorry, but what can I do? I eat as much as I can,' Katerina replied.

117

'Eat more. I shall have to see to it. Tell the servants to give us more suet.'

'Yes, Günter. But then you get too fat.'

'You don't have to worry about me. Worry about yourself. If you were fatter, you would not seem so tall. It does me no good to have a tall wife.'

'You should have married a Jew.'

'Shut up. Don't be so impudent. Don't argue with me.'

'I'm sorry, darling,' she said (firmly).

The endearing characteristics of Günter Strepper. He could never pull off his own boots. Time after time he tried it. Time after time Katerina caught him at it, red in the face. Then he would smile shyly at her as she pulled them off for him.

He slept flat on his face.

He always rubbed his gums with his forefinger after doing his teeth.

He blinked when he was nervous or excited: he always blinked at the Chancelry receptions.

He was coarse with her in the presence of Klaus: for example, the only thing to be said for her scraggy legs, he said, was that 'there was plenty of room between them'; Klaus was embarrassed; so was Katerina.

If something went wrong in Katerina's management of the household, as it did very often, Strepper would make her apologize to him in a most formal manner. There were variations to this game, which they had played since they were married, but for example, he would stand, his feet apart, his thumbs on the buckle of his belt. She would bow her head, apologize, kneel, look up, apologize. He would slap her hard, on her face, or push her over backwards with his knee. This was, of course, their way of making love; it is the way of many quite ordinary people; you or me (as they say).

The endearing things about Strepper. Now, after a year or two (ten) of marriage, there was nothing Katerina liked better than a bleeding collar bone, a few bruises anywhere around to be covered up with powder, or a few strands of hair loose on the bed cover. Blonde with streaks of brown. If Strepper did not provide his preliminaries, the love made was very inadequate for a marriage-bond bound mainly with the binding of *Mein Kampf*; but Strepper always did. For he too had difficulty not only with his boots. His joints were stiff—though once up and he was, of course, away. And no emotion aroused Günter Strepper more than anger and indignation.

Klaus, meanwhile, had his dreams of righteousness and Teutonic knighthood. Even now, after ten years in the Party, Klaus had his dreams.

While Günter and Katerina played their games in their house, he sat alone in his flat listening to gramophone records of the operas of Wagner, the symphonies of Brückner. He never went out except with Günter and Katerina. His work was his life. He was dedicated to (what was to him) the betterment of mankind. He was happy working with Strepper and doing whatever Strepper thought it best for him to do, whether summarizing reports or attending receptions at the Chancelry. He liked to see Katerina because she reminded him of his childhood in Pomerania and his brothers. These were the happy days.

On the tenth anniversary of their marriage, Günter and Katerina invited Klaus to dinner at the Kempinski hotel. Klaus and Günter wore their formal SS uniforms; Katerina wore a grey tailored dress and the grey with the black was elegant. They had just heard about Edward's Iron Cross; they drank his health in German champagne. Then they ate plovers' eggs and pheasant and green salad tossed in the French manner by the French chef. Through the window they could see the burnt hulk of the synagogue—if they looked.

'Klaus, my dear Klaus,' said Günter Strepper. 'You are my oldest friend so I wanted you to be here. You are also the oldest friend of my wife. You introduced us to each other, you brought us together, so it is quite right that you should be here to celebrate our happy ten years together.'

Katerina laughed and drank more German champagne.

'Please don't laugh, Katerina, I am serious.'

'I am as happy as you are,' said Klaus.

'Klaus,' said Günter, 'there are not so many men who can keep a young wife like Katty. I've kept her for ten years and I'll keep her forever.'

Katerina laughed again and leant more on her husband's shoulder.

'Katty, please don't drink quite so much so quickly,' he said. He went on. 'To me, our bond, Klaus, our brotherhood, is symbolic of the bond and brotherhood of all Germans. It will achieve miracles, miracles, miracles,' (louder and slaps on the table) 'as we have already seen miracles' (subsidence).

'Yes, Günter,' said Klaus. 'I think we should drink to that.' Katerina drank before they had raised their glasses.

'Please wait, Katerina,' said Günter. The waiter filled her glass. 'To our brotherhood.' The two men drank. Katerina did not. 'Would you drink the toast, please, my dear?' said Günter.

'Me too? Of course.' She drained her glass. The waiter filled it.

'I am a fulfilled man, Klaus,' said Günter Strepper. 'And
how many men can say that of themselves?'

'You are a man of the times, Günter, a man of the New
Order,' said Klaus.

'Yes, yes. Yes, yes.'

'Whereas others . . .'

'Yes.'

'Poor old Helmuth, for example . . .'

'Yes. Poor Helmuth. He is not a man of the times.'

'No.'

'But I think he deserves a toast, no?' said Günter.

'Poor Helmuth,' said Katerina.

They drained their glasses.

Helmuth von Rummelsberg: 1940

Helmuth von Rummelsberg was then ten thousand miles
away, attaché to the German Embassy in Tokyo. It had been
a journey of ten weeks in a Portuguese ship to get there. It
was his first journey of this kind and his first ten weeks in
ten years without a woman, a lover, a mistress, a girl-friend,
someone ringing up or writing, someone who talked to him
in that special asthmatic whisper—the tones of the beloved.
For if Helmuth had been known in the past years (by his
fellow diplomats) as a promising colleague, an excellent,
impartial civil servant, he was also known (by his fellow
diplomats) as the Casanova or Julien Sorel of the Wilhelmstrasse, as a man who charmed the mothers and seduced the
sisters, wives, housemaids, etc., of his colleagues and com-
panions. Of course they did not like this kind of thing—in
principle and in fact: even those who knew that there was
some business of an unhappy love in this Helmuth's youth

121

would gladly have excluded him somehow; but even if they could have disregarded his popularity among their wives and sisters, the pleasant opinions held of him by their mothers and housemaids outflanked them on both wings. And he was nice to the brothers and husbands too.

What was to be made of a reputation like that? Young diplomats in the Wilhelmstrasse were jealous because in their imagination they too would like to be incessantly playing with *des millions de joujoux, de bonbons merveilleux.*

Am I to say that they should curb their imaginations? I should think not. But think of for a time, without the imagination, or imagine in a disciplined way, twenty-five love affairs in ten years. Even if fifteen of these are just humorous liaisons with pretty housemaids who are bored by their work and their boy-friends (an aristocratic indulgence), the ten that remain with ten women he might have married, these are sad incidents—halting, stunted bursts of love—cowering gestures for a man.

A liner—as if a trip on the sea would cure, cleanse, or otherwise renew him.

Ten thousand miles, two thousand million people one way; the rest of the world the other—between Helmuth von Rummelsberg and his native country, his Katerina. It changed nothing.

Ten years. It changed nothing. It changed nothing in the head of this man. His ship arrived on the Inland Sea. His eyes alighted on the pillars standing in the water—the Shinto shrine of Miajima. It did nothing to the damage done to his brain (if one can be so specific about where the damage of love is done). To describe this damage, to catalogue this 'unhappy affair', this case of 'unrequited love' (of Helmuth von Rummelsberg for Katerina von Treblitz Strepper): for the month after he had felt sick. Then he had thought about it all the time, gnawing his knuckles in bitterness. For a year he had thought of her on most days. He had caught gonorrhoea three times and a needle from the doctor's syringe had broken off in his leg. By the end of thirteen months he had thought about her sporadically; her image had crossed his mind once a week, a month, every ten days. The nine years after that: he had thought about her less but always occasionally and when he did it was never dispassionately but always with a slow and pondering look in his eyes.

He landed at the port of Osaka and went to Tokyo by train. There he lived in the German Embassy.

Chapter Six

I

IF IT HAD BEEN NOTICED by other members of the British Community in Berlin that Suzi (no housemaid) came in and out of my house, I might have been in trouble. Security, morality and reputation. General C. and his wife lived opposite me in Charlottenburg. I therefore took a flat in the Savignyplatz, three minutes' walk from the Steinplatz. It was not furnished. The walls were white; there was a bed, a bathroom, and an electric kettle (cups, saucers, towels, sheets, a few provisions, etc.).

Suzi came to see me there, more often now that Helmuth was more often in West Germany. I asked her why he went there. She smiled and said it was to enable her to see me.

'Does he know that we meet together?' I asked.

'I think so, perhaps, I don't know. We don't talk about you.'

'Would he mind?'

'He does not seem to mind.'

'If he knows.'

'Yes, if he knows.'

'Do you still sleep with him?'

'Really,' she said, 'you have such a bad opinion of me. Isn't he my uncle?'

'Is he?'

She smiled. This was on our bed, in our flat.

She used to take me to the Dahlem Museum, or we would go to the cinema, to the theatre, to the opera. She liked to discuss each event afterwards—earnestly and comprehensively. Then for a week or ten days I would not see her or only see her once. She told me that she had to look after her 'uncle'. Then I would work very hard on my file; on the Almanach de Gotha; at digging up evidence; at trying to find a trace of a bastard or adopted child in the von Rummelsberg family.

I once took her on a tour of my favourite parts of the wall. We only got as far as the blocked-out bridge in Wedding.

'It is frightful, it is ugly,' she shouted, 'How can you enjoy such a sight?'

I shrugged my shoulders. 'I don't know,' I said. 'It is a monument of a kind . . . like the Great Wall of China.'

'You are perverted and cruel,' then, for the second time, she cried. I was embarrassed and drove her back to Zuntz for tea.

One Sunday I gave a cocktail party. It was all we did in the military and diplomatic circles, and it was my turn. My secretary invited all those people who had invited me over the past year, officers of the Allied forces within the orbit of my rank and department. I asked Suzi if she would like to come. She became very excited, said she would like it very much and then asked if Helmuth could also be invited. I did invite him and they both came. They talked to the few other Berliners I had asked; the British and Americans, too, talked amongst themselves. I talked to the few French who had come down from Tegel with Armand (lanky, pale Armand).

I hardly talked to the von Rummelsbergs—my Suzi and her Helmuth—and they left early, probably to get to the club.

'Who was that man?' the Political Adviser asked me.

'Helmuth von Rummelsberg,' I said. 'He was once in the German foreign service.'

'Oh, was he?'

'Strangely enough he is the brother of Klaus von Rummelsberg.'

'Is that so?'

Without looking at me, nor changing her expression, the Political Adviser's wife said: 'Fearfully common girl. It is awful the way these middle-aged Germans take their little mistresses around with them.'

'I think she is his niece,' I said.

'Yes,' said this English woman, 'they're always their nieces or secretaries or step-daughters.'

A remark like that from that kind of woman (my mother, my sister) might once have been enough to destroy my feelings of love for a girl—but Suzi had already lasted for longer than twenty-four hours. While I was not conscious of a particularly dramatic passion within me, she had somehow become part of me, part of my life. Again it was a negative approach, but a negative approach is often the most effective. If I had wanted to disengage from Suzi now, I would not have known how. I knew it could be done, I knew the answer—but not how, not what question to ask to get the answer.

She was cheerful and good-natured and put up with my bad moods or laughed at them. When she was in a bad temper it seemed rather endearing and sweet—she never diffused despair. She had a mind, an excellent mind: I never had to consider the depth of her comprehension in talking to her. Every remark of mine was understood, digested and returned in comment. After an initial intellectual shyness, she began to initiate comments and conversation—but always with feminine tact. For all her intelligence, she was feminine.

Her femininity: in the details of her clothes—always coloured or frilly, clean and sweet-smelling. There was no sense of utility in her style. Nothing was well-worn or old-fashioned. She would put on coloured underclothes and patterned stockings and developed quite unusual style (for a German girl) in her choice of dresses, skirts, blouses.

The flat: although we had little furniture and considered it as a temporary place to meet, she made it so charming that I much preferred being there than at my official residence. She chose the material for the curtains, a rug for the floor, a bedcover. She made paper flowers out of tissue paper which she put in a porcelain bowl. But most of all she herself decorated and lit up this room and any room she entered. There was a sense of delight in any space—a room, a yard, a street—when she was in one corner of it. That, and her voice—soft, expressive, soft, gentle—were the greatest of her qualities, though the list of them is long now: but *then*, with Armand, say, I just said that she was easy. I thought of it all as convenience. I did not realize that already, as a husband promises at a wedding, I worshipped her with my body. My mind might not have been lonely— ranging free and independent—but the body too, had its will—strong and unconscious. My body worshipped Suzi and worked on my mind.

It had been clear to me for some time that if I asked Suzi to live with me it would finish my career in the diplomatic service. It is tricky, in any case, for a diplomat in a sensitive post to marry or become involved with an alien, and my love was not (then) so absolute as to risk my career; for if I was not a diplomat, what was I?

She (Suzi) never asked me about my intentions, but once she said something about 'our child'—what the world would be like for him—then stopped, stuttered and blushed. I pretended not to notice and soon after she told me how much Helmuth needed her, depended on her; and how much she owed him. Between the two of us, however, we said enough about how tentative our friendship was, must be.

'How can I know you well,' I said, 'when we speak different languages?' (At Zuntz).

'But I speak English and you speak German,' she replied. It was like that. We discounted each other's excuses but made our own.

Incidents. Incident following incident. Suzi. Me. But I remained with engraved cuff-links and London suits. She still wore stockings on picnics in the Grünewald.

There were times when we met with Armand and later there were times when we met with Helmuth. They were the only ones to see us together. If Helmuth knew I was ... that ... about ... then he was well controlled. As well controlled as I. I was churned by my nerves when I met him; when sitting or standing a yard or two from him, I imagined his perfumed, marbled, loose stomach clammily pressed to hers; her acquiescent face under him. Could he see that in my face? In my expression? Always when we parted and she went home with him, she squeezed my hand as she shook it. Then I would drink a large whisky and try not to imagine his flaccid, buckling . . .

When she was with me, I never thought his thoughts might be the same. The young have a right to the young. He was the robber. Suzi was mine, even if the flat in the Karmerstrasse and not the bare room in the Savignyplatz was still her home. And when she was with me, I never remembered my own jealousy.

Once I asked Suzi a second time: 'What does Helmuth think we do together?'

'Oh, talk, go to the cinema. He is glad I go out with you.'

'Doesn't he even suspect?'

'Not at all. You see, he thinks, well, he thinks you and your friend Armand . . . he thinks you are . . . you know . . . that you don't like women.'

As she said that, I did like women, all for the sake of Suzi. Her eyes turned up but hid behind a lock of hair— their expression nervous lest I should be angry, relieved when I laughed. She turned, then and there, on the pavement, pirouetting on her foot, and kissed me. Of course her kisses now imitated mine—but this was the first kiss of her own accord. The innocence had gone but not the sweetness. There were times when her breath smelt of latrines or rotting liver; there were times when she was rough—but she was always sweet, sweet, though she wore stockings on picnics and would never eat sausages in the street. She grew sweeter but never sickeningly sweet; sweeter so that if I did not love her more, the love was more substantial—the glimpse of fleeting ankles was now a stare at the perfection which overflowed the flaws—a gaze at the charm of mind that distracted my (the other's) eye from any shortcomings.

Two months after she became my mistress, she began to take an interest in my work.

'What does a diplomat do?' she asked.

'He prepares reports . . . for his foreign office. He advises them . . . the government.'

'And on what do you report and advise?'

'Trade . . . that sort of thing.'

'Do you just do that all the time? It must be very boring,' she said.

'Well, it is,' I said. 'I am lucky to have other interests.'

'Me,' she laughed.

Then we were walking up the Kantstrasse to look at the photographs outside a cinema.

She returned to my work another time. 'You cannot study trade statistics all the time. There is not so much trade with Berlin.'

'I go to diplomatic receptions.'

'Yes, but what do you do in your office?'

'I investigate and report and advise.'

'What sort of thing? What are you doing now?'

I smiled. 'It's a secret.'

She did not smile. 'I am not curious, you know. I am only asking because I love you and would like to become interested in your work.'

We were then sitting drinking beer in a small café on the Stuttgarterplatz. It was August.

On a third occasion she said: 'You think I am elusive about my family. Well, you are more elusive about your work.'

'Diplomats have to keep secrets.'

'And girls too,' she said.

Then I was lying in the bath in the Savignyplatz flat and she was sitting on the lavatory.

Helmuth von Rummelsberg: 1941

There was evidence, I discovered, against Helmuth—
evidence that he supported the National Socialist régime:
but this evidence was slight and was never used against
him. There was also conflicting evidence, evidence for
Helmuth. He resigned from the German Foreign Service at
the end of the war of his own accord.

In Tokyo he received a letter from an old friend, Peter
Trübner, who had left the Foreign Office for the army, in
which he said: 'Our spirit here in Russia is fine but back at
home some people are getting fed up with the Nazis. Even
my little sister Betta ... is quite active against them ... in
secret.'

Helmuth had stayed with the Trübners on Lake Constance in 1936 and again in 1937. The father was a stolid
Catholic burgher of Uberlingen: Betta, he remembered, had
been a shopgirl with very fair hair in plaits. She had wanted
to be a vet.

It is not clear whether this letter is what led to Betta
Trübner's arrest (later). Probably not. However, Helmuth
did say in a letter to his brother Klaus: 'Trübner tells
me that even his little sister is plotting against your
lot.'

Then we know from the Americans that Helmuth was
instrumental in the arrest of their spy, Henrici. Looking for
a box of matches in the desk of the third secretary, Henrici,
he found instead a matchbox of microfilm of Embassy documents on the Japanese war shipping in Tokyo bay. He

reported this to the Ambassador and Henrici was returned to Germany under guard (later shot).

Helmuth barely noticed these incidents. It was at this time that he first met Shosuke Ienaga, a man of his own age in the Japanese Foreign Office. With Shosuke he began to leave the precincts of the German Embassy and lead a life beyond the formal one imposed by his profession. Up to now this had been difficult, because the Ambassador was a strict and fanatic National Socialist, a believer in the discipline and morality of the New Order.

However, since Japan was the ally of Germany and Shosuke's father was in the Tojo government, the Ambassador and senior embassy staff were pleased with his and Helmuth's friendship.

Though married, Shosuke still lived with his father in the Meguro district of Tokyo. Helmuth did not visit the house until some time after he had become a close friend of Shosuke. They would rather go out to Geisha houses in Tokyo; or visit Buddhist temples and Shinto shrines in Nara and Kyoto.

Shosuke was, like other Japanese, very small, but in Japan it was Helmuth who felt conspicuous and ridiculous. Shosuke was silent and reserved and for some time Helmuth found it impossible to assess his feelings and reactions. Later, however, he learnt to read the faint inflection of the lip or eyelid, the different degree of facial tenseness and relaxation, the colour of the skin on the cheek, the pressure of blood in the veins. He also learnt only to suggest what he would otherwise have said outright.

Shosuke spoke German, Helmuth no Japanese. Each sentence of the former in the foreign language was formulated in a long period of silence. Helmuth learnt to curb his enthusiasm in conversation, to think far more of each phrase he pronounced.

Gradually, too, he became used to such things as the flippant ministrations of the Geishas: their bird-like faces under thick powder topped by hair curled and shaped like carved and varnished wood. He learnt to sit cross-legged for hours at a time; to eat cubes of raw, unrecognizable matter and drink soups filled with floating spawn. Shosuke never drank more than three cups of saki; Helmuth sadly drank as many as twenty-five without feeling any effect.

The face of this Japanese friend of his was large and serious; his hair was black and cut short.

Sometimes they would go on from the Geisha dinners to baths and massage parlours and here too Helmuth had to learn, as a mental patient learns his treatment, what was of his body, what was of his mind; what was erotic pleasure and what was more profound compulsion.

Ise. They walked on gravel paths between hills hidden by thick tall trees.

'This is the sanctuary of the Shinto cult, the only part of Japan untouched by Buddhism,' said Shosuke. 'Elsewhere the two mix well together; Shintoism is for those who love life; Buddhism for those who think of death.'

Small Japanese children in the elaborate costumes of Samurai walked up the path to the shrine for the ceremony of their initiation.

'Perhaps it is like that in Germany?' Shosuke asked. 'National Socialism preoccupied with life and Christianity with death?'

'Not really,' said Helmuth. 'Not quite.'

'That is how it might have been in Russia, don't you

133

think? Or how it might be in Christian countries if the Bolsheviks finally take them?'

Helmuth, unaccustomed to the contemplation of any further spread of Communism, blushed and said nothing as he had learnt, in Japan, to say nothing.

And Shosuke, unlike a Japanese, explained himself. 'To the eastern mind, you see, the opposition of Communism to Christianity is very puzzling. Communism is apparently to us the child of Christianity. Asian Communism—it is just a further way of imitating the West.'

'To us,' said Helmuth, 'they seem very different.'

'Different, yet the same. And here,' Shosuke said, pointing to a rough log cabin surrounded by log palisades, up to which they had come through the wood, 'here is the extreme of our one opposite, yet it is the heart, the centre of Japan. It is the shrine of Ise. There lie the relics of our first emperor, son of God himself.'

Hakone. A large hotel built in the hills by Mount Fuji. The architecture, the furnishings, were all European of the Edwardian era. Helmuth felt that he could be in Baden Baden.

'This is a monument of the Meiji era,' said Shosuke, 'as typical as the Meiji shrine itself. For my grandfather this hotel might have been his first experience of the Western world. He was a war lord, a retainer of the Shogun. The life he led was the same as that his ancestor would have led in the middle ages. We did not want to become a modern, industrialized nation, you know. The Americans forced us to open up to their trade, they forced us with gunboats. So we imitated them. This war is only a further imitation—an imperialist war like the American war against Mexico or the wars between the British and the French.'

134

They walked in the Japanese garden beneath the hotel; exact paths, lawns, ponds and terraces steepening down to the gorge below. Fresh mists, half spray, came up from the river and curled around the trees.

'Of course we have not yet learnt to imitate their rules of the game. My father would seem cruel and savage to them, perhaps even to you. But he is no more savage and cruel than a European of the time of Shakespeare, Erasmus or Madame de Pompadour. It is possible to change the economic structure of a country more quickly than to change the habits of its people. But I know, if we lose this war, we shall be blamed for savagery and cruelty; our adversaries, I think, will blame their cruelty on machines.'

After six months of friendship, Helmuth was asked to visit Shosuke's family. Their house, from the outside, could have been in Zehlendorf or any European suburb: inside it was furnished partly in the European style, partly in the traditional Japanese style. The floor of the sitting-room was tatami matting and Helmuth removed his shoes; but there were armchairs and a sofa. The dining-room had a low table in the Japanese manner, but under the table was a pit for those who did not want to sit cross-legged. Shosuke's room was in the traditional style—the bedding was stored away behind sliding walls of paper and wood.

Shosuke's father, the minister, appeared for a short time; he spoke no German but laughed all the time and clapped Helmuth on the shoulder. His eyes were narrow; his hair was white; his mouth drooped in a sneer. Shosuke's mother was also there; quiet and silent. Both parents left after drinking some tea—the man leaving the house, the woman moving to some back room. Shosuke's wife, however, led them across the small garden to a hut, and they climbed in by a small door, more like a hen's entrance into a hen-hutch. There she put green powder into ceramic bowls, poured in hot water and beat the liquid into a froth with a whisk. Helmuth drank the tea as slowly and formally as it had been prepared.

Shosuke's wife was slightly taller than her husband and had long narrow eyes like her father-in-law.

'Tell me,' she said to Helmuth, as they re-crossed the lawn, 'what do you two do when you go out together?'

Helmuth blushed.

'Don't tell her,' said Shosuke, smiling.

'You know,' she said, lifting her kimono to enter the house, 'women in Japan are treated very badly.'

They drank more tea in the house and Shosuke's wife asked Helmuth if he had read Hermann Hesse. No, he said, he had not.

Then he left because there was warning of an air raid, and during air raids he was supposed to be in the Embassy. He wondered how such raids were in Germany—whether his brothers were in any danger—though now he rarely thought of Katerina, who rarely thought of him.

Klaus von Rummelsberg / Katerina von Treblitz / Günter Strepper: 1941

One day in June she (Katerina) went with her husband to see the Haus am Wannsee—the SS centre for experimental breeding. She thought of him (Helmuth) then because she was taken with Strepper by the director to see (through a two-way mirror) a selected girl mate for the first time.

'We find it better,' said the director, 'that the two partners

136

should not meet each other before they are mated. If they do then one or the other tends to form a psychological revulsion and they have to be re-paired. As it is, you see, they are made slightly drunk on white wine, then placed in this room with a mattress, dressed only in their underclothes. A mattress is better than a bed, we find, because it does not bend or buckle and makes the penetration of virgins easier. We tried them naked but that, more often than not, led to impotence in the male, which is curious, but there you are.'

The three of them sat in chairs, then stood closer to the mirror as first the man, then the girl, came into the room. There was no sound-lead between the two rooms so they could not hear what the two said to each other.

'You will notice,' said the director, 'that although the girl is a specific Aryan type with blonde hair and large limbs, the man is not so: he is brown-haired. This is because we attach more importance to the mental qualities in the male. This one is SS of course, and has fathered between thirty and forty. He is the one who is invariably impotent with nakedness. You see, he is having the girl undress herself; that is embarrassing to her which arouses him, yes, you see, and now, he even has her undress him which is lazy; he didn't do that last week. We use our best males twice a week; more often and their fertility decreases. Now, you see, he lays her on the mattress and rubs her with jelly and penetrates immediately. He also wastes no time in finishing it, I am afraid. But they are not doing it for fun.'

They came out into the garden which ran down from the brick mansion to the lake.

'You are here for the conference, I imagine, general?' the director asked Günter.

137

'Yes. This afternoon. My adjutant joins me after lunch and then we meet with Eichmann and the others.'

'Yes. You have a problem.'

'You have one too, I think,' said Günter.

'But a more pleasant and a more positive one.'

They passed several pregnant girls who smiled faintly. 'They are mostly country girls,' the director went on, 'so they get on quite well together. We keep one or two here for the full nine months; the others go to our house in Grünewald.'

'And are you pleased with the results?' Katerina asked.

'It is too early to say, countess,' the director replied. 'Our oldest child is only two months. Have you children, madame general, may I ask? We could not have thought of a better match than the two of you, if I may say so.'

'No,' she said, 'I am afraid we have no children.'

'She's too thin,' said Günter Strepper, 'she's miscarried three times.'

Katerina frowned.

After lunch with the director, Klaus arrived with a leather case of documents. The three of them then got into Günter's Mercedes and drove away from the Haus am Wannsee, past the S-Bahnhof, following the side of the lake northwards. Three or four miles north they came to another, larger, more isolated house on the lake. Several official cars were parked outside. Klaus handed Günter the document-case, then saluted. Günter entered the house: Klaus and Katerina walked round the house to the garden which also ran down to the lake.

'The SS have taken over the nicest houses in Berlin,' said Katerina.

'We only have these two on Wannsee, I think,' said Klaus.

138

'The Navy have five or six. This one'—his hand waved backwards—'used to belong to a Jewish publisher; you see, he did quite well for himself.'

'Now you're doing quite well for yourselves.'

'They belong to the state. This is used for conferences, and the other for experiments.'

'Have you ever seen those experiments?' Katerina asked.

'No. What were they like?'

'Disgusting. The whole idea is stupid.'

'They say we need the Aryran breed for the new lands in the East.'

'What nonsense. You know it's nonsense. Before, they said we needed the lands because there were too many Germans. Now it's the other way around.'

'Does Günter think it is nonsense?'

'Him? Of course not. He's as crazy as Hitler.'

'Be quiet.'

Katerina was silent.

'What is the conference about?' she asked.

'Jews.'

'As usual. What about the Jews? They seem to be more of a pest now than they ever were before.'

'Exactly. They're deciding what to do about them.'

'I thought they were being thrown out—pushed into Africa with the niggers or something like that.'

'We can't do that now because of the war.'

'So what are you going to do?'

'Exactly. That is what they're discussing.'

'Why not forget about them? Leave them alone. They're harmless now.'

'I know. But I don't think they will.'

'What?'

'Forget about them.'

'Why not?' She sat down and lay out flat in the sun. Klaus sat too, but upright, his hands clasped round his knees.

'You see,' he said, 'we never came across Jews in Pomerania, but I dare say, in the towns, in the big urban areas, some of our people suffered considerably from them.'

'How?' she asked, blinking into the sun.

'I don't quite know. Economically in some way. Having nothing to eat and seeing the Jews with plenty of their own food—kosher or whatever they call it. You see, the Jews always looked after themselves and did so right through the depression; but they kept squeezing money out of the Germans who owed it to them but had none, not even to buy food.'

'Was it like that?'

'Yes, it was. It must have been. That is why most of our people are quite irrational about the Jews. That and other things. They're probably cooking up something nasty in there.'

'Günter has nightmares about Jews,' Katerina said. 'Obscene nightmares. He wakes up puffing and in a real sweat.'

'Yes, he's like the others.'

Then they both said nothing. Klaus looked at the lake. Far to the left he could see a few heads of swimmers from the Wannsee beach.

'You're not really like the others,' Katerina said to him.

'No,' he answered, 'nor are you. But I try to understand them. I've got to.'

'Have you any news of Edward?'

'His unit is in France but I think he is to be appointed to

140

the General Staff with our cousin General von Osterhauen. We should see him soon.'

'And (gulp) what about Helmuth?'

'Yes. He's still in Tokyo. Doing well, I think.'

'I wonder if you will ever all be together again.'

'Oh, you know, Katty, we are grown up now.'

'Yes, I know. I mean, I wonder if anything of the old order will survive in the new.'

'I should say so. Doesn't Günter think so?'

'Yes, he does. So do I. But we are changing things so quickly. Nothing will be quite the same again, will it? So what will it be like? I haven't thought it out, this Aryan life. If I had a child, I would have no idea of how to bring it up as a member of the master race. Would you?'

'You would just bring him up as a German.'

'Yes, but that's not new. Germans, well, we have always thought we were superior but then, so do the French and the English, I imagine. They kick niggers around just as I used to kick the Poles and peasants at home. But I don't see that those stupid girls at that breeding farm down there are superior to our Polish servants at home—yet they're supposed to be our prize stud mares.'

'You should ask Günter to explain it to you,' said Klaus. 'I don't really understand it all myself.'

'Günter!' she said, her cheeks flushed, 'I am afraid his racial superiority does not extend to his brains.'

'Be quiet.'

Late in the afternoon Günter came down to where they were sitting: he had a faint smile on his face.

'Let's go,' he said, 'I'm hungry. Let's all three of us eat at that Bavarian restaurant. I could do with a good beer.'

They walked up the garden towards the car.

'If you see Eichmann, my dear, I think you should talk to him,' Günter said. 'He told me he had heard about you and would like to meet you.'

'Well,' said Katerina, when they were in the car, 'what are you going to do with the Jews?'

'The conference is secret, Kat, you shouldn't speak about it.'

'This car hasn't microphones,' she replied.

'Well,' said Günter, 'we are meeting again tomorrow but I think we've settled the Yids' lot once and for all.'

Edward von Rummelsberg: 1941–1942

As he returned with his unit through Poland, for re-deployment in the West, Edward had been shocked to see the destruction that had come after the war. He saw, from the train, whole villages of blackened stone and ashes; even, between Kutuo and Kolo, Deathshead SS burning cottages with flame-throwers.

Billeted in Posen for a night, and dining with an officer of the garrison, he asked what was the reason for the post-war destruction.

'Oh, it's nothing to do with us,' the officer replied, 'It's Frank's Government-General making damned fools of themselves.'

Then, next morning, while Edward was waiting in the train for Berlin, a goods train drew up alongside. Low droning moans came from the trucks. Edward leapt out onto the platform and shouted to a transport sergeant standing beside the train: 'Is something being done about those wounded, you blockhead?'

'Don't worry, captain,' said the transport sergeant,

'They're not our wounded. Poles, I should say, or Jews.' He laughed. 'Or both.'

Edward climbed back into his compartment and bit his finger-nails.

He spent two hours in Berlin, and tried but failed to telephone Klaus. Then his unit passed straight through to Frankfurt and was operational in Rundstedt's Army Group A by the end of April 1940—in time for the invasion of France.

Edward's part was to wait in an armoured column more than a hundred miles long and fifty miles wide (under General von Kleist) near the village of Dasburg—then drive through the northern tip of Luxembourg up into the wooded hills of the Ardennes. His Iron Cross was at his throat.

By 16 May he had reached the river Oise—a few charred English and Frenchmen behind him.

Then, though his unit went East again, Edward was appointed to the General Staff as adjutant to General von Osterhauen, a second cousin of his mother. There he found the thoughts and feelings of General Staff officers quite different from those of the young officers on the front. There they had felt calm pride in their victories and enthusiasm for battle. In Berlin, where they sat surrounded by marked and pinned maps of Europe, North Africa and the world, the officers, preoccupied with the strategy of the whole war, were gloomy and pessimistic. The victories in France and the signing of an armistice in Compiègne had been followed by no solution. Britain refused to come to terms; Spain would not join in the war. Their exact military minds were confused by their commander-in-chief's (Hitler's) intuitive strategy, which broke conventions but was often, as in France, brilliant and successful. The contingency plans for the invasion of Britain, the storming of Gibraltar, the occupation

143

of the Azores, the securing of French North Africa, the drive against Suez, the support of Italy in Greece, the buttressing of satellite states in the Balkans and, of course, the invasion of Russia, seemed (to them all) to be the classic blunder of a war on two fronts spilling over into war on a dozen. The senior staff officers walked round the building of the War Ministry with the pained expressions of people suffering from gastritis or explosive diarrhoea; they twitched at nothing and winced at any exchange of views with the enthusiastic National Socialists among their colleagues.

Von Osterhauen was a friend of Beck and always called his commander-in-chief 'That bugger'—a term (I know) used by his commander-in-chief.

'That bugger's going to land us all in the soup,' the General said to Edward almost every day.

'I think you underestimate our men, sir,' Edward replied. 'In my opinion, one German is worth ten of the enemy.'

'You may be right, my boy,' said the General, 'but first of all we are outnumbered by more than ten to one since that bugger has taken on the Bolshies as well as the British: and secondly, my boy, which enemy? Don't judge all of them by the Poles and the French. I helped to train the Red Army, damn it, so I know how good they are. That bugger doesn't...'

Edward's objections to the direction of the war, he told his elderly cousin, were ethical rather than military. What was the point of it? Were the conquered communities being furthered in any way by Germany? Frank was treating the Poles in the most abominable way, or so he gathered. It was a betrayal of the army not to treat the conquered people decently. His own men had always given their chocolate to the prisoners they had taken. Germany was a Christian nation and should behave like one. If Hitler was afraid of the Bolsheviks, then he should build up Poland; but instead, as far as he, Edward, could make out, they were pulling it down. The Poles were worse off than before the war. And the Jews. The government were making fools of themselves with the Jews who were now as harmless as household flies, whatever they had done before. To think that a special session of the Reichstag had been called at Nürnberg to forbid Jews employing German housemaids. How petty they were, the Nazis. They and their misty pagan nonsense, etc. etc.

'Oh, you're like Moltke and his Kreisau people,' said General O.

[*Helmuth James, Graf von Moltke. Born 11 March 1907, at Kreisau—his parents' estate in Silesia. A lawyer and his own estate agent. In 1939 he was the expert on martial and international law with the Supreme Command of the armed forces. Executed on 23 January 1945.*]

Edward was introduced to von Moltke and the latter invited him to his country house at Kreisau in the spring of 1942. The house reminded Edward of Kassow, which he had not visited since the death of his mother.

Moltke was very tall, taller even than Edward, and his hair receded from his forehead. Edward was shy with the older man—his brittle humour, his deadpan manner. He was also nervous in the company of the others staying at Kreisau—Peter Yorck von Wartenburg, Adam von Trott zu Solz. Their habits and mannerisms, however, were familiar: they had friends, relations and acquaintances in common. There were also Germans of a breed Edward had never

145

come across—the Social Democrat, Julius Leber; the Catholic priest, Father Delp. With these he was at first most ill at ease.

Von Moltke took Edward into the garden as soon as he arrived. 'I'm sure you don't have daffodils like that at Kassow,' he said, pointing to his own. 'Aren't those fine? But I like to have them in the ground. We don't pick them.'

'You needn't worry, Rummelsberg,' he said, 'We aren't doing any plotting down here. We're just thinking. All the same, I don't think that brother of yours ought to know ... just in case his friend Strepper gets wind of it.'

'No, sir. Of course not,' said Edward.

'I'm glad we met,' said the count. 'You see I'm afraid we're sure to lose the war and I'm afraid we deserve to. Nor is there much we can do about it—except wait for the end. But after the end, there will still be Germany and Germans and it's up to people like us to think of what that Germany will be like. If only they'd thought it out before 1918.'

His face was serious. His arms remained clasped behind his back.

'All my life,' he went on, 'even at school, I was against narrow-mindedness and violence—and presumption, intolerance and that absolute, pitiless regimentation which is so much part of our German character. It's that, I should say, which has found such perfect expression in this National Socialist state we have now. And I can tell you that from quite an early age I dedicated myself to overcome this spirit and all the harm it brings with it—excessive nationalism, racial persecution, unbelief and materialism.'

Edward nodded but said nothing.

'Have you noticed the smell of daffodils in a room?' von Moltke interposed. 'Heavy—sickly and heavy.'

146

'Perhaps you will say,' he said, smiling wryly, 'that I feel like this because I had an English mother . . .'

'Oh no . . .'

Von Moltke waved his hand. 'Perhaps it's true. I'm sure the Nazis would say so. In fact I don't mind if they do. You see, Rummelsberg, I don't think of myself so much as a German as a European. Germany is one part of the European body—a central, essential part, perhaps—the liver or the lungs—but no more than a part . . . and no less.'

Then he said, more quietly, 'And to be a European, that is just a means to being a man. And as a man I think I would just say I am a Christian, just a Christian and absolutely nothing else.'

'Now you must come and meet Freya, my wife, and my baby sons. I think you will like her . . . even though she's a Rhinelander.' He laughed.

After a time at Kreisau, Edward no longer felt ill at ease with the Catholics and Socialists but increasingly so in his uniform, in his black boots. Yet black boots seemed as integral a part of him as his calves and collar bone; as much an aspect of the world as bark on a tree. He was a professional soldier. He possessed hardly any clothes apart from his military uniform. Here at Kreisau the others wore sports jackets and wide, flapping trousers.

Chapter Seven

I

SUZI HAD A HANDBAG and in her handbag, like all Germans, she carried her identification papers. The handbag was black leather with false brass buckles and clasps: the identity card was I assume, grey linen like other West German identity cards, but I never saw this particular one. Though I knew it would tell me something of what I wanted to know, I never looked at it. This was our game now—that I did not quite know who she was. A girl must have her secrets.

She, on her part, did not quite know what I did in my office. She would try and wheedle that out of me. I thought that was our game. Of course I had good reasons for not having her know what I did: we wanted no leak to Klaus and the government in Bonn. Nevertheless I thought we were playing a game and this was her side of it, a game it was better to play while the whole thing was only an affair, a young English gentleman playing around with a foreign girl of pleasant habits and easy ways.

However, there were symptoms of a condition in me which suggested that the situation was changing. The affair had started with superficial attraction to a woman, or the idea of a woman, that was almost abstract. There was no change in the rate of blood-flow, no filling of empty arteries. It could have been a girl turning her head as she entered a shop across a street; a naked display dummy in a shop window; a skirt above the knee in an underground; an advertisement for a short-hand school; an actress in a film still; a princess in a history textbook—anything that was an image without reality or reality so brief that there is no second look. She had been a girl sitting at another table in a café, vague through the steam and cigarette smoke. How many thousands of them there had been.

Then came the second state: immediate sexual attraction. Face to face and alone. The first chance to back down because, after all, what was that blouse she was wearing to me? The pattern and the colour were alien yet they were her choice. The scarf tied round her neck seemed pretentious. She was a different person from the one I had imagined—different voice, different opinions, different ideas of right and wrong. Coarse, perhaps, or prudish or lecherous. Emphatically different. What outrage and absurdity to think of any closeness, confidence, intimacy with this other person or . . .

How nice it would be to bump her bosom against my chest, to kiss her lips and her nose, to lay my hand on the underhang of her buttock, etc. In fact I wanted to have her, I did, that was over, and to see her again, well, that was another question, another stage, another instinct.

The pleasantness of her femininity: she was gay, sweet. She had a different nature from mine. She talked on about other things. She scraped potatoes for me to eat. She fried onions at lunchtime. She wiped the table clean after I had eaten. She made tea at teatime. She made the bed. She tidied the room. Secretly she put scent under her ears, behind her knees, which wafted around her and in her room, her bed. There were pretty bottles in the bathroom and tubes of stuff I would never use: little packages of things particular to her, a girl, a woman. And there was her mind, working quite differently—sticking and clamping at certain points, flying over others; powerfully, secretly obsessed; compulsive, uneasy, furious, strange—strange to me. She had a realism, a conservatism, that went far deeper than my caution. She had dreams, hopes, fantasies, that went much higher than my ambition—and all dropped and died and grew again in a rhythm that I could not feel.

This is what held me to her after the simple act of sexual intercourse which was all I thought I wanted. I reached the stage when I found it unpleasant to be without her. A trip to a new city began with reflex excitement but the streets seemed flat, the people dull because she was not there. Listlessness. Boredom. Disinterest. At night there was an indeterminate but diffuse pain all through my body. During the day, an alternation in my mind between obsession with the thought of her and paralysis. I needed her advice not, perhaps, because I would have taken it but because I wanted to hear it. In fact I had become used to her—her companionship, her thoughts, her reactions, her presence. I was no longer an integral person. Necessary organs had been removed. When she was not there, my body wilted.

Up till then I had made friends wherever I was. I did not know what it was like to be lonely. Now I still had friends but I was lonely all the same. I started to think how nice it would be if we were together all the time, to move in a pair. And I began to have the image of a son or a daughter in front of me. I felt that I was aging. I noticed that there were periods when we did not make love as frequently as before. I started to fear for the son and the daughter. I started to fear for the permanency of my relations with Suzi. I wanted to project our partnership far into the future. I repeated to myself the arguments that love becomes squalid when you have boils on your back from which she would have to squeeze the pus; and when she would have piles which would agonize the action of our bodies. I told myself that her limbs would lose their consistency and her flesh would sag all over. I knew that I would have a sporadic and unhappy thrust at some high-school girl or get stuck into some cultured widow who travelled in Libya. I knew that she would have a particular and special friendship with a priest or a doctor; but, when it came down to it, she was the girl to whom I wanted to be unfaithful. Her legs and arms were the ones I wanted to see loosen on the bone. I wanted to shout meanness and amateur brutality at her. She was the one I wanted to embarrass at dinner with friends whom she liked and I did not. It was with her that I wanted to bicker over household costs of five and a penny— and God help me if she dies before I do and I am without it all, this woman.

At the same time, in the worst possible contrast, Helmuth von Rummelsberg and I became friends. The more I loved Suzi, the more I had to admit that he was charming, kind and intelligent. He was also funny, which is rare enough for a German—funny in a caustic, cynical way, funny because he laughed at everything. I had learnt so much about him that I felt I knew him well. Through the experience of love for Suzi I could understand how much he had suffered from his unhappy love in early life but only when I disciplined myself to think this way did I do so. Otherwise the

Helmuth who came from the file and my imagination was not the same person as my rival and friend.

The first time we met together without Suzi was when I bumped into him in the Kurfürstendamm one day at eleven in the morning. (Suzi I knew was at her lectures at the hospital.)

'Won't you have a drink?' he asked. 'Have you time?'

I said I had. We went into the nearest bar—a small place without a name which I have never noticed since but it was next to a camera shop.

'It is good you see so much of Suzanne,' he said. 'I am afraid though she exploits you to improve her English.'

'I am afraid it is the other way around,' I said. 'She helps me with my job.'

'Your job. Yes. It used to be mine, you know?'

'Yes . . . I remember . . .'

'But now I'm in show business. It is more interesting and more rewarding, I can tell you.'

'I quite believe it.'

'Dancing may be the lowest art form but for me it is the most powerful and penetrating. Dancing in the widest sense. Have you ever watched a parade? Of course you have. The Queen's Birthday parade here in Berlin. Don't you find there is a power in those things? Have you seen a torch-light procession? The Nazis came to power, you know, perhaps because they put on the best shows. It was Julius Caesar's maxim—bread and circuses.'

'I wouldn't know how to begin . . . in show business,' I said. We were both drinking beer.

'Neither did I, I can tell you. But I was trained as a soldier, you know. If you can drill a troop of men, why not a troupe of women? And I loved women, girls, for themselves.

That is important and rare enough. Most men want women to relieve them of a temporary urge or one single woman as a support and damn the rest. I like their natures quite apart from their reproductive functions or my own emotional needs.'

'You aren't married?'

'No. I am not mad. Suzi looks after me now that I am an old man . . . and the girls at the club.'

'A wife wouldn't like you to have a troupe of dancing girls—is that it?'

'If I had a wife, I might not have developed my taste for women.'

We asked for two more glasses of beer.

'I wish you would tell me about Suzi's parents,' I said. 'She's very evasive herself.'

Helmuth looked at me sharply, then at his beer. He pondered for a few seconds. 'I don't think I ought to tell you, really. She'll tell you herself some time. Her parents are divorced, you know. Her childhood was very broken up and spent in different places. Her mother . . . well, she never really settled on one man after her marriage . . . or before it, for that matter.'

'Are you her mother's brother?' I asked.

'No.' He laughed. 'I am not a real uncle, you see. More an adoptive one . . . but since she is studying here in Berlin she stays with me. She has been making a great mystery, has she? Yes. She likes to do that. She is quite young. Girls of her age—they have the bodies of women but often the minds of children.'

That evening I saw Suzi. We skipped the cinema and went straight to bed, eating bread and sausage where we were and watching the television Suzi had asked for and I

153

had installed. Later I asked her to leave Helmuth and come away with me.

'Yes,' she said.

But later she withdrew into herself and as I talked of leaving the Foreign Office and taking a position in some other branch of the civil service, she said nothing.

'You would like it in England,' I said.

She said nothing until she said: 'No. I don't know. I am German, you know, and there is Helmuth . . .'

'German, English—what does it matter? Europe will be united soon enough.'

'Yes, I know but . . .'

'Do you love me?'

'Yes. I do.'

'Well then?'

'What about Helmuth?'

'What about him? He doesn't really love you. You only pretend that he does.'

'I don't pretend.'

'He told me himself he loves all women and not one.'

'When did he tell you that?'

'This morning.'

'Did you see him this morning?'

'Yes, I did. We met and had a drink.'

'Did you talk about me?'

'He said you came to see me to improve your English.'

'Yes. I told him that.'

'And he told me he didn't love any one woman.'

'He may not be telling the truth.'

'No. But it is quite possible. He had an unhappy affair and it marked him.'

'Did he tell you that?'

'No.'

'Then how do you know?'

'I know . . . I was told about it. It is true, isn't it?'

'I don't know. I think it is.'

'Will you marry me?'

'I . . . don't know.'

'Why not?'

'My parents are divorced.'

'So what?'

'I was unhappy.'

'I would make you happy.'

'Yes, but you see I want to be very sure.'

'And Helmuth?'

'And there's Helmuth.'

'Do you love him or me?'

'You.' She was near to tears but she did not cry, I embraced her and worked my fingers round the curling channel of the inside of her ear. Her lips were sticking out in a sultry way as if she had been caught at doing something she knew was considered wrong but thought was right—biting her nails or eating between meals. But her fingers gently tapped my other hand. Resentment and affection.

'You see,' she said, then hesitated: 'you see we don't know each other completely, do we?' She looked up at me, evenly, as if she had stumbled on it.

I sighed. 'No, but . . . we know each other well enough. There's not much to know about me. I'm a simple person.'

She smiled and kissed me shortly. 'Are you?'

'Yes. And I know you well enough to want to marry you.'

She smiled again.

All this time we were in Berlin, West Berlin, surrounded

·by its wall, the wall by East Germany, East Germany by another wall, that wall by Europe. And each moment was a moment in history, history which had made the walls, the states, the governments; history which had gathered the peoples and settled them where they were. (All I cared about was Suzi.)

The Berlin Records Office. Records and Files. Names which recur in lists, little spots tracing a life. Linked to places, times, organizations. Born Pomerania. Born Pomerania. Born Pomerania. They were all born in Pomerania. But then one is a diplomat—Japan. Another a soldier—Poland, France, the Vistula, the Oise. The third a party policeman following the armies—Poland, France, Russia and Germany, Wannsee, Dachau, Auschwitz, Biedefeld, Munster. This and that post, recorded in the official gazettes, the lists, the records, the registers. The names remain the same—von Rummelsberg; the first names vary—Klaus, Klaus, Helmuth, Klaus, Edward, Edward. After hours in days among the records, the word von Rummelsberg springs out of a page as I turn onto it. Or the name Strepper—and that springs out more often.

The smell of the dust and books. The polite officials of the library. The rising ranks of my subjects. Edward becomes a lieutenant, then a captain. Günter Strepper, with Klaus always a rank or two behind as his adjutant, begins as a Hauptsturmführer, the equivalent of a captain, then rises quickly through the ranks of Sturmbannführer, Obersturmbannführer, Standartenführer, Oberführer, to Brigadeführer, or major-general, where he sticks.

A mass of initials. For Klaus and Strepper—SS and SD: and the more complex HSSPF, RuSHA, SSFHA, SSHA, EGr,

Ek. For Helmuth AA, RAM, VAA. For Edward—OKW, OKH, OK, OB, GK. I mastered the terms—linked the certainties of their meanings with dates and place names.

The Political Adviser asked me to report on my progress. He was a diligent, dutiful man with that musty pride in his profession of the older kind of diplomat. He exuded distinction. A dull, a limited, a decent man.

'What do you think of our Klaus von Rummelsberg?' he asked me.

'It is difficult to find anything unwholesome that is his personal responsibility,' I said.

'Yes. That's what I thought.'

'But I haven't yet followed him to the end of the war.'

'No. Quite. And I want you to keep at it. This Strepper, you see, was one of the worst of the war criminals—a real scoundrel—and it is difficult to see how von Rummelsberg was not involved with the atrocities in some way as Strepper's ADC.'

'It is.'

'And I'll tell you something else. There's a new dimension in the business. We've heard from the Americans that Klaus von Rummelsberg may be up to something doubtful with the West German Right. We always think that these things end with the war but of course they don't.'

'What might he be up to?'

'I don't know. That's just what I hoped you might find out. There's an increase in right-wing activities in the Federal Republic, you know. The small, nationalist parties have combined into the National Democratic Party. Nothing much yet but enough to put out some people ... well, the Americans anyway, ... for various reasons ... but we're in it with them, we're open to the criticism that we encouraged it, you see, by not going through with the denazification. I'll let you know if anything else comes in.'

I left the Political Adviser and did not waste another minute on Klaus von Rummelsberg who, since he remained unmarried until the 1950s and was almost certainly chaste up to the end of the war, could not be the father of Suzi.

Helmuth himself, in the way he had behaved in this respect, was the most likely father for the natural child I loved, but the middle-aged secretary to the German Ambassador in Tokyo returned to Germany barren, as she was to remain until her death in a car-crash in 1952. There is no evidence that Helmuth had any European mistresses other than this woman while in Tokyo. There was a favourite geisha but Suzi is not half-Japanese, however delicate her ankles.

II

Helmuth von Rummelsberg: 1943

It was at this time (April) that there is evidence in favour of Helmuth. The indiscreet Trübner was involved again: 'There's a rumour,' he wrote to Helmuth, 'that last month when Hitler came to Smolensk, one of the people who don't like him at the headquarters of Army Group Centre— probably Schlabrendorff or Treschow—put a bomb in a bottle of brandy and then gave it to Colonel Brandt as he got into the aeroplane going back to Rastenberg. And it didn't go off!'

Helmuth folded this letter into a thin strip and put it in the binding of an anthology of erotic poetry. He mentioned it to no one.

The spring in Japan was wetter than it had been in Pomerania, but its effect was as beautiful. Helmuth went for a week with Shosuke and his wife to where they had sent their son to save him from the bombing raids on Tokyo. The journey was overnight and took fourteen hours—the trains were slow and held up by smashed sidings and debris on the line. However, once they were through Osaka and the sky grew light, Helmuth could see the shapes of islands in the Inland Sea, which had been his first and most beautiful sight of Japan. The sun came up behind the mountains as they drove in an official car from the station where they had disembarked. They left the town, the road following the sea for a few miles, and turned into a house with a garden running to the shore.

Women came out of the house and bowed deeply to Shosuke, his wife and Helmuth—who also bowed. Then the five-year-old boy ran out from the woman who had been holding him and hugged his parents. He bowed quickly at Helmuth and then returned to hugging and talking in a high excited voice.

They entered the house and, after removing their shoes and putting on slippers, went through to a room that looked out over the sea.

'On the island there,' said Shosuke, pointing to the shape in the water a mile or so away that was now sufficiently illuminated by the sun to be seen to be wooded, 'on that island but over to the right of us, is the shrine of Miajima; a shrine to the deities of the sea. Perhaps you saw it when you arrived?'

'I did,' said Helmuth. 'It is very beautiful.'

They sat down. The women brought in tea and for Helmuth some coffee with rice cakes.

159

'Well, we needn't be afraid of bombs,' said Shosuke. 'We're well out of the town and it is not one with war industries.'

Edward von Rummelsberg: 1942

Edward was now aware of the different varieties in anti-Nazi opinion. There were those, like von Moltke, who were pacifists—against the killing of anyone, even Hitler, not only for moral reasons but for the practical consideration that any act considered treasonable would lead Germans to believe that treason had lost the war. It would exculpate Hitler and the National Socialist Party.

There were others who were in favour of violent action against Hitler and the government. Some, like Hans Oster, had been in league with the enemy since the beginning—had warned them of the invasion of the West in which Edward himself had taken part. Others, like Claus von Stauffenberg, had come to oppose the government more recently but were hatching plots of assassination and revolution.

Many of the conspirators were Christians, like Edward—some Catholic, others Protestant. Most of them only acted against the elected government because, like Edward, their duty was to a living God rather than a living leader of the people.

[*Claus Schenk, Graf von Stauffenberg. Born 15 November 1907. Member of the Swabian aristocracy, related to the Yorck and Gneisenau families. Considered a soldier of genius. He was wounded in the face, hands and legs in North Africa. Appointed Chief of Staff to the army Ordnance Department. Planted a bomb near Hitler in Rastenberg, East Prussia, which exploded but did not kill Hitler. Stauf-*

160

fenberg was shot in the court of the War Office in the Bendlerstrasse, 20 July 1944.]

'My dear Rummelsberg,' said von Stauffenberg one morning as they walked together from the War Office to Unter den Linden, 'it's like this. Or at least this is how I see it. We have a conscience and for the sake of that conscience we must put ourselves to the test before God.'

'We cannot put ourselves to the test on every issue...' Edward muttered.

'No. Not on every issue. On very few. But on this issue, yes, I am sure of it because Hitler, to my mind anyway, Hitler is evil... evil incarnate.'

Evil incarnate. Von Stauffenberg was a Roman Catholic. Edward believed in the existence of evil, but he did not really know what it was, so he found it hard to conceive of evil incarnate.

'Shouldn't we be like Moltke, just think and pray?' he asked.

'Yes. Pray, by all means. But we must act too. The most terrible evil is being inflicted on human beings at this moment,' Stauffenberg said, 'and at the last judgment God will ask each one of us Germans what he did about it. History, too, will ask the nation what it did against Hitler.' He stopped and sucked at his teeth. 'I don't know if we'll ever succeed in getting rid of him. Only God can beat the devil and... but you see we must make the gesture. Not just for the sake of our consciences but for the sake of Germany.'

They reached the corner of Unter den Linden. The one man with his straight nose, wavy black hair and heavy brow smiled at the other, Edward. They parted. Von Stauffenberg went towards the Brandenburg Gate, Edward in the opposite direction towards the Opera House.

There were notes scribbled in the margin of Edward's Bible:

'Stauffenberg talks of evil incarnate, but what is it? In what way does the Devil work? If Hitler is evil, then what about the others? Did they know what he would do? Did they know what they themselves would do? Strepper, perhaps, but not Klaus.

'Why did Strepper and Klaus become Nazis? Frustration. Why were they frustrated? Is it the natural state since the Fall? This is fatalistic Christianity. It must be possible to lead a fulfilled life. But this involves social action, political action.

'If the Nazis were either evil or in error, who does it leave (if one takes, as one must, those elections of 1930 all over again)? Wouldn't Stauffenberg and von Moltke still vote for some ridiculous and ineffectual party in the Centre or on the Right? Out of a kind of snobbery? A Christian should be humble enough to share the political consciousness of the poorest people. What did they vote? S.P.D. Also ineffective. The Communists . . . Why does one react with superstition to the word Communism? More than four million people voted Communist. I must read Marx . . .'

Again, in Edward's copy of *Capital*, his habit of writing in the margin shows us the progression that led him to Communism.

'False consciousness. That, of course, is the clue to frustration. We feel estranged from the product of our hands. Klaus: not the product but the society in which he lives.

162

Confused as to his function. He has a distorted picture of reality because of the falsity of his economic status. How does he, do we react? By inventing ideologies. The Nazis invent a racist scheme that explains everything—the frustration, the alienation—so Klaus and Strepper believe in it and join the others in sculpting the world to fit their dream. But the world is different: and you cannot carve living tissue. You are left with a wound.

'What causes false consciousness? The alienation of man in a class society.

'Communism. Is it really pure reason or is it another ideology?

'I have only my Faith. My consciousness is the product of my Faith. I test every Marxist hypothesis from the standpoint of my Faith and every hypothesis passes the test. Is Communism, then, not only the expression of Reason but also the expression of Faith? Does it only need simplicity and humility to see this?'

Edward evidently decided that it did because by the spring of 1942 he was in touch with Harro Schultze-Boysen.

[*Harro Schultze-Boysen. Son of Admiral Schultze-Boysen. His mother and his wife's mother were both friends of Hermann Goering. Thus he was employed in Goering's own intelligence service, the Air Force Research Office. He was, at the same time, leader of the 'Red Orchestra', a large network of German Communists working against the National Socialist Government in cooperation with the Soviet Union. He was executed in 1942.*]

Edward knew that Harro Schultze-Boysen was still involved with the Communists. He had met him in the autumn of 1941 through Katerina Strepper, who knew Harro's wife, Libertas, through the latter's mother, Countess Eulenberg. Edward approached him and was told, at first, to study the work of Marx, Engels, Lenin and Stalin. Edward did so, and came to accept their economic theories and interpretation of history because there seemed to him no reason why this should not be the way in which God worked. Moreover the basic assumptions of justice and equality for all men seemed (to him) compatible with, and part of, Christian belief.

In August 1942 a Russian agent was captured by the German secret police and under torture he betrayed members of the 'Red Orchestra'. While Edward was only in tentative touch with the organization, it was rooted out by the Security Services and Military Intelligence working in conjunction. Harro Schultze-Boysen among a hundred others was arrested, tortured and executed.

Edward himself might have been arrested, since it was known by the Secret Police that he had met with Schultze-Boysen, but it was also known that he had met him through Katerina Strepper and so the file on Edward was passed on to Günter by the investigating officer. Günter in turn passed it on to his adjutant, Klaus, who removed it from the office.

However, Edward's case would not be forgotten so long as he remained in Berlin and on the General Staff. The quickest transfer that could be arranged was to the Eastern Front. (It may be that Günter Strepper and Klaus von Rummelsberg suspected that Edward was in touch with the 'Red Orchestra' and wanted him out of the way for their own sakes as much as for his.)

Klaus von Rummelsberg / Günter Strepper / Katerina Strepper: 1943–1944

Soon after Edward's posting to the east, Strepper was himself transferred from the headquarters of the General SS to the SS Economic and Administrative Main Office. It was in this position that he committed his crimes—notably the liquidation of three hundred Russian prisoners-of-war to ease a shortage of accommodation for which he was responsible; the personal torture and molestation of a Jewish woman; the verbal order that led to her death; the ordering and organization of medical experiments of his own concoction and compelling a German woman to take part in them. The first and third crimes were uncovered in official memorandums—one regretting the loss of a labour force, the other querying the relevance of the medical experiments to the war effort. The second crime which, as far as is known, was the only personal crime, was disclosed by a lieutenant (Untersturmführer) of the Deathshead Battalion on duty in the camp when the crime occurred.

The first crime. Throughout the night before in the guest room of the camp commandant's house, Katerina had complained to her husband. 'I hope you realize,' she said, 'that your new job is just a way of getting you out of the way. You are only duplicating Glueck's work and getting in *his* way.'

'Please be quiet,' Günter said. 'I think they can hear you.'

'I am sure they can. In these shoddy wartime houses the walls are as thin as paper. But it doesn't matter. The commandant is sure to know you've been shunted into this job and I should think by now he can guess why.'

165

'Shut up.'

'No I won't.' Katerina sat at the dressing table, looking at herself in the mirror. Günter sat very much to the edge of the one bed in his pyjamas.

'I've a good mind to ask for another bed,' Katerina said.

'Please, Kat. They probably haven't got another.'

'Well, the sofa, then. You know I can't sleep in the same bed as you these days. And if I can't sleep I get awful headaches.'

'I'm sorry . . . but please . . . just tonight.'

'You'd think that a major-general in the SS would be asked about his sleeping arrangements.'

'I dare say they asked Klaus.'

'You're blaming him?'

'He doesn't know we don't sleep in the same bed.'

'Well, tell him.'

'I'd rather not.'

'Then I will.'

'Please don't.'

Katerina sighed and almost laughed but kept a glum expression on her face.

'Well, here goes, I suppose.' She stood up and crossed to the bed, climbed in it and sat in the middle. 'How are you going to cover up your blunder tomorrow?' she asked.

'What blunder?'

'The Russian prisoners.'

'I don't know. Shoot them.'

'What a stupid idea.'

'It's been done before.'

Next morning. It was so hot that the field-grey uniforms were soon covered with dust up to the waist. The Russian prisoners who had been kept out in the open all night now stood. The commandant of the concentration camp was arguing with Günter Strepper.

'You see, general, we need these Russians here to meet our quota of industrial production set by your own department. And we have had specific orders not to liquidate prisoners with a productive capacity.'

'I know, I know,' said Günter. 'But my dear colonel, it is a question of cost-effectiveness. You admit you have nowhere to house them. We cannot have them without huts. It would cost more to transport them elsewhere than it would to liquidate them.'

'But the production quota . . .'

'Colonel, I take full responsibility.'

A score of the prisoners had fainted in the heat.

'You see,' said Günter, 'they are not strong. They would not last you long. They would hardly survive to build their own huts.'

Katerina was with the camp commandant's wife looking at her garden.

'I don't think they should be shot,' said Klaus.

'Why on earth not, you fool?' Strepper shouted. 'They are Russians, aren't they? We have two action teams in the camp who can do it. We get rid of Slavs and Bolsheviks at the same time, two birds with one stone. Why on earth not?'

Klaus said nothing but looked straight ahead.

'Yes, shoot them,' said Günter to the commandant, 'on my responsibility. We have no room for them.'

The second crime. The concentration camp at S. The commandant's office.

'Do you know who they have here?' said Klaus to Günter

167

Strepper as they looked through the lists. 'A woman called Rosika Stein. I think she must be the sister of that chap Helmuth used to know in Berlin.'

'Well, we'll see if it is,' Strepper said. They sent a lieutenant of the camp guard to fetch her. He returned with the woman after half an hour, saying he had had her washed.

Rosika Stein. Her age at the time must have been more than thirty but she was as small as before and still looked like a child. She was thin but not emaciated: this, the lieutenant explained, was because she had a position in the brothel. She was dressed in the normal striped smock of an inmate, but it was clean.

Her behaviour was normal. When Klaus asked her if she was the sister of Gerhard Stein, she smiled and said she was. Strepper sat on the desk and continued to read the lists. Klaus explained that he was Helmuth von Rummelsberg's brother. She smiled again. Klaus offered her some chocolate which she accepted. He asked her what had become of her brother. She said she did not know but thought he was in America. Strepper spat. Then she left and Strepper and his adjutant continued their perusal of the lists.

As they left the office, Klaus waited until Strepper had gone ahead, then said to the lieutenant that he hoped he would secure some kind of decent treatment for Rosika Stein.

'She couldn't be better off than she is now,' the lieutenant replied.

'This brothel sounds rather squalid,' said Klaus.

'If it's not the brothel, it's the oven,' the lieutenant replied, and laughed. Klaus left the block.

There was a special house at S. for officials of the SS Economic and Administrative Main Office and those of the

Concentration Camp Inspectorate. Günter, Klaus and Katerina dined there together that night.

'I must say,' said Katerina, 'I regard this gassing of Jews as a despicable business.'

'Please don't talk about that again,' said Günter.

'It's despicable and cowardly,' she went on. 'It is impossible to imagine someone like my father, or like yours, Klaus, who were tough enough as soldiers, lowering themselves to such cowardice as to kill people in gas chambers and ovens.'

'Your cardinal error,' said Günter in an unusually loud and high-pitched voice, turning his fork round and round in his hand, 'is to consider the Jews as opponents susceptible to concepts of honour and bravery. They are not men, they are vermin. They are vermin like rats or foxes or anything else.'

'What nonsense,' said Katerina. 'Of course you, my dear, have never opened a book but luckily you have an adjutant who has heard of Heinrich Heine, for example. Have you read Heine, Klaus?'

'Yes,' said Klaus quietly.

'And would you describe him as vermin?'

'No.'

'Oh, Klaus is romantic,' said Günter Strepper, blinking.

'And what about Christ,' Katerina continued, 'was he vermin too?'

'Yes,' shouted Strepper, 'if he was a Jew, he was vermin.'

'No,' whispered Klaus.

They were silent.

'I wish you would not speak about things you know nothing about,' Günter said to Katerina. 'You do it simply to make me argue with Klaus.'

'Well, I am more interested in what Klaus has to say than in your Nazi clichés,' his wife replied.

Strepper's ears went red and he had an acute attack of blinking. 'Very well,' he said, in a loud voice again, 'I will not interrupt your conversation.' He got to his feet, walked out of the dining-room and out of the house.

Katerina and Klaus neither said anything nor looked at each other for some time. An orderly entered and asked if they would like more coffee.

'It isn't coffee,' Katerina said.

The orderly went out.

'I'm sick of it all,' she said.

'I know,' said Klaus.

'Don't you often wish you could go home?'

'Yes. We will sometime.'

'I'm going soon.'

'Leaving Günter?'

'Yes.'

'Perhaps it's best.'

'I'm a little afraid.'

'Yes. We're going to lose the war. A lot of people won't forgive what's happening in places like this.'

'What about you? Why don't you come home?'

'No. I've got to stay with Günter. He'll be out of his depth.'

'I shouldn't if I were you. He's a fool.'

'No. You go home. I'll look after him for you.'

Strepper, when he left the house, went up to the lieutenant of the camp guard who was outside.

'I should like to see the Jewish woman again,' he said.

'Yes, General,' the lieutenant replied. 'Shall I bring her to you?'

'No, take me to her.'

They walked from behind the commandant's house through the military compound and to the area before the camp fences. The dust of the day was now held together by moisture from the air. The air smelt.

'This is the brothel block,' the lieutenant said, pointing to the standard issue hut ahead of them. 'If you hear a shot, don't worry. It will be Major Kartevski. He likes to practise with his pistols on the whores—he gets a nice profile and then knocks off the nipples . . . a crack shot.'

They climbed the steps. 'There's a special room for senior officers,' the lieutenant said. 'It's kept for the commandant but he never uses it. His wife won't let him, I don't suppose. If you'll wait there, General.'

Strepper did wait there, looking at the walls, plain, cream papered. There was a small table next to the rudimentary bed; bed and mattress were obviously made in the camp workshop, because the bed was made of wood and rope and the mattress of sacking and straw. On the bed-side table there was a small pot with a plastic flower—an orange daisy. On the mattress a green counterpane that covered only the centre of it. That was all there was in the room. It was very clean.

The lieutenant returned with Rosika Stein. He said nothing further but pushed her into the room and closed the door.

Günter turned and looked at her, his eyes slightly bulging, his lids blinking, his hands held together behind his back, still in full uniform of a major-general in the SS—belt, pistol and bayonet.

171

She smiled with her lips. She wore the same shift as before but it was no longer clean.

'Do you want me for pleasure?' she asked. She did not falter on this word: it was a term used in the camp.

'Yes, take it off.'

As she did, Strepper himself undid his belt, his tunic and the buttons of his breeches. Rosika was undressed but did not behave in a way that would suggest she was embarrassed, save that she held her shoulders with her hands, covering her bosom with her elbows. That may have been because she was cold.

Strepper stepped forward, his belly now exposed too. He took her hair, which was not cropped, and had grown to a moderate length.

'Please don't hurt me,' she said.

Strepper emitted a laugh of some kind and passed the hand not holding her hair down her neck, forcing her arms apart, then passing it over her right breast. There the enormous horny palm pressed against the breast, but either because the skin of his hand was thick or because this breast was miniature, he felt nothing. So he placed the tip of his index finger on the tip of her breast and pushed it as if it were a crystallized cherry on a plate of junket.

This may have hurt her. Puffing, he was (as they say) properly aroused. His hand passed further downward on her body, but the finger, the small sensitive patch of his finger on its tip, as it passed the outer ring of the promontory it had been prodding, was touched by certain hairs which were growing there for the protection of this soft spot which might have nourished a child. The hand shot up again to her face, took her chin and held her face so that the eyes could look into hers. He was not large but she was

172

very small—her feet were three inches off the ground, the weight of her body was held by his hand and the roots of the hair on her head.

'Are you a Jew?' he said, panting between the words.

Rosika made a slight sound of no significance: her eyes, perhaps, moved sideways to express futility or despair.

'Of course you are,' he spluttered. He dropped her so that she fell on her knees. He went to the door, turned and the sight of her on her knees brought him back across the room.

'You poisonous bitch,' he said.

He picked her up by the neck and threw her face down on the bed, her legs still dragging on the floor; and with a loud wheezing coming from his mouth, he tried to push into the orifice between her buttocks whose contents were (to us all) foul but (to him) harmless. There seemed, however, to be some difficulty, and however hard he tried, he could not do it.

'Shit and blood,' he muttered, unbuckling his bayonet. He stuck it in up to its hilt, withdrew it and followed the bayonet, dropping it eventually to the floor. The blood eased his way until it was sopped up by the grey cloth of his breeches.

'Lieutenant,' he said as he left the block, 'she is to be liquidated tomorrow.'

The lieutenant nodded and saw to it that she was (and terror forced the liquid excrement to break through the clotted blood as she saw the faint wisps first leave their nozzles in the cement ceiling).

It is not possible to say if Günter Strepper committed other atrocities of this kind. Personal crimes such as this were only uncovered where the victim survived, or where statements made by other war criminals incriminated third parties. On the other hand crimes which involved administration, such as the third of Günter Strepper, were pedantically registered in the records of certain departments of the government or the SS.

Katerina had for some time refused to sleep in the same bed as her husband, and she would not play any of their usual games. Strepper told her that she had become frigid: she replied, 'Yes ... perhaps ... with you, anyway.' Strepper pondered over this: he asked doctors about frigidity, the cause of it, whether it could be selective as well as general. Their answers were always the same: very little was known about frigidity or any other aspect of female sexuality. So Günter Strepper began his own research into the subject. He invited a certain Dr Christiansen from Sweden where he had been recently expelled from a medical university for doing just the kind of research that Strepper had in mind. As guinea-pig Strepper offered Dr Christiansen a racially pure German girl, a political prisoner whose arrest and internment he himself had arranged.

Christiansen's laboratory was attached to a small concentration camp in Bavaria. There he developed the coital, automanipulative and mechanical techniques he had started in Sweden. He started the detailed filming in colour of the girl's reaction to sexual stimulation; a radiophysicist on his staff is said to have created the artificial coital equipment which enabled them to discover so much that was hitherto unknown.

However, in the autumn of 1943, when Katerina left her husband and returned to Pomerania, Günter Strepper lost interest in the experiment. He sent Klaus, who had until

174

then known nothing of the programme, to order the cessation of research and the liquidation of the girl. Klaus arrived at the camp and went straight to Christiansen's laboratory—a bare room in an ordinary hut full of complex equipment and smelling of talcum powder. A girl (the girl) was laid out on a plastic-covered table, her arms and legs stretched apart and tied to metal rings at the table's four corners. Her fair hair stuck to her face with perspiration. It was the first time that Klaus had seen a naked woman.

'Do you mean to say the girl is a German?' Klaus said to Christiansen when he saw her shoulder-length blonde hair.

'Of course, captain. She is one of your little white roses . . . though her rose is rather red now.'

'What is her name?'

'Trübner. Betta Trübner. Don't you know about her?'

He did, since he was the one who had told Strepper about her activities in the Catholic resistance in her university. He went over to her. She was very young—he could tell by the look of the skin on her leg, by the freckles on her face.

She blinked at him. 'Are you higher up than him?' she asked. 'I wish you'd make him loosen these. They're very tight. I won't struggle, I promise.'

Klaus did not answer her but walked back across the laboratory to Christiansen. 'She is to be rendered unconscious,' he said.

'That's easy,' said the doctor, picking up a syringe.

'Only unconscious . . . for an hour or two.'

'Of course,' said Christiansen. Betta Trübner struggled as he pushed the needle into her flattened thigh, but her breathing immediately became more regular and her struggling stopped.

'Liquidation,' said Christiansen, 'is as simple as that. They stop struggling, then they stop breathing. I've never done it but I've seen it done. Her breathing won't stop. Don't worry. You're taking her away, are you? Pity. She's a pretty little thing.' He patted the stomach of the unconscious girl.

Klaus von Rummelsberg picked up a telephone and ordered an ambulance on Strepper's authority to take Betta Trübner from the camp to a civilian hospital where she was to be entered as a light bombing casualty. After three days in hospital she was to be returned to her home on Lake Constance.

Then he turned to Christiansen. 'Your research is to be stopped. Your team is to report to the SS Administrative Main Office for different duties.'

Christiansen, a tall, thin man with cropped hair, shrugged his shoulders, slapped his hands on his legs. 'I knew it wouldn't last,' he said. 'I knew it was too much to expect.'

'My advice to you is to disappear, change your name. Get back to Sweden, if you can.' Short words, as if Klaus was holding his breath. Christiansen noticed the pressure behind the other man's way of speaking. He smiled.

'Ah, you think I am what the allies call a "war criminal"? You're not . . . no, of course not . . . you're not one yourself; you saved the girl. A spectator.'

Klaus's face stiffened and he turned away from the doctor.

'Just let me say,' Christiansen went on, 'that what you have seen here is not a "war crime". The girl was better treated than she would have been anywhere else and the research was . . . worthwhile . . . the most worthwhile research to come out of the Third Reich: if she hadn't been used here she might have been put to reviving the frozen bodies of airmen . . . the Air Force are trying that . . .'

Klaus turned. 'What do you mean . . . worthwhile? This . . .

176

pornography.' His hand stretched out towards the empty plastic-covered table.

'Pornography . . . yes . . . will you listen a moment? Let me explain my work before I disappear and change my name? Before I am written off as a pornographer . . . a war criminal.'

'Of course. I'm listening.'

Christiansen went over to the table and leant against it facing Klaus. 'Sex, captain. Sex is the key to . . . well, in my opinion, it is the key to almost every human act. Freud, of course, already suggested certain sexual patterns in the subconscious, but I am convinced that our instincts to procreate, to continue the race, have much . . . cruder ramifications than Freud envisaged. The demands of the race—the human race—are much nearer the surface than we think. We have minds, we do have minds, but it is strange that with our minds and our belief in free will, we behave very like certain species of animals—geese, for instance, or rats . . . anyway . . .'

He paused. He seemed (to Klaus) to be thinking to himself. Klaus said nothing.

'Orgasm,' Christiansen said. 'My research is into orgasm in the female. I worked in Stockholm . . . I was dismissed . . . then I was asked here. I continued. Strepper offered me unique facilities—the optical equipment, the girl—before, you know, I depended on prostitutes. Now I must stop again. Do you know what orgasm is, captain? Are you a married man?'

'No,' said Klaus, 'I am not married.'

'Orgasm, in a layman's language, is the moment of maximum pleasure for a woman when she is making love. Unlike the man's orgasm which is the same as his ejaculation,

177

the woman's orgasm has no primary function in the processes of reproduction. It is pure pleasure: the clitoris has no other function than to induce it. Now the degree of pleasure experienced by a woman in orgasm is not simply quantitative—not just the most: no, it is different, qualitatively different. Some women never experience it. It is, you see, it is a sense of release, a beautiful suffusion of warmth—I don't know—these are just descriptions—I have never experienced it. Me, a man, I have my orgasm but it is simple, mechanical, automatic. A woman's orgasm is like the pains of childbirth—something a man can never experience and hardly imagine. It is, for a woman—this orgasm—it is like a vision, a drug—one can see that: to be swept into unconsciousness by pleasure, to abdicate personality through joy, yes—no wonder they are always looking for it. It is the point, the essence of their natures as women.'

Another silence between the two men. Suddenly, quickly, Christiansen started speaking again.

'I'll tell you. We developed equipment—penises of plastic with the same optics as plate glass. Cold-light illumination which allows observation and recording without distortion. It can all be adjusted to physical variations in size, weight —the speed and depth of thrust—all controlled by the woman. It is driven by an electric motor—an ingenious thing—only you Germans could have done it. Anyway . . . we have discovered just what physical changes are involved in orgasm. You see—during sexual intercourse a congestion of blood vessels and a tension in muscles builds up. When they are released—suddenly—that is orgasm.'

'Then it is just as mechanical as a man's,' said Klaus.

'Physically, yes. But the effects of this release of blood and muscles are vastly different . . . they are never the same . . .

178

sensually, emotionally . . . and that is where we have reached in our research, in our knowledge. For if, as we now know, there is no physical, anatomical difference in different orgasms, between what used to be called—quite incorrectly —the clitoral and the vaginal orgasms, then we are left with only the psychological factor to account for the variation, a psychological factor which is itself totally bound up with the social factor. No. The fallacies are exploded. It does not much matter how a lover performs: it is *who* he is that governs the orgasm, that decides whether a woman will have this . . . this mystical experience, or just a local gratification. But what type for what woman? That is the question we must answer.'

'I don't see why it matters,' said Klaus. 'People have a chance to choose, these days.'

'Exactly . . . as they like. But why does one girl prefer one man? What strange evolutionary function is at work in the choice of a young girl's "heart"? What are the social consequences of her preferences? Do you remember 1914? No girl would look at a man who was not a soldier. A man with a medal could have as many of them as he wanted. Now, in cities, the women hate their men to wear uniforms—and you see if, after the war, they don't shy away from soldiers. They'll be ashamed to be seen with them. Stendhal tried to make a science of love—he came near to it—but now, with all modern developments in scientific technique—like our plastic camera—can't we advance on Stendhal?'

'It seems to me that you are just evolving an elaborate form of marriage guidance . . .' said Klaus, making towards the door.

'Marriage guidance! Ha! Marriage guidance could save us from wars.'

'How do you mean?' asked Klaus, turning.

'Just as I said. If girls start fancying pacifists instead of soldiers. That is the first step. And then if a jilted man can be shown how to make himself appealing—because when a girl jilts a man, she makes him dangerous. It's the same when a woman leaves her husband. An impotent man ... look at Hitler. But a girl does not jilt at random; she jilts for instinctive reasons, because the man does not possess the qualities that would dominate her, would push her to that experience where she disintegrates into her own feminine essence. She knows. She has intuition that seeps from her ovaries into her mind. But what is the function? Can we trace the pattern, the meaning of her intuition's judgment? If we could know the nature of submission in women, then we could control its concomitant, aggression, in men. Women could be chosen and trained to fulfil men—men could be unleashed upon their quivering, yearning masochist-mates, instead of upon each other. That is my aim ...'

Klaus opened the door of the hut and said, in an expressionless tone of voice, neither angry, as before, nor understanding: 'Yes, well ... goodbye.' And as he left the laboratory, he heard the Swedish doctor Christiansen saying, 'I don't know ... after the war ... perhaps, America ...'

Chapter Eight

I

HELMUTH VON RUMMELSBERG dressed impeccably. His clothes were always clean and exact. The cuffs of his shirts poked out of the jacket sleeve one inch on both arms and on all occasions. His shoes were always as well polished as they had been that first time I saw them next to Suzi's ankles.

We used to meet now quite regularly for a drink, and he would talk about his life in show business. He was evasive, as they all are, about what he did before and during the war. He also said he no longer took any interest in current affairs. His study of show girls was his life.

'People with an obsession are as lucky as those with a vocation,' he would say. 'There is really something to their lives. Otherwise, I think, human beings are generally bored. I was very bored as a diplomat and might have gone on that way until I died if it hadn't been for our defeat in the war. At the end, you know, a lot of us thought again. It was a bad moment when we realized that such terrible things had happened in our time and many of them in our name; and that we had done nothing about it, even those of us in positions of some influence. Maybe there was nothing we could have done. I don't know. Anyway, I had to admit to myself that being a diplomat had not helped at all: I also had to admit that my main interest had never been foreign affairs but always women's legs. There you are.'

'Have you no family?' I asked.

His casing remained impeccable but his eyes became glazed for a moment. It was in the café of the hotel Bristol-Kempinski. I could see the Jewish memorial where the synagogue had stood.

'Yes, I have a sort of family. Haven't you heard of my infamous brother Klaus?'

'Yes, of course . . . your brother.'

'But we were all scattered after the war. We don't see so much of each other. What about you?'

'I have a sister.'

'And do you see much of her?'

'When I go home.'

'Yes. You see, we have no home to go to. It is on the other side of the river Oder.'

'In Poland?'

'Well, yes.'

'I see.'

Then we saw Suzi coming towards us. 'That,' he said, 'is my family,' and the friendliness I felt towards him turned to the old loathing as he said it, as he odiously claimed the girl who approached—so that I had to hold the cup of hot chocolate to my face and blow the heat into my eyes as if to cool it, all to give some explanation for a red face and watering eyes.

'Hello, you two,' Suzi said and sat down, swinging one leg over the other.

She had become used to our seeing each other without

her. She also seemed to like being there with the two of us —presiding over her two lovers—and she carried her chin lower like a young broody. When I told her (afterwards) how upset I always became at the thought that she went back to him every night, she stuck out her lips and became soothing, or what she thought was soothing. 'Poor darling, she said, with a suggestion of irony as if my complaints were really a joke, 'I wish I could be with you always but you know I can't leave him just yet. He's like a father to me, you see. He's been so kind. He's got no one else. How can you possibly imagine that he's my boy-friend? It's a ridiculous idea,' etc.

Of course the more I got to know Helmuth von Rummelsberg, the more probable it became that he was her lover. He was handsome, charming; he admitted, professed, advertised, that it was women—girls—their legs, their ...— that interested him. They were his hobby, his profession, his only interest, his only preoccupation, his total, life-long obsession. He savoured them, he drilled them, and having got as far as that, it is likely that he made love to them as much as his physical constitution allowed—and as to that, he looked the product of an excellent gymnasium in every sense and had sunburnt skin that went very well with his white Mercedes-Benz.

I could quite well imagine him evolving a routine at his club where he said to one of the girls before the show, a girl who happened to take his fancy that night, 'Let's have a drink afterwards,' and let her in (afterwards) to his double-bedded office behind the scenes. Suzi said he never brought them home—and the irritation with which she received the suggestion that he might was evidence (to me) that she would have been jealous had he done so.

183

'I wouldn't mind if he did,' she said, 'but he would be afraid to shock me.'

To shock her, who had not shown much shock when I had stuck my hand up under her skirt. More likely he did not want to lose a nice, fresh, young, home-grown sample of the species waiting dutifully in his silk-lined lair.

Since he was so open about liking the legs of women, I wanted to confront him with Suzi's. One Sunday afternoon in summer we went to the Wannsee beach. There we found a patch of sand among all the pasty-skinned Berliners and we sat down, also in our costumes. Suzi in her costume—!!!!!!—it was a one-piece affair, black and modest. I would like to say that her limbs came out of her torso like shafts of pale light but they were nothing like that, however nice it sounds. They were simply her legs and arms, which was enough for me. Suzi's costume. It was like a child's costume, this black one-piece affair—and she seemed so innocent that I hardly dared say what I had prepared to say to Helmuth. Her arms were sticking out backwards and propping her body from the palms of her hands so that the body was at forty-five degrees to the sand and her legs bent slightly over it. Her head was dropped so that her hair fell down on either side of it and hid her face.

'You should enter a beauty contest, Suzi,' I said. 'With your legs you'd be sure to win.'

Suzi did not move her head.

'Do you think they are fine legs?' said Helmuth. 'I find them too thin.' He laughed. 'Perhaps it is because I am a German and the Germans, like their women to be fat... like the Turks.'

Suzi looked up and smiled without conviction.

'Helmuth is a cunning devil,' I said to her (afterwards).

Suzi thought it could go on this way. I thought it could not and I was right. However I was right for the wrong reasons. The crisis, as it were, did not happen in the way I expected.

The way I expected (1): The happiness and unhappiness in our relationship being for me equally balanced, I would present Suzi with an ultimatum which she would not accept. I would steel myself and no longer see her—that is to say I would make no future assignments, avoid cafés Zuntz and Kempinski at tea-time and burn all photographs and letters.

I had some fine daydreams about such tragedies but it did not turn out that way.

The way I expected (2): Suzi would let slip some remark such as 'once at school I thought I was pregnant,' or 'young men fancy themselves but older men are just as good.' Then I would have caught her out. A tirade of abuse—'You wretched little lying bitch, you whore, you stinking, grasping cow,' because women seem to mind words, and then a cool break—'Let's avoid any further unpleasantness and call it a day. We've had some good times together.' What poignant dreams. They brought tears to my eyes.

Of course, now, from the point from which I am telling this story of my adventures (a point you will have to guess at), all sorts of ambiguous interpretations present themselves: was my mind trying to shake off the grasping demands of sexual instincts? Did I sense that Suzi was not the girl for me? That a German girl was all right for an affair but not the sort to introduce to one's mother as a bride? That frustrated love cannot last long? Did my common sense balk at such a girl without family or background?

Anyone might give these explanations if they did not know what I discovered. But if they did know then I would

185

say that any ordinary, decent Englishman—even any American or European—would have behaved in the same way—not for the fact itself but for the revelation, the interpretation, the classification it provided of this girl Suzi.

It was one afternoon of quite a bright day. I was gay enough. Helmuth was in West Germany. Suzi and I were to meet at Zuntz at the usual time but the weather was so fine that I told my secretary that I was going to the Records Office and I set out for the Karmerstrasse flat on the off-chance that Suzi might be there and free to go out to the lakes.

I ran up the stairs to the flat, rang the bell and heard her footsteps coming to the door. I was happy that she was there.

She opened the door and looked as happy as I felt.

'I took the afternoon off,' I said. 'I thought we could go out to the lakes for tea.'

'How nice,' she said and kissed me. Then she turned and said, 'Just a minute, I'll change my shoes.' She went back into the flat, singing.

I waited and looked into the post box. There was one letter. I picked it out and looked at it. It was in a sloping, feminine hand and addressed to Suzanne Strepper.

She came out of her room, still singing.

'There's a letter for you,' I said.

'Oh, it'll be from my mother.' I handed it to her. 'Yes, it is,' she said.

'Your name is Suzi Strepper then?'

'Oh . . . yes, it is.' Her expression became sad and baffled; her face went very red.

'I hope you're not related to Günter Strepper.'

'Yes,' she said, 'he is my father.'

186

Katerina Strepper: 1943

Katerina Strepper went back to Pomerania in the autumn of 1943. Her mother and father were both dead by then, but this did not spoil her feelings upon her return home. For her home was not made up of the people but of the land.

The railway lines to the east from Berlin were closed to civilian traffic, so she took a train north to Neubrandenburg and from there was given a lift in a supply truck that was going from there through Anklam to Swinemünde.

Already, in Swinemünde, she was there, at home. She went towards the sea front, past the hotels that were full of the wounded to the one where they had stayed. They remembered her and found her a bed and the next day the woman who had been a housemaid but now acted as a nurse arranged for Katerina to travel in a trawler along the coast to Stolpmünde.

On the trawler she sat on the deck looking at the white shore and the line of pine trees. That was the view of her home. The view of her: she was older, of course, now aged about thirty-five—but still tall, with the same coloured hair (blonde, brown-streaked). Her eyes were still deep blue. Her beauty had increased with harassment—her skin was best burnt by the sun and she was naturally thin. Her beauty was tough, at ease sitting legs apart on the deck of a fishing boat.

Since she had telegraphed from Swinemünde to say she was coming back to what now belonged to her, there was an old man from the estate at Stolpmünde. He had a horse and cart—not the old car that now had no petrol—and it took them the rest of that day and the day after it to reach her home. At junctions with roads going east they often had to wait an hour at a time for convoys to pass.

The old man, who had known Katerina since the days when she had cut down the rose plants, since the days even when she only screamed for her own way, grumbled lightly and steadily about the war, the death of his son on the front, the impossibility of obtaining petrol, fertilizer, sacking or twine.

'You can use dung for manure, can't you?' Katerina said.

'No,' he replied. 'The beasts were taken away four months ago.'

They were lucky, he thought, to have their supply of potatoes growing in the rose beds.

They reached the house in the evening and Katerina did not care that the house was empty, the estate dilapidated. She went to her room, which the remaining servants had prepared as best they could, and lay on her back on her bed.

The trees she could see from her window were the same. The smell of the air at that window and the smell in the room itself were the same. The way her bed sagged in the middle was just the same—even the pink cover on her bed was one she knew quite well from before the war.

Maria, her maid, who had left to get married in Stolp to a certain Peter Stefan (a grocer's son) before the war, was now back because her husband had been killed. She brought Katerina some coffee, apologizing that it was not real coffee.

Günter Strepper: 1944

Günter Strepper, after his wife had left him, not only lost interest in his experiments with Betta Trübner on frigidity and orgasm, but became apathetic towards all his duties as SS Standartenführer in the SS Economic and Administrative Main Office. He left his adjutant, Klaus von Rummelsberg, to cover up his inactivity as best he could.

Then, in the early spring of 1944, six months after Katerina's departure, he deserted his post and disappeared.

He reappeared in Stettin, where he requisitioned a car from the SS Economic and Administrative sub-office and again in Koslin where he requisitioned petrol. He reappeared...

Katerina Strepper / Günter Strepper: 1944

Katerina was talking to Maria as the latter dug up potatoes to store them in the cellars. They could hear the guns of Reinhardt's and Rokossovski's armies around Schneidemühl. It was a feeling in the air as much as a sound. Then they heard the more specific sound of a car draw up and they turned. Katerina saw her husband come towards her. Maria backed away.

'You,' Katerina said to Günter Strepper. 'What are you doing here?'

'Katerina,' he said in a flat voice, 'you must come back. We're in this together.'

'If I were you,' she replied, 'I'd get away while you can. We expect the Russians any minute.'

'You must get away with me.'

'Don't be ridiculous. The worst that can happen to me here is getting raped by a few Russians.'

'No, no,' Strepper said less flatly, 'that mustn't happen. You must come.'

'I'd rather the Russians than you and the incendiary bombs in Berlin.'

'No, not Berlin. We'll get away.'

'No. I'm not going anywhere with you.'

'You must. Come inside and talk to me. You'll see it's the best thing to do.'

'You might as well go now while you can. The Russians will shoot you out of hand if you are caught in that uniform.'

'Come inside,' he shouted and took her by the arm, squeezing it with his hand.

'You're hurting me.'

'Come inside.'

He pulled her across the potato patch to the garden door of the drawing room. They went in. It was almost empty. What pieces of furniture there were, were covered with dust sheets.

'I need you,' he said, backing her towards the wall. 'We belong together.'

'No, we don't, you . . . guttersnipe. How can we belong together when I loathe you, when I despise you?'

'I need you,' he said.

'I don't care. I don't need you. You're common and repulsive. You . . . you defile this house.'

She wore an apron over her brown woollen dress, the only woollen dress she had. Strepper tore at the apron. She hit his face but he walloped her back so hard that she found herself stepping backwards.

'Don't do that,' she said quietly.

'You are my wife,' he said, as quietly.

Then he grasped her arms behind her back with one

190

huge palm of his and tore open her dress but it stuck and she struggled so he simply flung her onto the floor so that she was stunned for a moment but found when she recovered that her skirt was caught in a bunch at her waist, that he was on top of her, his breeches round his ankles.

At once after this, what seems to have been the legitimate conception of Suzi, Strepper stood up, buttoned up and left. Katerina wondered what she could wear now that her brown dress and slip were torn. She thought quite rightly that if she changed into any other clothes, say something of Maria's, it would be likely torn again—so she simply straightened what she had on.

Edward von Rummelsberg: 1944–1945

On his way back to the Eastern front, Edward von Rummelsberg had been billeted for a second time in Posen. The town was a different place now—partly damaged by Russian raids and seething with a chaotic mass of soldiers of the German army who were, as often as not, Albanians, Romanians, Scandinavians, French or Walloons in the uniform of the Armed SS.

Edward was totally dejected, going as he was to an almost certain death at the hands of his comrades. While before he had never been afraid to die for his country in a cause he believed was just, he was now terrified of being killed on the wrong side.

He had no way of finding out who was in Posen at the time, so he went out alone to a small restaurant in the town. The place was quite crowded but he sat down at a table where another man, a middle-aged civilian, seemed almost finished.

A blustering, jolly woman came up to him. 'A dark beer or a light one?' she asked.

'A dark,' he replied.

'And it's sausage and cabbage. That's all there is.'

'That'll do fine.'

'We had some pork but it went in ten minutes. We're lucky to have the sausages.'

She went away. Edward nodded to the man opposite him who nodded back but looked depressed.

The waitress came back with his beer. 'You're lucky to be on leave,' she said.

'I'm not,' he said. 'I'm on my way out.'

Whereupon her manner changed. She became quieter, less sharp—in fact she behaved like a nurse.

'I don't envy you,' said the middle-aged man. 'Are you going east for the first time?'

'No,' Edward replied, 'I've been on leave.'

'Well, it's nasty now, sir, I don't mind telling you.'

'How do you know what it's like since you are a civilian? You shouldn't spread rumours like that when you know nothing about it,' Edward said in an irritable way.

'They aren't rumours, sir. I'm only an engineer, I know, but it's the things that are going on behind the lines I'm talking about and I've seen them. For the sake of your soul, sir, best get yourself killed right away.'

'What are you talking about?'

'Well, I can tell you if you want but it'll put you off your dinner.'

'Go on. You might as well tell me since you've begun.'

'Well, I'm an engineer, as I said, and I've a small company which has been on contract to the Reich Ministry for the Occupied Eastern Territories since the beginning of the war. Last month we were putting up some weapon-locker huts for the SS near Minsk when we heard shots from some pits several hundred yards from our site. We were quite a way behind the lines so I went to the pits with my foreman to see what was going on. There we saw a line of lorries and people getting off them—men, women and children of all ages. Then there was this man from the SS standing there with a riding whip . . . or a dog whip . . . I don't know which. He made them undress. They had to put down their clothes in fixed places according to what they were, you see—shoes, shirts, petticoats. The heap of shoes—well, there must have been eight hundred or a thousand pairs—and great piles of clothes.

'The people undressed without screaming or crying or anything and then just stood around in family groups kissing each other, saying goodbye—funny when you think about it. Then another SS man made a sign with his whip and they went off towards the pit without a sound. No asking for mercy or anything like that.

'There was an old woman with white hair who was holding a one-year-old child in her arms and singing to it and tickling it. The child was gurgling, you know, very happy. The parents were looking on with tears in their eyes. The father was holding the hand of a boy about ten years old and speaking to him quietly. The boy was fighting back his tears. The father pointed to the sky, stroked his head and seemed to explain something to him.

'Then the SS man at the pit shouted to his friend. The friend counted off about twenty and told them to go behind the earth mound. I remember one girl, thin with black hair, who as she passed close to me pointed to herself and said, "Twenty-three years old."

'My foreman and I, we went around the mound and there—there was just an enormous grave. People were wedged together and lying on top of each other so that only their heads were showing. Nearly all had blood running over their shoulders from their heads. Some of them were still moving. Some were lifting their arms and turning their heads to show that they were still alive. The pit was already two-thirds full. There must have been about a thousand people in it. I looked for the man who did the shooting —he was an SS man who sat at the narrow end of the pit, his feet dangling into it. He had a machine-gun on his knees and was smoking a cigarette.

'The people, without any clothes on, went down some steps and clambered over the heads of the people lying there to the place to which the SS man directed them. They lay down in front of the dead or wounded people. Some caressed those who were still alive and spoke to them in a low voice. Then I heard a series of shots. I looked into the pit and saw the bodies twitching on top of those already lying motionless on the bodies that lay beneath them. Blood was running from their necks.

'The next lot was already approaching. They went down into the pit, lined themselves up against the previous victims, and were shot.'

The engineer, who introduced himself to Edward as Herman Graebe, stopped and took a swig of his beer.

Edward was silent: then he said, 'Impossible ...'

'I swear before God that it's the absolute truth,' said the engineer. 'I couldn't invent something like that.'

The waitress brought Edward a plate of sausage, cabbage and roast potatoes which he ate because he was hungry.

*

Edward was now convinced of his duty, but it was difficult to execute. He was in command of a depleted squadron of Panther tanks manned half by veterans, half by new, ill-trained recruits. They were attached to the 111th Panzer Army which together with two infantry divisions defended a line south of Marienwerder on the right bank of the Vistula. The whole division was under strength and (we now know) the Russians, first under Zhukov, then under Rokossovski, had a superiority of three to one in gun power and even greater advantage in mobility. Consequently the outcome of the battle which was fought was not in doubt. Moreover Himmler's command of Army Group Vistula was chaotic, his signals service failed to function and, after the start of the Russian attack on the morning of 26 January, 111th Panzer was unable to make contact with Army Group Headquarters.

Edward's squadron was far back from the front line. On the afternoon of the 26th, though there was still no sign of the enemy, Edward ordered his squadron to provide an artillery barrage at an indeterminate distance forward. He knew that the shells were probably falling on the advance line of German tanks. The result was that all his tanks were soon out of ammunition since they had been in short supply from the first. When a junior tank commander suggested that the barrage was wasteful, Edward told him not to question orders; then, when each tank requested new supplies of ammunition, Edward told them that there was no contact with Army Group Headquarters.

They received the order to withdraw westwards during the night, but Edward delayed his transmission of the order so that, when the second Russian Armoured Brigade began its attack on the morning of the 27th, his unit was totally cut off from the rest of 111th Panzer and had no alternative but to surrender.

Even when they were standing in rows as prisoners-of-war it did not occur to the men of Edward's squadron that they had been the victims of anything but the incompetence of Himmler and Army Group Headquarters.

The Russians, however, were more curious and Edward was asked by the political commissar attached to Rokossovski's headquarters why his unit had not withdrawn with the rest of 111th Panzer and why it had not fired a shot. Edward's Iron Cross did not suggest that he was a coward.

'No,' said Edward awkwardly, 'it was because I believe the Soviet army to be the vanguard of the proletarian revolution in Germany and would be the last to stand in its path.'

'Then,' said the Commissar, watching him closely, 'you will be pleased to hear that Soviet tanks are past Marienburg in the north and have reached into Pomerania in the centre.'

The thought of Russian soldiers on Pomeranian soil. Edward's face did not move.

'Yes,' he said, 'I am glad to hear it.'

Within a week, though he remained at Rokossovski's headquarters, Edward was in touch with the Committee for German Liberation in Moscow which had known about him through the 'Red Orchestra' for some time.

Helmuth von Rummelsberg / Klaus von Rummelsberg: 1945

A child lay dead in the road leading to Hamburg. Helmuth told the driver of the Foreign Ministry car to stop to see what could be done.

'Senseless, sir,' the driver said. 'The chances are she's a case of typhoid. We might catch it ourselves.'

Helmuth could tell by the way the little girl was settled in her sprawled position that she had been dead for some time. 'Do you mean that there's an epidemic?' he asked.

'A result of the raid, sir. We had one of the heaviest last week. A real Ami blanket. I don't know what chance we have of getting through the town even now.'

They were stopped by a civil defence officer at a street intersection.

'You can't get through this way,' he said. 'There's still a fire storm in the centre.'

'Officer,' said Helmuth, 'there's the body of a child on the Wedel road.'

'I don't know where you've been, sir,' the officer said. 'There are the bodies of tens of thousands of men, women and children in there'—he jerked his thumb over his shoulder—'and there were tens of thousands more burnt alive.'

'He was in a submarine,' said the driver. 'High priority Foreign Office.'

'Well,' said the officer, 'we've had two of the heaviest raids yet. The whole town is gutted . . . there never was a chance of putting out the fire. We couldn't even stop it spreading because any of our men who tried got sucked into it. Your best chance is to try and get round onto the Lübeck road.'

There was black smoke in the sky ahead. They swung to the left of it. The streets they followed were empty and more grey. Every second block, even here, was gutted and those still standing were deserted.

'Were you caught in the raid?' Helmuth asked the driver.

'Don't worry about me, sir,' he replied. 'I've seen it all. Did you hear about Dresden? I was there too except I was

197

out of town, in one of the suburbs up above the town with my sister who married a professor there. Well, they came over two nights running and set the whole damn place on fire, so the only place for the people to go was the parks. Tight packed, they were, because the town was full of refugees as well as the townspeople. And damn me if those British planes didn't fly over and machine-gun the people in the park. We could see it clear as anything from where we were. Well, we went down afterwards to help clear up—but in the end they stopped piling up the bodies and just burnt out the cellars with flame-throwers. It was the only thing to do to stop the epidemics.'

'Did they bomb the Zwinger?' asked Helmuth.

'They bombed everything, sir. Churches, hospitals, houses. Bang. And bullets too. Some of those people we piled up afterwards had great big holes in them, sir, I can tell you. I hope someone settles up with those murderers afterwards—though I suppose it'll have to be God, won't it, sir, since we're going to lose the war.'

As they passed through the eastern suburbs of the city and crossed the Lübeck road, they saw the temporary hospitals that had been set up in the villas of the Hanseatic merchants. People were propped against the steps.

When he reached Berlin, Helmuth went straight to the Foreign Office to report. The whole building was in chaos but eventually one of Ribbentrop's permanent secretaries came up to him.

'Von Rummelsberg, is it? We're very glad you're back but you know things have changed so quickly. There's nothing to be done in the office. The foreign minister talks of a diplomatic solution but I don't see what it is to be. I suggest you take some semi-permanent leave. Pop in now

198

and then if you like to see what's going on ... while the building is still standing.'

The permanent secretary looked up at him. He was a prim man, a lesser civil servant, who, like the civil defence officer, was at his best now that a superstructure was redundant and all that was necessary was to keep going at the lowest level of administration.

Helmuth left the Foreign Office building. He must have looked an extraordinary figure (to passers-by) because his clothes had been kept in excellent condition in Japan and while everyone else in Germany wore worn and filthy uniforms of one kind and another, he was dressed in a pin-striped suit, a stiff collar and a long grey overcoat.

The Foreign Office had booked him a room in the Adlon hotel which he found difficult to reach because of the guards surrounding the approaches to the Chancelry and its bunker. He left his luggage there and then walked through the streets to the Headquarters of the SS Economic and Administrative Main Office, where he asked for his brother, Klaus von Rummelsberg.

They looked at him sullenly but eventually sent for Klaus who raised his eyebrows and said, 'My dear boy, how nice to see you. How well you look.' Klaus held in his hands a sheaf of papers.

'You're probably busy now,' said Helmuth. 'Could we meet some time for a drink? I'm staying at the Adlon.'

'Yes, of course,' said Klaus. 'In fact I can come with you now.'

He fetched his coat and they left the SS office. Walking with his brother back to the hotel, Helmuth said 'Things look rather nasty back there.'

'Yes, they are,' said Klaus. 'How were they in Japan?'

'They can't win the war . . . either.'

'No.'

'Have you heard about Edward?'

'He's lost on the eastern front, I'm afraid, like so many others.'

'And Katerina?'

'There's a problem there, Helmuth. I think you're our only chance.'

'How do you mean?'

'Günter has to get away, you see.'

Helmuth's face stiffened. 'I'm sure he's arranged it all.'

'Like the others? I wish he had. No. It never occurred to him that we'd lose the war. I think he was the only Nazi who believed every word of their own propaganda.'

'So what is he going to do?'

'He's too stupid to do anything for himself. Katerina's left him, you see.'

'Has she?'

'Yes. He went to get her back . . .'

'She went home?'

'Yes, God help her. The Russians are already there.'

'And wouldn't she go with him?'

'No.'

'So what did Strepper do?'

'He came back here and joined those of our people who like hanging anyone they imagine a deserter. But I put a stop to that.'

'How?'

'Well, he deserted himself. Now they're all packing their bags but most of them have been preparing this holiday for the last two years. Not our Günter Strepper I'm afraid. You could fix us up with visas, couldn't you?'

'Yes. But are you going with him?'
'Yes, I must.'
'Why?'
'The Russians shoot SS on sight.'
'You can get rid of the uniform.'
'Yes . . . but one's got to see some things through.'
'Yes,' said Helmuth, 'yes, you have.'

Chapter Nine

I

WE DID NOT SAY MUCH to each other, Suzi and I, that afternoon by the lakes. We chose Schlachtensee and walked right round it in the trees that ran down to its banks. She was sullen (as if she had been caught biting her nails or eating between meals) but then probably only because our game was over and she had lost. I was sad, then angry that I was upset by an immaterial accident of birth that in no way affected the girl I loved.

'Why didn't you tell me before?' I asked her, watching the dead leaves I kicked as we walked.

'Oh . . . you know . . . you foreigners get so upset about the Nazis and the SS and that sort of thing.'

'But sooner or later I was sure to find out.'

'Yes . . . sooner or later. Now you have found out. Do you mind?'

'Of course not.'

'But your mother will mind?'

'No. I don't see why she should. Anyway, it doesn't matter if she does.'

'No.'

'It must be terrible for you, though,' I added.

Suzi said nothing but breathed in as if to sigh but stopped
and held her breath for some paces.

'No, it's not terrible,' she said. 'Why should it be?'

'It must be terrible to know that your father was a war
criminal.'

'There were lots of war criminals. Helmuth says that
every soldier, sailor and airman is a war criminal.'

'That's quibbling. Your father was one of the worst.'

'That's not true. It's just that they picked on him. Everyone was a Nazi. Lots of people knew what was going on. My
father did some of the dirty work for them and got the blame.'

'You don't even know your father. You haven't even met
him.'

'How do you know?'

'You mean you know where Strepper is hiding?'

She shut up immediately—then said: 'I can still love
him, can't I, if he's my father?'

'How can you love a mass-murderer—even if he is your
father?'

'Well, I do. And for all you know your father dropped
the bombs on Dresden.'

'That's quite different. Anyway, my father is dead and
he was in the Colonial Service.'

'Why is it different . . . to kill people with bombs rather
than guns?'

'It wasn't cold-blooded.'

'It was.'

'They weren't innocent civilians.'

'They were.'

'You started it all.'

'I was not born.'

'The Germans.'

'It was the Treaty of Versailles.'

'Nonsense.' I was angry now, for whatever disgust I had felt at the knowledge of her paternity was multiplied by this childish defence of her monstrous father.

'I suppose it means you don't love me any more,' she said suddenly.

'Of course it doesn't mean that,' I said. 'I love you just as much.'

Love is not something you can decide upon. There are different ways of approach and departure; but always some mechanism of the mind correlates the quite disparate compulsions and inclinations of the man and itself decides. I drifted into love for Suzi—from a casual admiration of her ankles at Zuntz one afternoon I started an adventure—my adventure became an obsession and my love as fanatical as it could have been from the first if it had happened that way. And now, as I said that I loved her, I felt a faint ache in the front of my neck as if I had to force the words from my larynx with reluctant muscles ordered from the brain. It was not just that I was still irritated with her and that this mood did not suit the words. It was that as I said them I thought to myself what meaning these common, bandied words must have had for me, without my knowing it, if a shade less meaning was so fearful.

In the weeks that followed I refused to admit that I loved her less, but soon the muscles ached on my face too as I more often had to force myself to smile when I saw her. When I kissed her or when we made love I had to work up a venereal compulsion—think not of her but of her genitals. My caresses became a crude rubbing of her various minor organs against the skin of my hand. So she too withdrew and became as dry as a chalk box.

Further, from being irritated by her ridiculous defence of her father, I became irritated by what she chose on the menu (the way she could not decide), by the way she suggested going to films she knew I had seen before, by her alternating moods of sullenness and grovelling, panic-stricken affection.

I refused to believe that this disengagement had anything to do with her parentage or her attitude towards it. It was just, I felt, that an inherent incompatibility had manifested itself at last, that her different age, nationality, social class, all combined for the disintegration of the tenuous ties of an affection based on random sexual choice. She was after all, a pick-up off the streets, living with a man of established immorality.

We never talked any more about her father but I could not help seeing some of her characteristics in a new light —roughness, vulgarity. I remembered her crying at the Berlin wall—what hideous hypocrisy in someone whose father was a mass-murderer! I remembered her saying, 'Jews are rather awful, aren't they?'—a remark I had not objected to when she had said it but which seemed in retrospect loathsome.

I had fallen in love with her gradually. My love had reached a peak when I had asked her to marry me. It might have happened suddenly, as suddenly I ceased to love her. My mind at this time was full of the atrocities of the Germans during the war, more especially those of Günter Strepper, because in my research into Klaus von Rummelsberg I read about them over and over again. Suzi's stubborn ignoring of their enormity, of their implications for her and her people, drove me into a quiet fury. She saw what was happening but persisted. When, for example, I made some remark about the death of five million Jews in the concentration camps, she replied 'Five million Jews! People forget the twenty million Germans!' I hit her then but she just set her jaw and went red in the face. I fell out of love with her as, I maintain, anyone can fall out of love—even with his wife—after one year or twenty years. Or, I suppose, it can last forever.

A result of this, aggravated by what I now knew about her father, was the terror that she would conceive. We had, of course, seen to it that she would not—on those first occasions I had taken that responsibility without any mechanical assistance but that was unsatisfactory so I took to the usual device. (There was a time when Suzi had herself fitted up but with that contraption and its smeared white poison nature took its revenge by giving Suzi a pained expression that inhibited me every time she scurried off to put it in—so we threw it away.) However our habit was, as it is probably the habit among millions of other couples, to do without anything during those parts of the month when Suzi was unlikely to conceive.

The point of this is that when it now came to the day she told me it was safe, I was reluctant to do away with the contraceptive but could think of no excuse, so I did; but on the point of ejaculation I felt a strong impulse to withdraw —and did so. The impulse was the product of a thought in my mind that though called safe, the period was not certainly safe and possibly, quite possibly, Suzi would conceive a child that would be both my son and the grandson of Günter Strepper. The thought that this was possible—that I should find myself in a situation where this was possible —so appalled me that the one impulse to withdraw from Suzi at that one moment became persistent inhibition—so I avoided being alone with Suzi and soon decided that I had better break off with her altogether.

After we had met for tea at Zuntz, we walked up the Kurfürstendamm wondering, she thought, what to do that evening. Then I said to her, 'Suzi, dear. I cannot help it but I am afraid I don't love you any more.'

She stopped and turned and said: 'How do you mean?'

'I can't help it,' I repeated. 'Love is involuntary—you know it. I am still very fond of you but I don't love you.'

'Do you want to stop seeing me?'

'I think it would be best . . . for a while.'

She said nothing. The muscles round her jaws trembled but tears too are involuntary and she cried very slightly—this was the third time.

'I thought it best to tell you,' I said. 'I hope you understand.'

'I know,' she said.

'Let's go to a film now, anyway.'

We walked on. Then she said: 'No. I'd like to go home.'

'I'll see you home then,' I said.

'No. I'd like to go alone.'

I stood there. We looked at each other. She started to go back down the Kurfürstendamm, then said: 'I think I will never like Englishmen . . . now.' Then she went and I continued on up the Kurfürstendamm and went to see a film on my own. I felt (I remember) relieved, but I wished I had put it another way. I should have asked her if her feelings towards me had changed because surely they had too. But I could not go back again and ask her.

(It was now possible to get down to my work in a more professional spirit and it quickly lost its association with Suzi Strepper.)

Katerina Strepper / Edward von Rummelsberg: 1944–1945

Pomerania. On the Tuesday a shell hit the stables and
sent splinters into the leg of the old man. Katerina and
Maria bandaged it up. So far as they knew German troops
had withdrawn and the fighting was to the northwest on the
coast around Colberg. They did not know whether Koslin or
Stolp were in Russian or German hands. It was a week since
Strepper had left them and they still had not seen a Russian.

The village was deserted because most of its inhabitants
had left. Only the old man with splinters in his leg and
Maria remained with Katerina.

After the shell had hit the stables, they rushed into the
cellar where they had stored potatoes, half a barrel of salted
herrings and six buckets of water; but it was a stray shot so
they came out again.

Maria thought Katerina should change out of her torn
clothes but Katerina would not.

'It might put them off,' she said.

There was an unusual affinity between the two women at
the prospect of being raped by the Russians.

'It can't be much worse than being raped by one's husband,' said Katerina.

'Oh, madam,' said Maria, 'I wasn't raped by my husband.
Old Stefan was ever so gentle.'

'Well, the Ivans may be gentle too.'

It occurred to Katerina that they might disguise themselves as men (she with her flat chest) or as old bags but
somehow she said nothing and did nothing about it. The

apathy demonstrated by her torn, and now stinking, clothes affected all her projected actions: now that they had the potatoes and the herrings in the cellar, there seemed nothing else to do but wait, for weeks or months, feet on the soil. She spent the days walking round the house, into the farm, through the garden, crumbling away the woodwork of the gate posts and window frames where it was rotten, breaking off dead branches of trees that were within her reach; looking into outhouses, and sheds; or going into corners of the garden that she had not visited since she had played in them as a child. It seemed extraordinary (to her) that, for example, she had not set foot in the old summerhouse, which was less than five hundred yards from the house, for ten or fifteen years. Now, when she did, a vague recollection came back to her of when she had been there before, when she had wheeled out the straw chair which was there still and used it as a carriage for her dolls. Her father had stopped her, saying it was not a toy, and she had put it back in this summerhouse—but now, she thought, could she have spoilt it so much as it had been spoilt, left to rot in a rotting hut?

Behind the summerhouse was the animal graveyard—the corner of the garden where she had buried grey squirrels shot by her father or mice the cats had caught, played with, killed but not eaten.

On another day she went into the part of the house that her mother and father had used. She herself had never moved out of the room she had had as a child, nor used any but the nursery bathroom. The rooms here were also half empty; the staff had thought of putting the furniture in the cellar and had started to do so until they had realized that they would need the cellar for themselves.

She looked at the bathroom door and remembered the day her mother had had to hammer on it to wake up her father who had fallen asleep in his bath. She remembered how awesome and extraordinary it was that someone should fall asleep in their bath—how chaotic and uncertain the world must be where one's own father could do such a thing.

Then, on the Friday, when she was in the morning room at the corner of the house which also held its memories, she heard Maria shout: 'Madam, madam—they're here. Three Ivans in the garden.'

She ran to the window and there, sure enough, were three Russian soldiers with machine-guns coming across the garden.

They were an extraordinary sight (to her) because they were so plump, so well fed. One of them was almost Tartar in appearance but the others quite European. Katerina stood quite still behind the curtain and they did not see her but came into the house and immediately found Maria who was half-way down the stairs. She shrieked in rather a whooping way as they pulled her downstairs and into the drawing-room.

Katerina started forward—involuntarily, I am sure, because she knew there was nothing she could do to save Maria—and her movement caught the eye of the last and most handsome of the three Russians. He darted back across the hall into the morning room on tip-toe—hoping, perhaps, that his comrades would not notice.

Katerina backed into the room; but when the soldier found himself face to face with her, his face dropped.

'*Kultura,*' he said sadly. ('Not for the likes of me.')

Katerina did not know what he meant, but backed towards the sofa since she wanted to avoid being raped on the hard floor.

Disconcertingly the Russian—a dark, sallow chap who could not have been more than twenty and now, close to, looked more Slav than he had seemed from a distance—opened the flap of his pocket in his tunic and took out a small bottle with a very worn and dirty label.

'Vodka,' he said and sat down heavily on a delicate chair that creaked.

Katerina came forward again and he thrust out the bottle. She took it, timidly, drank a little, and handed it back to him. He took a heavy swig and grinned up at her.

'You ... *kultura*,' he said, a single word in halting German. She smiled hopelessly.

Sounds came from the drawing-room. The Russian jumped up and closed the door. His uniform was clean—his tunic pressed, the baggy breeches starched and the boots polished where they were not covered in mud. He sat down again and offered her the bottle. She shook her head so he took another swig, grinned up at her again and pointed to a medal on his breast.

'Stalingrad,' he said; then made the noise of a gun like a child playing at war.

Katerina's (conscious) mind was working fast. Here, she thought, was quite a decent Russian; much better commit herself to him and hope for some protection than await the attention of his more predatory friends once they were through with Maria. It was the Tartar she dreaded.

So she moved up to her friend and laid her hand on his shoulder. He jumped to his feet with the gun and repeated '*Kultura*' in an interrogatory and less emphatic tone of voice.

Katerina now backed away again towards the sofa, her dress falling away at the neck where it had been torn. Her eyes (smouldering) never left the Russian's and with a great grin on his face he followed her slowly with his hands raised.

She sat down and back with one knee bent on the sofa and he, also putting one knee on the sofa, mounted it and . . .

But the door opened and there was a man at the door in a German staff-officer's coat who shouted 'Halt' in finest high-German. Then 'Ukas Stalina' (Stalin's orders) in bad Russian. The Russian stood up slowly and turned. The German had his hands in his pockets and the Russian could see both that he was not armed and that the star of the Red Army was on his uniform.

'Husband . . . husband?' he asked, in German.

'Yes,' said the man at the door.

'Huh,' snorted the Russian, picking up his bottle of vodka which he had dropped on the floor. He went quite quickly from the morning room to the drawing-room.

The German was not Katerina's husband. He was Edward von Rummelsberg.

'Oh Edward,' said Katerina, somewhat sourly, 'thank you. You saved me.'

'Yes,' he replied, somewhat sardonically, 'in the nick of time.'

'But what are you doing here? I thought our troops had withdrawn.'

'Yes,' he said and blushed; 'I'm attached to the other side.' At that moment a Russian officer came in the front door. 'The German Committee,' Edward went on, 'we're helping them clear Pomerania.'

'How do you mean?'

'I'm with the Russians.'

'Good evening,' said the Russian in German, peering over Edward's shoulder.

Katerina stood up off the sofa and smiled. The three men came out of the drawing-room. They chatted with the officer and then all the Russians left, the officer saying to Edward, 'I'll come back in an hour or two.'

Maria came out of the drawing-room. 'Oh count,' she said on seeing Edward, 'how good to see you. I hope they haven't hurt you.'

'I'm all right,' said Edward. 'What about you?'

'Oh,' she said. 'I got it. Did you get it, madam? I wish it hadn't been three times, that's all. But still. I suppose it's better than an Ami blanket.'

'The filthy things,' said Katerina.

'I'm sorry it happened to you,' said Edward, 'but I'm afraid to say they behave like angels compared to what our men did in their country.'

'I must say,' said Maria, 'I wouldn't mind being raped if it saved a few lives. I'd have done it to save Stefan.'

'Maria, would you leave please,' said Katerina. 'I would like to talk to the count alone.'

Maria hobbled out.

'I hope you won't call me count any longer,' said Edward. 'It might confuse our new masters.' He smiled.

'Yes,' Katerina said, returning to the sofa and lying on it. 'Oh, I am so tired.'

'Yes. Everyone is tired.'

'Won't you sit down, then?'

He drew up the frail chair and sat facing her. Katerina began to sway her legs slightly so that the cloth of her skirt rubbed against her skin.

'It is extraordinary that they let you change sides like that.'

'There have been Russians fighting on the German side, you know. Dirlewanger's people, for instance. And many Germans working for the Soviets.'

'Weren't they traitors?' she asked.

He smiled. 'It depends what you mean. Am I a traitor?'

'Perhaps. I don't know. I don't care any more.' She passed her tongue over her lips. 'I have left Günter, you know.'

'I didn't know.'

'I've no one. Only this place but it's empty. I'm vacant too.'

There was a silence. She swung her knees backwards and forwards. Edward looked at her.

'Did the Russian tear your dress like that?'

She looked down. 'Ah . . . yes . . . partly.'

'I see. I didn't notice.'

There was another silence—a space for the finer feelings of embarrassment which in both of them had long since been scarce.

'You wouldn't like . . . ?' she began; then said, 'No.'

Edward stood up. 'I think you and Maria had both better come with me.'

'Why? Where to? Can't you stay here or at Kassow?'

'No. We must go to Berlin; or at least cross the Oder.'

'Why?'

'Unless you want to stay and face the Poles?'

'The Poles? Why the Poles?'

'I thought you understood. Pomerania is to be ceded to Poland.'

'Of course not. Why?'

'It was agreed among the allies.'

'But I can stay here, can't I? They won't turn me out of my home?'

'Yes. They certainly will. That is what I'm here to explain

214

to you and to our people at Kassow. The alternative is to stay here and become Polish.'

'I am German.'

'Yes. I know. That's why I don't advise you to stay here. The Polish partisans have been behaving much worse than the Russians. They suffered enormously too.'

'But are we ever to come back?' Katerina had now mounted up onto her knees on the sofa. Her eyes, once smouldering (like peat), were now cold (like a tap running in a dark room).

Edward was standing still looking ahead out of the window in the direction of his own home.

'I don't know,' he said. 'I doubt it.'

'Oh Edward,' she shouted, 'how can you do that? How can you let them turn us away from here? Take away our land, our homes?'

'There is nothing I can do. It is just the price Germany has to pay . . .'

'Damn Germany. This is more than Germany. It's Pomerania. It's our home land. How can you stand there like a priest preaching this hell and disaster without raising a hand except against your own people?'

Edward smiled again sardonically. 'You can stay,' he said.

'A Pole? How can I become a Pole? What will they do to me? No, you must protect me.'

'Yes,' he said, 'I will look after you but you must come with me. You are allowed to take three hundred marks and anything you can carry.'

Katerina suddenly, calmly stepped onto the floor.

'When?' she asked.

'I should think,' said Edward, looking at his watch, 'that

215

they'll be back in an hour. I'm afraid you will only be able to take a small bag.'

'Are you leaving all your things at Kassow?'

'Of course.'

'All the furniture and pictures; the blue plates?'

'Yes.'

'I will be ready, you'll see. I must borrow some of my old clothes from Maria.'

A stray shell. As Katerina's home had been isolated from the life of others before the war, so it had escaped the fighting and destruction. The towns they passed through on the way to Berlin, towns which she knew quite well, were flattened. Quite literally the constructions of man, Pomeranian man, for shelter, work, worship and rule, had come down into a pile of their materials—rubble of brick and beams. Where there had been fires, this junk was blackened; and there were small holes in these haphazard heaps where the men and women, Pomeranians, had crawled out. Now it was hard to understand what they did without homes; the tents belonged to the Red Army and were well guarded. The people clustered into what rooms remained intact or built themselves makeshift shelters. Many stopped in ditches where the front had overtaken them as they fled, and some started now or continued the trek westward.

'What I wouldn't do,' thought Katerina to herself, 'for a pot of real coffee and a chocolate butterfly bun filled with real cream.'

Then Berlin—the chaos lifting under the stolid Russian command. The minor civil servants already coming out from under the rubble to reassume authority. Crippled husbands steadying their stomachs with bits of old chalk plundered from kindergarten classrooms as they re-enter their wives who so recently stayed the Russian advance. Water pipes hastily bound together lest the whole system disintegrates—but water already flows from the taps again. Berlin has been saved the American raid—it is only Russian guns that have knocked holes in the houses. The buildings are falling down but the telephone still works.

Scraggy, pallid virgins emerge from the lofts where they have been hiding. Russian trucks, two types, move along the streets with troops, with food, with boxed machine-tools unscrewed from the factory floor. Lines of people, the women in blue aprons, make their way out of the town towards home—home from which they fled, home which they imagine, home in the east.

Queues form around district town halls. Groups of petitioners cluster around the casual commandment from Minsk or Kharkov. A café is reopened stocked with the plunder from a police station. Red flags fly from the Reichstag, the Brandenburg Gate. Red flags are made from the corner of Old National Socialist banners. The Amis, the Tommies arrive. There is a victory parade.

Katerina and Edward found lodgings in an abandoned flat near the Red Town Hall. Maria was given work and a place to sleep as a civilian employee at the Russian cavalry stables in the Glienicke palace. From the start, Edward was away all day at work with the National Committee and the Communist Party. Katerina, for the first days, remained in the flat making the beds they had constructed on the floor out of piles of newspaper, sweeping the two rooms denuded of furniture, washing the few plates in the trickle of cold water that came out of the tap, planting lettuce

217

seeds in the window-box, and thinking of what she who had hardly cooked a meal in her life before could make of the pieces of bread and tinned fish-paste that were often all they had to eat.

Later, however, Edward brought back slightly better food which (Katerina suspected) was given to him as a Party member. He said nothing about where he got it, but simply that it had been made available. Katerina looked much happier and quickly learnt to make various dishes with what she was given.

Also she began to leave the flat, at first just to walk in the streets around the block in which they lived, then past the town hall, and the ruins of the Bode Museum, the Cathedral, the Opera house, the Academy.

The nasty, indeterminate smell that had still been in the air when they first arrived was now gone. She risked longer journeys and eventually reached as far as Tiergarten or Schöneberg to see if any friends of hers were still to be found in the houses they had previously inhabited. But most of these friends had been connected with the National Socialist Party and were gone, their houses and flats deserted, destroyed or lived in by strange families. One vague acquaintance, the wife of an SS Sturmbannführer, was still in her house in Steglitz, which was intact; but she was not pleased to see Katerina. She said that her husband had fled or been killed, that she did not care because in her heart of hearts she had never agreed with his ideas and now had a very decent Ivan who brought her food. This was said through the front doorway, the door ajar, and Katerina left without entering the house.

Edward always came back late in the evening and talked to her rather politely about the old days, their childhood;

sometimes he would talk in a haze about the future, about how (he imagined) it would be. 'An honest, just start to our new national life,' he would say. 'Historical and practical justice for the German people.' But he was talking to himself, not to Katerina, for if she asked him a question or even said something in agreement, his eyes would snap onto her and he would change the subject.

Katerina was confused and perplexed by living with a man like this. It was not that she thought now, as she had for an instant in Pomerania, that she loved Edward. Of course Edward was just a childhood friend who was looking after her as would any of the von Rummelsberg brothers who thought of her as a sister. The love she thought she had felt as he saved her from the impetuous Russian was just an excess of gratitude and relief. Nevertheless, there was something irritating (to her) in the way he had put her pile of newspaper in one room and his in the other; in the way he left her alone in the kitchen to wash each night as if they were hearty, chivalrous Hitler Youth and German Maidenhood on a camping expedition. Why (she wondered) did he never use the lavatory in the flat when she was in the room next to it? She had once had a sharp attack of some kind of squitters in the middle of their make-shift dinner and when she had returned to the room where they were eating, Edward had had a red face and a look of acute embarrassment.

She knew that Edward had never lived in a house with a woman other than his mother before—and certainly never with a girl. But she imagined he had had some kind of tumble with a girl in France or Poland. She was not cold between army blankets at night; but that the heat of her body should simply radiate around her body seemed (to

219

her) a waste—that the smell of her body that came with the heat should not mingle with another's (his) seemed a pity.

Edward always asked her each evening if she had been all right, what she had done that day. He never discussed his own work.

One evening he said to her: 'You know, Helmuth is in Berlin. He's been in a flat near the Adlon all this time.'

'But I thought he was in Japan,' Katerina said.

'I know. So did I. But it seems he came back before the end of the war.'

'What is he doing?'

'He is working with the Americans.'

Katerina Strepper / Helmuth von Rummelsberg: 1945

Katerina went one evening at six to the Hotel Adlon, which was miraculously still standing between the demolished Chancelry and the Brandenburg Gate. At the desk there was even a porter with cross keys on his tunic.

'Could you tell me where I could find Count Helmuth von Rummelsberg?' she asked.

'What is your name?' the porter asked.

'Countess Katerina von Treblitz.'

'Well, countess,' the porter said, 'I'm afraid he's not here any more because the Russian officers have moved in, but I have his address.'

He took out a battered black notebook. 'This, countess,' he said to her, 'has the last known addresses of all the big boys—including Adolf himself. Our friends upstairs would like this little book, countess, but I can't part with my discretion for simple politics, can I? You never know what twists and turns we're in for.'

He wrote an address on a piece of paper for Katerina. 'I should think you'll find him in now, countess, and it's only a ten-minute walk from here. I'd call you a cab if there were any.'

She walked there quickly. It seemed unlikely that there would be a building in the street which was distinguishable in the rubble or which she remembered from before—so destroyed was this part of Berlin. But from several blocks away she saw one building standing out from the ruins and knew that that must be the number on her piece of paper. It bore no number but she went into it and up to the third floor. There she knocked on the right-hand door. It was opened by Helmuth.

His shock was short, but long enough for him not to notice her misty expression. Politeness, the same politeness as his brother's, soon expressed itself in his face and directed his action.

'Katerina, how nice to see you, won't you come in?' etc.

His flat was rather like hers—small, under the roof, with two rooms and a little kitchen. It was a garret but she knew that to have it he was as privileged as Edward. However, Helmuth had decorated his garret, first by stripping the flowered wallpaper which left the walls a mottled white and brown (plaster and glue). On this he had hung six Japanese scrolls—four of calligraphy and two with Sengai ink drawings.

'How nice you have made it here,' said Katerina.

This flat too had no furniture—the former inhabitants must have stored it in the cellar—but Helmuth had taken down the door between the two rooms and laid it on pillars of bricks to make a desk; and he evidently used an oil drum as a stool.

'I am afraid there is nowhere to sit except on the floor,' said Helmuth.

'May I look in here?' asked Katerina, peering into the second room.

'Of course,' said Helmuth.

'Oh, you have a nice bed,' she said. It was a mattress on the floor, with blankets marked in blue with 'Hotel Adlon'. It was clear from the articles piled on the floor that Helmuth lived here alone.

'Yes,' said Helmuth, 'they managed to sneak it out for me from the hotel.'

'May I sit here?' Katerina asked, sitting on the mattress.

'Yes, of course,' Helmuth brought in the oil drum. 'Would you like some coffee?' he asked.

'Have you coffee?'

'Yes.'

'Is it real coffee?'

'Yes. It's American.'

'How lucky you are.'

'No. It's just that I'm working with the Americans. I have an old friend among them who gave me a job.'

'Who was that? I had no idea you had American friends.'

'He was here, you see; but he went to America; and now he's back with the occupation force.'

'What was his name?'

'Stein.'

'Oh yes. I remember. A Jew.'

'Yes.'

'And he's with the Amis?'

'Yes.'

Katerina sat on the bed. Helmuth went into the kitchen

and while he boiled the water, Katerina shouted: 'How was Japan?'

'Fine,' he replied.

Then he came back with coffee in a saucepan and two cups.

'I am staying with Edward,' said Katerina

'Are you?'

'We're living in a little place just like this one ... over by the town hall.'

'I thought that you were back at home.'

'I was but I had to leave. We all had to leave. Edward turned up just in time to save me from the Russians. But then we had to get out ... before the Poles came.'

'What was Edward doing there?'

'He works with the Russians. He's part of the National Committee.'

'The Communists.'

'Of course,' said Katerina. 'He's sensible.'

'Perhaps.'

'But then so are you. This is the first real coffee I've had since before the war.'

'I saw Klaus and Günter out of the country,' said Helmuth.

'Oh, did you?'

'Yes. They got away to Switzerland.'

'That's good.'

'I expect they'll go to Argentina now.'

'Why Argentina?'

'We have cousins with a cattle-ranch in the Rio Negro. They can hide out there.'

'You're very good to ... Günter.'

'Well ... he's one of us ... in a way.'

'Yes . . . well, he was. I thought he'd be caught.'

'He wasn't.'

'No. Not that I'd have minded. I'm going to divorce him, you know. I was going to for some time but I had to put it off.'

'Oh yes.'

Katerina was silent. She looked at Helmuth with glistening eyes. He was caught by her glance. The oil drum felt like an extension of his spine.

'Oh Helmuth,' she said quietly.

He sat up sharply, 'Why?' he asked. 'Why were you going to divorce him? You were married for fifteen years.'

'I always hated him. It went wrong from the start.'

Helmuth looked at her.

Sexual attraction oozes out from the wrinkles around the eyes—then it trickles from the other creases and cracks in the skin, the muscles around the folds sagging so that the mouth, for example, forms a vapid smile. And after it is emitted, this attraction forms an atmosphere around its planet so that body and expression together form a haze.

'Oh Helmuth,' she said. 'If only you hadn't left me alone there that autumn in Pomerania. I was so alone. I was so frightened. Do you remember? Did you ever know what it was like for me? My father threatened to kill himself. We had no money. I needed comfort and you were away. How often I have cursed myself since that I did not wait for you to come back, but I so needed protection, love and protection, and . . . that Günter was there, always around me, begging me, pleading, pushing, barraging me with his demands. I was blinded, Helmuth, can you believe that? I was blinded by my fear. Do you remember those times? When we all felt that Germany was falling down around us?

224

I was such a young girl, Helmuth: I was frightened and I made an awful mistake.'

Helmuth heard what she said, but, at the same time he tried to remember if he had really not seen her since that occasion in Pomerania when they had parted. The memory was so faint. Was this the same girl? Of course. It was so emphatically someone he knew well. He thought she looked old—her face was covered in wrinkles (out of which . . .). But he thought that she was quite extraordinarily beautiful. He even laughed to himself thinking, 'I had fine taste in women from the beginning.'

Katerina was leaning back on her arm on the mattress. Helmuth, on his drum, was above her. He could not see her nostrils. She wore no stockings, of course, but a decent grey skirt (one she had once given Maria but that Maria had never worn because it was too small) and a dark blue blouse. Helmuth could not see her nostrils but he could see the crevice between her breasts. Even now, he thought to himself, in these times of scarcity, she has found some padding for her bosom. Then the vague memories of his hand on her flat breasts like drop scones—he had never seen a woman since who was like that, who had such thin legs and blonde hair with a dash of brown. But in those days the very base of the two breasts would always be kept half an inch apart by the curve of the skin that joined the mammary gland to the breast bone and breast bone to mammary gland; but now the skin was loose and the closed crack (out of which . . .) went straight to the bone.

Her shoes were very worn.

Katerina asked him a question. 'I think, don't you,' she said, 'that everyone should be allowed to make one mistake.'

'Yes, I suppose so,' he replied.

'A mistake which you needn't count, however bad it is?'

'Yes.'

He wondered if the colour was still a faded orange.

'Do you think . . . do you think it will ever be possible to forget the last fifteen years?' (Katerina asked him) 'Do you . . . will you forgive me, do you think, sometime? If we scrub them out? We're young enough, aren't we? We have a long life to live. Germany has to begin again. Can't we do it too?'

'Yes . . . I don't know.'

'Please don't think badly of me if I say it,' she went on, clearing her throat a little, 'but if I don't say it now, I never will. I love you, Helmuth, I don't think I have ever really stopped loving you since we first kissed each other in the forest. Do you remember the logs, Helmuth? I remember them as well as I remember your eyes looking at me, your hair falling over your face and your hand ice cold rushing down . . . there; and I didn't dare start or shudder with the sudden cold in case you noticed, Helmuth, in case you noticed and misunderstood and didn't love me then.'

Helmuth covered his face with his hands: but her soft, sweet voice went on.

'I know there will always have been the years with Günter, Helmuth, that even if we forget them they will still have been there. But I want you to know one thing, even if you turn me out afterwards, as I deserve. I want you to know that with Günter it was never the same. That was why we never had children. I couldn't bear it. That great lump. It was a travesty. I won't say I never did it with him, Helmuth, because that wouldn't be true. But I never liked it; I never moved with him and after a time I wouldn't let him. He used to do it to himself but I didn't care. If ever I thought about it again, it was remembering those times with you.'

'I don't mind about all that,' said Helmuth. 'What happened, happened. We have all made mistakes.' And certainly, he did not care.

'Yes, Helmuth, but my love, my real love for you, has preserved itself through my mistake, through the fifteen years. I know I have no right to expect you to believe that —that it would be a miracle if you did; but it is miracles we have to expect, isn't it? Now that I see you again I am so sick with love that I can hardly speak'—she cleared her throat again—'but I feel so happy because I feel pure. You were my only lover and now I feel as if I am further back still, that we are still children and I am a virgin child playing with you again in the woods.'

They were both silent. Helmuth looked down at the empty cups with their dry dregs of coffee.

'Will you kiss me?' Katerina said.

He looked up.

'Just once . . . please?'

He leant forward and kissed her lightly on the lips. She put her hand behind his neck and drove their mouths together with such force that rather than sense her passion he looked to save himself from falling off his oil drum, which he only did by raising himself from it and—lips still sealed to hers—coming forward onto his knees on the mattress.

'Oh, my love, my love,' she said.

'Yes,' he said; and they kissed. His hand was now warm but she shuddered and he teetered on the brink of oblivion; but he never fell. Each button and buckle was clear in its relation to his finger, the air, the light from the window. Her skin was a texture like the corner of the mattress, her swaying caresses and writhing reaction to his were as exact as pistons under steam. There was no correlation between

227

what he saw before him now and his memory of his first love. He could see that the body was of a thirty-five-year-old woman—the flesh looser, the pigmented skin browner than they would have been on a younger woman: but the comparison was with a geisha girl or half-a-dozen other women. The first was too long ago.

As he made love he felt two separate sensations—the specific genital and spinal sensation which was common and expected; but also a strange and unusual ache in every nerve of his body and in his head, as if a heavy anaesthetic was about to plunge him in unconsciousness. But gradually the former sensation overcame the latter; he became detached; he wondered when it would finish, how she felt; he noticed how her half-open mouth and glazed eyes, the look of mystical concentration, were just as they always were on any woman in such a position.

Afterwards he felt her breathing stop, then flutter down on terraces beneath him. She said: 'Oh darling, I am happy.'

When it was past nine o'clock, when the ripples (as it were) had reached the shore and they were talking together about the scarcity of vegetables, he interrupted her and said: 'Katerina, my dear, I think I had better say this now rather than later. I was confused when I saw you this evening. I liked what we have just done; but we would be off to a false start if I didn't say that I don't love you, not as before or again. I'm afraid it was too long ago. I can love you, I am sure, as an old friend ... or as a sister; you've always been a sister to us all, anyway; but I can't love you as a lover or a husband.'

She said nothing.

'I'd be no use to you, anyway. I'm not going back to the Foreign Office. I did no good while I was there. I have plans of my own which mean living alone. I'm used to living alone.'

In a tone of voice which (to Helmuth) was surprisingly ordinary, Katerina said: 'I'm quite a good cook, now, you know. Wouldn't you like me to come and cook for you sometimes?'

'I don't think so.'

'We don't have to do . . . that.'

'No. I know. But it'd be better not to see each other alone . . . just now.'

'Won't you come and see Edward?'

'I'd like to see him, yes. So we'll meet that way. But if he's working for the Russians, I'll have to be careful or I'll lose my job with the Americans.'

'I hope you'll bring us some of that Ami coffee,' she said.

'Yes, of course,' he said, relieved that she had (as they say) taken it so well. 'Take a packet with you.'

'I will . . . now . . . I'd better go . . . because if I'm not staying here the night, I must get back before it's dark. I don't want to bump into a randy Ivan.'

So she left Helmuth's flat and went back to her own and Edward.

Part Three

Chapter Ten

I

Early in the year, just before I returned to England on leave, control of the Calvert Group of companies passed out of the hands of the Calvert family into those of an American public company. This affected me only because a Calvert daughter was my next girl. Sarah.

If the bolt is in the slot on the door of a public lavatory, the sign on the outside reads 'engaged'; if not, it reads 'vacaɪ ʾ. I met Sarah through my sister and her eyes read 'vacant as clearly as that. My sister told me why this girl, among others, was available: she had been engaged to and living with a man who was a partner in a merchant bank. This bank had financed the take-over of the Calvert group for the American company. The Calvert family had fought the take-over and when the merchant banker had refused to dissociate himself from his bank's part in it, Sarah had broken off the engagement.

She must have been twenty-five or -six when I met her. She looked unhappy and beautiful. Her body was so fine in a conventional sense that it might have seemed vulgar—like a model's—if not for her animated face. When she spoke —when she was interested in what she said—she hurled herself at you through this face with the physical energy of an athlete doing a long jump. When she was bored, tired or depressed, there was the opposite effect—of a long-jumper not jumping.

The second time I met her was at a large party in a London hotel. She was talking to a Labour member of parliament and this man was suffering from her lack of interest. He was that classless kind of Englishman whose classlessness amounts to provincial airs given an American veneer. He looked as if he had tried to pick her up.

'I am a member of parliament, you know,' he was saying to her. 'I govern you, my girl, whether you like it or not.' This line did not take him far: Sarah muttered something about her father not having a vote but without it more power than the whole Labour party. Then she smiled at me and we left the other man.

I felt great sympathy for her, being in some ways in the same situation. Sympathy was the basis of our relationship —and it was not really enough. I was also a little afraid of London and she seemed to know her way around. I had, after all, spent my life until then in my parents' house in the country, in a boarding-school, in a small university town, and abroad. I had never lived in London except for the eighteen months when I was training in Whitehall. Its people seemed quite strange—their clothes, their customs. This often happens to diplomats: their image of the country they are representing is quite different from the reality. England is no longer a country of people who play in cricket matches or go to church on Sunday—yet we have been trained to behave as if it was. How extraordinary that throughout my education as a child and my career as a diplomat I had been isolated from any individual or group of people whose lives could be called typical of those being led by my own people in my own country. Now I watched the short skirts, expensive cars and sharp personalities around me with the naïve mixture of envy and disapproval of a real country boy. Sarah seemed a tangible and immediate embodiment of this fast, smart world I did not know.

The affair started immediately. That night at the party we danced together all the time. I wondered if I should not be self-effacing but there seemed to be no one else in the crowd of people, glittering in my eyes, that she wanted to dance with. Nor did it seem to occur to her that I should want to dance with anyone else. When it came to four in the morning and we were dancing slowly and closely in semi-darkness, the alcohol in my blood had induced a rhythm, a chant in my mind. 'In my own country with a girl of my own kind. In my own country with a girl of my own kind.'

We did not talk much. Rather awkwardly I asked her about her father and the take-over. She may have been tired of the subject but she did not show it. She said the main trouble was that her father and uncle now had nothing to do. That was her objection—not that the Americans had bought the company but that it was unkind, extremely unkind. I could not think of anything to say to that—either way.

We danced together and then I took her home. It was perhaps an extraordinary assumption that she wanted me to do so. Neither of us had talked about it or made a gesture of any kind. I did feel that she wanted to attract me but hardly had the energy: her body itself had been so buffeted, frustrated and disappointed so often that it rebelled against her mind—that mind which normally threw her into her long jump.

At the dance, in the taxi, she smoked. Her hands would fumble at her handbag and take out a packet (a cigarette from the packet) and an old lighter. It was only when the lighter was in her hand that her eyes would look down at what she was doing. She would never allow me to light her cigarettes. She used her own lighter. After she had lit a cigarette, she clutched the lighter for some time in her fist but when the cigarette was half smoked she put the lighter back in her bag. When she was not smoking her hand tightened and relaxed involuntarily on the handbag or my hand.

The skin on her shoulder, her face, her hands, was flawless, like a synthetic fibre developed by one of the companies in the Calvert group. I was curious, at the dance, to know if it continued like that all over her body.

A girl in a ball gown is gift-wrapped. One hardly likes to undo the pretty bow. Before I did, of course, I came into her flat, poured her, myself, a drink. And so on. All without direct words on the subject. I did not ask to come in; she did not invite me. It was simply something that was done between two of a kind. It would not have surprised me if she had gone into her bedroom to turn down the bed or had sat by the mirror rubbing her face with cleansing cream. However she played the game—we both played the game quite correctly. She smoked her cigarettes on the sofa while I drank my whisky and soda and talked about the pictures on the wall, admired the yellow chintz. Girls, I knew, were unhappy in flats on their own: they prefer to build a home around a husband. Sarah—and this is a sign of her character —had ignored the urge to wait and had done up the place prettily, conventionally, well. Also—and again a sign of her character—I could see that she had a double bed. Few girls

236

of our class in my experience would so openly declare their habits and values even if their lives were like that of the professional whore.

I became nervous as I often do but she became emphatic in her gestures so I unwrapped the gift wrapping. The skin was indeed the same lustreless, flawless white all over her body.

After a week of my company, Sarah became more cheerful. She told me about the young banker—but nothing that seemed to give him any character. She said the difficulty, after living with someone for two years, was getting used to sleeping alone.

'I think one's body gets used to the warmth of another person, don't you?'

I agreed.

'But I couldn't go back with him . . . the take-over, you know, it was just symptomatic. I mean I don't know my father so well. My mother left him when I was eight. But . . . you know . . . the callousness . . . the ruthlessness . . . just because my father's a millionaire doesn't mean to say he has no feelings . . .'

'No,' I said.

'It's very modern, I know, but the way these business people completely dissociate their work from their ordinary lives . . . Henry—that was his name—he couldn't understand what I was talking about. It was a good deal for his bank so it had to go through. A.B.C.D. But, you see, he really rather disapproved of me for sleeping with him. He put off getting married . . . I think, because of that . . . so when I left him I suppose he thought . . . I don't know . . . a tart reverting to type.'

Sarah seemed to like my company—the warmth of my body in her bed—but she was restive when making love. She liked making breakfast: often, before I was awake, she was up in the kitchen preparing it—crushing the oranges, scrambling the eggs, grilling bacon, boiling milk, making coffee and toast—juggling with all these different things so that all were ready at the same time. Then she would put it all on a trolley and wheel it into our bedroom. Sometimes there were even primroses wreathed between the knives, forks and pots of honey and marmalade. If I was not awake she would shake my shoulders—impatient for us both to sample her art before it was spoilt. She refused to cook any other meal in the house and had an Irish woman called Mrs Blake who came in the afternoon to clear up.

After breakfast Sarah would have a bath and dress. I liked watching her dress because she had a large number of clothes—she bought something new almost every day—and because she wore strangely martial underclothes that I had never seen before either on a woman or in an advertisement. She told me that they came from New York. Certainly this may be what made her figure seem so excellent when she was dressed: naked, her trunk seemed disproportionate to its appurtenances.

She did not mind my watching her because she hardly noticed. She was wholly concentrated. She always wore clean clothes (only on our first night did she not put the day's underclothes straight into a wicker basket) and she was ruthlessly fashionable in the clothes she wore. Through her I came to realize how exacting it is to be fashionable. Certainly she had the money to buy what she liked, but she was not a creator of fashion—nor did she follow so far behind as to buy what was illustrated in fashion magazines.

The fashion, she said, was dead as soon as it was in the possession of the public—it was, to her, a mild antidote to democracy. The position between leader and follower; between the eccentric and the common. To know not what the fashion is, but what it will be. This was Sarah's main preoccupation, the end to which she used her intellectual ability.

Sometimes I went with Sarah on her shopping expeditions —into the big stores or the small dress-making shops she patronized. I sat in the same back-room while she took off and put on the different dresses. The dress-makers did not seem to mind. I imagine the young banker had done the same.

Sarah never talked to me about my work: she never mentioned Germany except once when she asked me why I lived there.

'Because I was posted there.'

'Couldn't you have changed your job?'

'You don't resign from the service just because you don't like one posting.'

'I'd rather live ... God ... in Canada ... anywhere rather than Germany.'

'I quite like it.'

'I'm sure it would be very nice if the Germans weren't so awful.'

'I had some quite good friends.'

'I don't know any Germans, thank God.'

On abortion, hanging, homosexuality, Sarah's opinions were liberal.

In the evening Sarah was endearing as girls are endearing. She lay back smiling on the bed; she danced around the room on her own to a gramophone record; she would burrow her hands under the cushions of the sofa as if to hold them back but they would break loose and hug me hard; she bought me ties; she fumbled in her handbag for her cigarettes; she deliberately dropped half-crowns on the floor of her car so that they were there when she needed them for cigarette machines.

I can say that I was endearing to her. I was kind, gentle, courteous, amusing. I was punctual. I dressed well. I could explain to her what she did not know about politics and the arts; and listen when she taught me what I did not know about fashion and films.

After about three weeks she began to be contrary, disagreeing petulantly with any suggestion I made. She did not hide this change in mood: she said it was a good sign, that she was becoming less inhibited with me.

I had noticed before that she seemed dissatisfied in making love. We do not know what it is that will satisfy and satiate and I had always considered it nonsensical for a man to worry about such things but incumbent upon him to sympathize enough to do his best. Sarah's breathing never halted: her consciousness was never suspended; and rather than lie still after making love, she tossed about as if sleepless in a hot and uncomfortable bed. At first, when I asked her, she said she did not know why she reacted in this way: I presumed that, like the smoking, it was part of the return on an unhappy childhood and uncertain home.

Secrets of the bedchamber. One evening after the first three weeks, an evening when we had had dinner quietly together and gone to bed early, her inhibition must have relaxed still further; for as we made love I heard her murmur something but could not make out what it was. A few

240

moments later she murmured it louder, more insistently, and this time I could make it out. 'Hurt me,' she said, 'hurt me.' The embarrassment I felt was certainly a fine variation of that emotion but I complied as best I could, feeling ridiculous in doing so as well as embarrassed, because naturally I am a gentle man and gentle is what I had always thought a man was expected to be. However it is easy enough to scratch and bite someone you are lying on, naked like that: I was even able to hit her a little, pull her hair—but I felt more and more awkward. I had no way of knowing how far she wanted me to go, though whether I pulled her hair or scratched her back, she never discouraged me and when it was over she seemed to have enjoyed it more than usual because she did lie still.

'Do you like . . . being hurt like that?' I asked her.

'Yes, I'm afraid I do rather. How did you know?' she answered.

'You said so.'

'Oh, did I?' She smiled up at me. 'Did you like it?'

'I didn't mind.'

'Henry was very rough,' she said. 'Do you know, he once beat a girl-friend of his so much that she couldn't go out of the house. I went to see her, to bring her groceries and things. She was a friend of mine, you see. She had great bruises on her cheek—it was quite black. That was when I met Henry.'

I am sure I would have adapted myself to Sarah's tastes. I suppose it is natural for a woman to want a man to be rough and brutal, like the female cichlid which, if not faced with a brutal male, does not react to him at all. That night as Sarah, my mistress, lost all her inhibitions, she introduced me to different ways of doing things which, she said, Henry

241

had taught her. It fascinated me how easily adopted were these variations, these perversions. In a book, I thought, Sarah might seem diabolical but here she was, and I knew her, an ordinary English girl whose only qualities in any way unusual were richness and neurosis.

I say this emphatically—that she was normal, ordinary, like many others—because I did leave her after that, not because of her but because of myself, my own neurosis, the dream I had in her bed.

II

Edward von Rummelsberg / Katerina Strepper: 1948

I was (I dreamt) in Edward's flat in Berlin. Piles of newspaper covered the whole floor. Suzi, a small, squat Suzi sat in the corner with wide eyes staring into the room. Edward was standing looking out of the window, his hands on the sill. Katerina sat on the newspapers, leaning against the wall, looking at her feet stretched out in front of her. These two people, whom I only knew from the photographs taken of them in their youth, were more real to me in this dream than were people in my life awake.

Katerina was speaking to Edward in an even tone, as if reading from a book. 'Strepper,' she said, 'would never kiss me. He was like a negro and he had a negro's hair. He would never bother to kiss me or unbutton my clothes. He would just tear off my dress and so there was always mending to be done. He would tear me, too. He didn't care. If it wouldn't go in, he'd blame me and hit me as hard as he could, throw me down on the floor, even, kick me, then pick

242

me up again by the hair and try again—in front or behind, he didn't care. I don't suppose he could feel the difference. I wasn't allowed to care. He didn't notice if I liked it or not, but you see, I did. It was the thing I liked most; the only thing I really liked. It made my dull life worth living. It was something to wait for, to think about, to look forward to. Sometimes I'd bait him, whine for it; he'd kick me over, throw me a broom and tell me to do it myself. But I'd crawl back and in the end he'd throw me to the floor, pick me up by one leg, stamp my clothes off with his boot...' She turned to face Edward. 'And you?' she said, 'and you ... and you ... and you?'

Edward remained looking out of the window.

Then (I dreamt) they were both gone from the room and I myself came into it. Suzi crawled out of the corner on the newspaper, leering at me over her shoulder. I could not make out whether she was a child or a dwarf. She lay down in the middle of the floor, flat on her stomach, her legs apart; then she lifted her child's frock from her bare bottom. She leered at me again over her shoulders, a dwarf or a child. My eyes were fixed on her legs—short, fat, stubby—a child's or a dwarf's.

I either woke up then or the rest was still part of my dream. I lay still and gradually thoughts and feelings came into my mind. I wished that I had buggered Suzi or that I could bugger her now: and I wished I had never met the girl who lay next to me in the bed.

Chapter Eleven

I

On my way back to Berlin I was asked to look in on our Embassy in Bonn. There was at that time what was called the Rightist crisis: the National Democratic Party, a conservative political party in Germany led by former National Socialists, had made gains in the state elections in certain parts of the country—especially in the cities of Bayreuth and Erlangen in Northern Bavaria where their share of the vote was up to ten per cent.

Our Ambassador, Sir Peter Dodd, was a man very like the Political Adviser in Berlin but at a further stage in his career, ripened as it were to that over-ripeness which is the mark of an Englishman in authority.

'We're not disturbed,' he said. 'It would be absurd to be disturbed by these little fluctuations in voting pattern. They still have such . . . such a small percentage.'

'Yes,' I replied. 'All the same . . .'

'All the same, we have to keep our fingers on the pulse, don't we? Hitler started with less.'

He explained that the next day there would be a conference at the American Embassy with our Political Adviser and the American Political Adviser and I would be called upon to say what I knew of the activities of Klaus von Rummelsberg. I explained that I had been investigating this man's past life and knew little about his present one.

'It doesn't matter,' said the Ambassador, 'it doesn't matter. You see, we aren't worried about this thing. It's more for form's sake—something to put in a report.'

I had dinner in the Embassy that night and was back in the slow world of diplomats—the meticulous serving of elaborate food, the conversation of Lady Dodd which avoided any reference to our profession—to politics or foreign affairs. She described the facilities for sports among the diplomatic community in Bonn and told me how good the Belgian Ambassador was at tennis.

The bedroom in the Embassy—clean walls, a beige carpet and large white government towels. No pictures on the wall. I lay awake trying to think of what I could say about Klaus von Rummelsberg. It would not help my career in the service if I said nothing. Though my researches were quite recent, I had so emphatically forgotten that part of my life that they came back to me like recollections of an uncle I had known as a child.

He was the eldest: there were three of them. He had been a National Socialist, he had escaped to Argentina at the end with Günter Strepper and later returned. He was a power in the refugee movement, allied to the extreme Right. The refugees wanted to return to the territories ceded to Poland at the end of the war—which was part of the programme of the National Democratic Party. A return to Silesia, the Sudetenland, East Prussia and Pomerania, a return home for the Germans who were in Duisburg, in Johannesburg, in Bogotà.

It is a good thing to have a profession—an occupation

that coasts along from day to day, year to year. If I had only to eat or to love women or to look at pictures and listen to music, my mind would fester and ferment as it had done in this short leave. Perhaps if I had been working when I had met Sarah it would have come out all right. If I had even been a postman it would have meant some hours in each day spent carrying the sack, sorting the letters out, ordering them to come to the top of the pile as I reached each house; watching the people change, the houses change; some get a new coat of paint, others grow tattered as the occupants get older or the smell behind the door becomes one of stale beer and smoke and the eyes of the opener blearier and blearier.

Otherwise, with no work, breakfast still lies in the stomach when fatty slabs of meat are served up for lunch and the evening noodles curl onto the strawberry tart of teatime.

In this sense the diplomat's life is almost as good as the postman's. Somehow communities which are nations want to order their humdrum affairs in fancy phrases and fancy thoughts, and men like me do it for them. All you need is a liberal education, an order to hang around your neck and, of course, a flag for the flag-post.

There I was. There was a development in foreign affairs. Shopkeepers and tenant farmers in parts of Northern Bavaria had voted for the Right, the extreme Right, the Radical Right. From boredom, from irritation or from nostalgia, they had thrown a vote or two at the old-style barrel-thumpers, the injured pensioners of the Arms-bearing SS— perhaps just not to have to vote any more. So we, the Englishmen, ex-enemies, fast friends, gather round with the Americans, ex-enemies, fast friends, to ask ourselves— what is it? What can be done? We must not make those

246

same mistakes as were made before. The table has a fine polish: there are sharpened pencils in front of us, clean blotting paper and fine crested paper. Some have the lion and the unicorn—others the eagle. My thoughts are crested too, and surely in the minds of the Americans there is a claw clutching olive branch and arrows at the same time.

The American Ambassador sat at the head of the table: our Ambassador sat at the other end. Each of them had his first secretary on one side and on the other the Political Adviser to the Commander-in-Chief of his army in West Berlin—my superior, Mr Perkins and my acquaintance, Gerry Stone. I sat between the two groups on one side; on the other sat the American Ambassador's secretary.

'Well,' said the American Ambassador, who chewed like a film star, and was certainly as tall and lean as a cowboy, 'I'm not going to do much talking because I don't see there's much to say.'

'Yes,' said Sir Peter, 'I'm sure you're right, Ambassador. However, there is a certain element of public opinion in our country if not in yours who would like some reassurance from our government that there is no ... no return of National Socialism.'

'I don't think American opinion is much interested in Germany just now,' said the American first secretary.

'No sir,' said the American Ambassador.

'No,' said Sir Peter, our Ambassador.

'The opinion of the Federal Government is that there is nothing to concern us,' said the American first secretary, 'and that should be good enough for us.'

'Yes,' said Perkins.

'I think,' said Gerry Stone, and everyone at the table

listened to him, 'I think this segment of public opinion in your country, Great Britain, are the Nazi witch-hunters, aren't they? They see a Nazi behind every tree and many of them are socialists, aren't they, and many of them socialists with good friends in the Soviet Zone?'

'That is true of some of them,' said our first secretary.

'Yes, but I say,' said Sir Peter, 'there is something in what they say, isn't there? You can't get away from these election results. The National Democratic Party sounds very much like the National Socialist party to people reading the newspapers in England.'

'Correct, Ambassador,' said Gerry Stone, 'but the question surely is not why are the Germans voting for a party with an extremist right-wing platform and ex-Nazi leaders, but why does the Christian Democratic party no longer attract the votes of these people?'

'The Federal Government is Christian Democrat, they're good friends of ours, and they say they aren't worried,' said the American first secretary.

'Of course they say they aren't worried,' said Gerry Stone, 'because if they were worried it would be to admit their own failure. Let me recapitulate on our policy towards Germany, gentlemen, if I may, because its . . . its theme . . . is sometimes forgotten. After the unconditional surrender of German armed forces in 1945, we were faced with the reconstruction of Germany, were we not? Such reconstruction had to be administered by Germans, good Germans, if we were not to make Germany a colony. The British Labour Government, am I not right, Ambassador, experimented with Social Democratic administrations, but it became clear to us in the American zone, and the British soon came to accept our point of view, that Social Democratic administrations were mostly unacceptable both because of their weak attitude towards Communism and because of their ... their rustiness—after all, most of them had been in concentration camps or in hiding for ten years. They had lost touch. The alternative that presented itself, you will remember, was the formation of Christian Democratic administrations—the Christian Democrats being in part, and basing their support on, those Germans who may have inclined towards National Socialism once, who may have voted for the National Socialist ticket, but had presumably suffered a change of heart ... along with all else.'

A bleary look came over Sir Peter's eyes: our first secretary shifted in his chair. The Americans leaned forward.

Stone went on, his large hand gesticulating on the end of his short forearm, poised on its elbow on the table. 'We realized, didn't we, that you cannot reconstruct or administer a country, even one that has unconditionally surrendered, against the will of the majority of its citizens unless you create a totalitarian state as they did in the Russian zone. Therefore we went with the majority, the same majority of course which had voted for Hitler, believed in Hitler, but with their ideas modified, leavened you might say, by the Catholic Christianity of some of their leaders. But we had too, of course—I am merely recapitulating—to accept the majority's prejudices and the logic of their change of heart. We forgave them so we had to forgive the perpetrators, wasn't that so? We released the war criminals; we commuted their sentences. And we built a stable state. Communism was discredited, isolated. The Soviets advanced no further. The Social Democrats remained what they had mostly been, a gentle opposition forced by the public opinion we had created to accept our views and interests.'

Gerry Stone hesitated. He looked at the Ambassador's secretary who took down in shorthand what he had said.

'Would you agree with that, gentlemen?'

I said nothing. Sir Peter grunted. The Americans nodded their heads. Perkins said, 'Yes, I suppose so.'

'The question,' Stone went on, 'is therefore—why does the Christian Democratic Party, led by our friends in the Federal Government, no longer absorb the Right as it did and was intended to do?'

'Yes,' said the American first secretary, 'that I guess is the crunch.'

'It is a point of view,' said our first secretary.

'Now from this point on, I am expressing my personal opinion,' said Gerry Stone.

'Go on, boy, go on,' said the American Ambassador.

'In my opinion, sir, the section of the Christian Democratic Party represented by our friends in the Federal Government, though perfectly loyal to the alliance and our interests, is veering towards compliance with certain socialistic ideas—this to secure its own position in the party leadership through supposed popularity among the people. Now it certainly is not in our interest to see them lose control of their party to the anti-Americans but it seems to me that our friends have a mistaken assessment of the correct strategy in the situation. After all, the influence of United States interests in the Federal economy, and above all in the general field of communications and mass media, together with that of like-minded West German citizens, is so overwhelming that this electoral posturing is unnecessary. And from our point of view, does it matter if they do lose votes to the Social Democrats whose present leadership is as committed to our interests as they are? The danger

250

gentlemen, is not of losing votes to the Left but, as we have seen, of losing votes to the Right—because the National Democratic Party is not committed to the defence of our interests. Quite the contrary.'

'I go along with that,' said the American Ambassador.

'So do I, so do I,' said the American first secretary.

There was silence from our side until Sir Peter said: 'What do you think should be done?'

'I think you, sirs, should intimate to our friends in the Federal Government that we, the Allies, take these electoral results extremely seriously. It would be ... unwise to give the exact reasons. Use the Nazi argument. Suggest that their policies return from centre-left to centre-right. I think they should discourage any further prosecution of war criminals —even to the extent of interfering with the judiciary. We ourselves could close the Tribunal files to the state public prosecutors. It should also be suggested that they should not make any contacts with Iron Curtain countries where that conflicts with the real or imagined interests of the refugees.'

'We have our man ...' said Sir Peter, waving his hand at me.

'Yes, young man,' said the American Ambassador, 'you haven't said anything.'

I opened my mouth. Gerry Stone watched me. 'How is your Klaus von Rummelsberg?' he asked.

'As far as I know,' I said, 'as far as I can judge, Klaus von Rummelsberg is not so militant as to, for instance, obstruct allied policy towards Eastern Europe.'

'If I may dissent,' said Stone with a firm face, 'I think you are not quite right there. Of course I am not the expert on von Rummelsbergs that you are'—he smiled 'but his public pronouncements are certainly very militant.'

'I think that might be just . . . letting off steam,' I said.

'You are optimistic. To the whole group of us, this course of playing into the hands of the Right parties and not the Right of the Christian Democrats is more perilous than it seems. It is not just that ground lost on the Right must be gained on the Left which starts a drift Left-wards and leads gradually to Socialism. . .'

'Salami tactics,' said the American Ambassador.

'Quite, Ambassador,' Stone said. 'Worse than that, the support increases in the same ratio for those right-wing parties, especially the National Democrats and Refugee Movements, whose leaders are extreme nationalists and enemies of our interests. We are quite aware that these personalities are working with the French and that they would not hesitate to reach agreement with the Soviets if they thought this would unite Germany. These men, whether they are ex-Nazis or not, are the real enemies of our countries. They are little von Papens for the Bolsheviks and their plans are quite plausible—for are we sure that the Soviets would not make concessions and re-unite Germany if they thought it would neutralize West Germany, and see us driven out of Europe? The German Right and the Soviets have a traditional understanding going back to 1917. Nationalists like von Rummelsberg are as unhappy as the Gaullists about our predominant interest in their economy. We should not underestimate these dinosaurs.'

Our first secretary leaned towards me and said in a low voice, 'I wish he wasn't so damn sure that our interests were the same as theirs.'

'What are our interests?' I whispered back.

He shrugged his shoulders, and looked at Sir Peter, whose face was redder than usual but he said nothing more.

'Listen son,' said the American Ambassador to me, 'I'm afraid there may be something to what Mr Stone says. Couldn't you try and find out a little more about this Klaus von Rummelsberg? Just where he stands on the Soviets and on us? That is, if that's all right with your Ambassador?'

'Yes, of course,' said Sir Peter. 'Yes, of course.'

My meeting with Klaus von Rummelsberg was arranged by a third person, a Mr Benender, who was acquainted with von Rummelsberg and had done odd things for us since the war. He drove me out from Bonn in the afternoon on the road to Bad Godesberg. The house we reached was medium sized and recently built—there was an ordinary view of the Rhine and a garage for two cars. The total comfort of this kind of house seemed to me typical of a West German but not of a von Rummelsberg as I had imagined them. From it (I thought) I could guess at the type of woman his wife must be.

We were met at the door by Klaus von Rummelsberg. Benender introduced us and then drove back to Bonn. It was the first time that I had met Klaus, but of course I imagined I knew him quite well. I knew him as a child, as a young man. I was now to see what he was like now that he was older.

He was, he had become, like his house, a West German— that is to say he was sunburnt from holidays in Jugoslavia and his hair was greyish and curled at the bottom of his neck. He smelt of cologne and cigars: there was the sheen of a businessman on his skin. Only he was tall, exceptionally tall, much taller than the other West Germans who were brown from holidays in Jugoslavia and sleek from vegetable juices extracted in their electric juice-extractors.

253

Klaus von Rummelsberg took me into his sitting-room which was (as I had imagined it) comfortable, contemporary —with many pure-grained woods and low-slung leather chairs.

'It is very good of you to see me,' I said, speaking German, 'but you see the Embassy likes to keep in touch with the various leaders of different parties. I cannot think why we haven't bothered you before.'

'It is a pleasure,' he replied, 'it shows how thorough you British diplomats still are. No other Embassy is anything but embarrassed by our refugees.'

'I would like this to be off the record,' I said, 'as the journalists call it. Whatever you may say will be treated by me as . . . as a diplomatic secret.'

'That is just as well,' he replied, laughing. 'With the refugees you have to be careful. It is what you are said to have said that matters—much more than what you do.'

'Don't they expect much . . . action?'

'No. I don't think so. There are very few who are ready to leave their comfortable homes and large salaries to march back to their grocers' shops in little Silesian villages. But you cannot say that sort of thing, except off the record as you call it. Then everyone says it.'

He laughed. He had large hands and long arms which he stretched out in a kind gesture as if inviting a child to walk into them. For an instant I remembered that he had been, following the annals and evidence, an enthusiastic National Socialist, an officer of their protection squads, the impassive witness of mass murder. Now that did not seem so much unlikely or unbelievable as meaningless—it was a meaningless memory. The places are still there—I had seen them:

there is the stadium at Nürnberg; the outhouses at Dachau; the hooks at Plotzensee. There are weeds between the paving stones of the stadium; flowers growing in the execution ditches and rust on the hooks, but those are the same places: whereas this man's body had renewed itself several times since then—the white skin of autumn winds in 1944 is scattered as dead cells into dust: and the brain, the mechanism of conscience, will, ideals—that too has passed by blood through the kidneys and urine to the earth.

'Is there anything you would like to know?' he asked.

'Well, I think you have already told me. There is an element among our people, you see, which is really afraid of that march east.'

'Yes, yes,' Klaus replied. His forehead wrinkled slightly; that is to say, he frowned. 'But I do not see why the public pronouncements of German politicians should be interpreted more literally than those of politicians in any other democracy. We are a democracy now, aren't we, and that means to bark rather than to bite, doesn't it?'

'I know,' I said, 'that was my view.'

'Then it is quite genuine, this fear of a return to Nazism?'

'Yes, I think it is . . . among certain people.'

'It is difficult for us to understand that. I had thought it was . . . cultivated for other reasons. I was a Nazi, you know. I was in the SS. Of course, you know all about that. But, you see, since I went through it once, since I lived a National Socialist life for the first thirty or forty years, it astonishes me that anyone seriously considers a repetition of it all. The condition of our people is so different: the way of thought is different—even if we had not had the experience. And that itself would be enough.'

'I think,' I said, 'it is just that the second world war was presented as a repetition of the first and so . . . some people fear a third . . . over Germany.'

'The first war and the second war. You see, to us they were the same war.' Klaus said this quietly and (it seemed to me) he did not expect an argument or answer. His chair was low: his knees almost came up to the level of his chin, so long were his legs. 'To think of a first, then a second, then a—third—the old animosities—that is the dangerous mistake.' He said this, again, as if to himself. Then he realized that I must have heard. 'I am sorry,' he said. 'That is not very polite: especially to someone of your generation. The faults of the British are not to be compared . . .'

He smiled. I expected to feel irritated that this ex-Nazi should talk about our mistakes but I did not. What did I care about the failings of one side or the other? Had I not learnt, bitterly enough, that others, younger than I and more innocent, believed as strongly that their fathers had been right and ours wrong? Had I not sacrificed enough to that vendetta? I liked Klaus von Rummelsberg as instinctively as I liked his brother, and I saw no reason to give up either of them as friends.

Klaus may have noticed the brief expression of irritation and he seemed relieved when I said that as far as I could tell he was right, that the experience of defeat had freed a large number of Germans from many prejudices when the experience of victory had only confirmed the British in theirs. Their attitude to Germany was an instance of this.

'I think you must be an exception,' he said.

'No,' I replied, 'but I know something of the Germans. What we do not know,' I went on, 'is what your real political objectives are.'

'If they are not to march over the Oder?' He smiled; that

is to say, his face creased, the sockets of his eyes moved, into a momentary expression of humour. 'Wouldn't it be enough if it were to stop others marching over the Oder?'

'It would certainly be enough and that would make *you* exceptional.'

'But your . . . element would not believe it.'

'No.'

'They might be right. I am a Pomeranian. The refugees are my people. They have been torn from their homeland through collective but not individual guilt. It is difficult to understand, these days, what that can be like. So few people have roots of any kind. But we were country people. We lived almost as if we were in the middle ages. Do you know what it is to love a view or a wood or a certain kind of mist? Can you imagine what it is to love them more than a woman; or even to love a woman because her eyes, too, have seen the same view; knew the wood—to love her not because she had a fine bust but because the lungs behind it had breathed in the same air?

'I myself can remember the horizon in all the four directions from our home and when I am tired of that plain view of the Rhine I imagine them: there were fir trees to the south—a hill near to us to the north behind, fielded hills far away to the east and to the west the valley—the tree tops of the valley.

'For others, of course, it may be some street they have known for most of their lives. They remember it as well as I remember what was to be seen out of the top windows. The sausage shop, perhaps, and the people who went in and out of it. Of course it's all rubble—and my fir trees are probably down. The shape of the hills may not have changed much—but I doubt whether I'd like to go back to see now.'

257

'I can understand that it is a pity,' I said.

'Well ... Germany deserved to be punished. I have no doubts about that. It was a pity that the Pomeranians and Silesians and Prussians were singled out, because we were not the most guilty.'

'If you accept that you have lost your land, then what is it you want?'

'Are you a modern man? If you are you may not understand. What have you got, in your head, do you think? Is there something more than a machine?'

'I don't know. I hadn't thought. I am agnostic, more or less.'

'Well, you see, I am full of spirit and soul. Pomerania was more than a geographical home. It was the object of our loyalties—like Germany. Loyalty, you know, was our quality. The East Prussians were known for being brave; the Pomeranians were loyal, always loyal. Now our loyalty is ... a little frustrated.'

'You still have Germany.'

'Germany? What Germany? Do you consider this trading area worthy of our historic loyalties? No, don't you see that Germany has gone almost as surely as Pomerania? The name remains—what is it called? West Germany. An area, an area where they work hard and can be relied upon to screw nuts into bolts as no other collection of people.'

'Then you are a nationalist,' I said. I did not understand what he was saying. I felt queasy in my stomach as if my suspicions released acids into it—and this latest, the sharpest acid.

'No, I am not a nationalist,' Klaus said quietly, as before, 'because this is not 1870 nor 1914. If we lived then, I probably would be, strutting along the pavement with an

258

officer's sword and everyone would make way; and you would be in a white uniform administering your justice to the Africans or the Indians. But I am still a patriot as Luther was a patriot and Heine was a patriot. And my political objective is to live in a country worthy of that feeling but let me say that that country is as much yours as mine because it is not only Pomerania, it is not only Germany. It is Europe.'

I did not understand what he meant, so I could not discuss it further. I was only filled with the suspicion that this must have been the way he and his fellow countrymen justified their National Socialism—that matter may renew itself but this soul he believed in remained the same—incorrigible.

He may have seen that I had nothing more to say because he stood up and said: 'I hope that you will have some coffee. My wife is preparing it.' He went out of the room. I was left alone for a few minutes. Then he came back into the room and behind him came a woman, almost as tall as he was, carrying a tray with coffee and cake on it. It struck me that she was extraordinarily thin for a middle-aged German woman, but otherwise her appearance was as one might expect. She wore a tailored beige suit and a white blouse. Her hair was grey but clearly dyed that colour. I stood up when she came into the room but sat down when she invited me to do so. She put the tray on a low table by my chair and as she stood up I noticed the nostrils of her nose. At the same time she said: 'I believe you know my daughter, Suzi.'

It had not occurred to me that Klaus might be married to Katerina Strepper, but now that I knew it hardly surprised me. If I was taken aback, it was at finally being face to face with this woman.

'Yes,' I replied to her, 'I knew her quite well in Berlin.'

'Yes,' said Frau von Rummelsberg, 'she told us all about you. She was here for a time, a few months ago.'

'How was she?' I asked.

'She had been in Baden-Baden, you know, in a clinic. She had not been so well. But now she is better. She is back in Berlin.'

'With . . . with . . .'

'Yes . . . with my brother-in-law.'

II

Edward von Rummelsberg / Katerina Strepper: 1953

June 16. Berlin. A procession of construction workers marched down the Stalinallee to demand that the increase in work norms be rescinded. By the time they had reached the Alexanderplatz, the column had become a crowd of several thousand. Waldemar Schmidt, Chief of Police in East Berlin, was prevented from arresting certain demonstrators by the Soviet Military Authorities.

From a window of the flat where she had lived since the war, Katerina Strepper could see the men walking to join the crowd. Her view of the demonstration itself was blocked by the blank wall of a gutted building—the gutted building that had stood there since the end of the war. She continued to watch the men, who walked quickly, some trotting for a few paces, as if late for work. Her child, Suzi, played with wooden bricks on the floor of the room behind her.

At ten past seven, Edward came into the flat. He bent over and kissed Suzi. Katerina remained looking out of the window. Edward put down his leather bag which was battered, as were his shoes, and went into the kitchen. He came out holding three pieces of black bread which he ate—an empty triple-tiered sandwich.

'Aren't you cooking anything tonight?' he asked.

Katerina turned in from the window.

'There's nothing to cook,' she said.

'Why not?'

'Why not? Because there's nothing in the shops.'

'You are exaggerating.'

'And I suppose they are all exaggerating too,' she threw her hand back towards the window.

'Yes.'

'Huh. Is that what the Party is going to tell them?'

'I admit there are shortages but there certainly isn't famine.'

'Oh yes. That's true. There's no one dying in the street. What a triumph for socialism that is.'

'Katerina, you cannot do what we are doing . . . what we are trying to do . . . without making some sacrifices.'

'Then I don't see why we are doing it. And they don't, I can tell you.'

'You know that the best of us aren't out there.'

'I don't care if they're the best or the worst. They're the same sort as I am. Haven't we suffered enough for one generation? Must we have a whole life of misery so Suzi can hypothetically have a whole life of happiness? Or Suzi's children? Or her grandchildren? Aren't they to suffer a little too?'

'It is no use arguing. You have . . . you have simply lost your optimism . . . your faith.'

'It is no use arguing, as you say, so please don't argue

about this. I've decided to go to the West. I can't stand it here and I don't want my daughter to grow up with a blue uniform and a red flag the only colour in her life.'

'Suzi would be happier here . . . in the long run. I am sure of it.'

'You don't care if I go. All you care about is Suzi—all you want is a child to father like an old hen. Well, there's more to being a father than patting a child on the head, so I'm damned if I'll leave her with you.'

'You're free to go if you want to. You're not my wife. Even if you were my sister, you would be quite free to go. I suppose it's my fault. I'm never at home and you get bored. But I shall miss you and Suzi.'

'You'll miss her more than you'll miss me.'

'I feel like her father. She calls me father.'

'Then for God's sake why don't you come with us? You must realize that the Party's finished over here. You'll probably all be strung up by a mob. We could be together over there, just as we are here. We'd be much happier.'

'You know I couldn't. I want to see it through over here. You know I must do that. I owe it.'

At ten that night Edward drove Katerina and Suzi through the Brandenburg Gate and left them with three suitcases at the Hotel am Zoo on the Kurfürstendamm. He drove back into the Eastern sector of the city.

June 17. The revolt had spread to other parts of East Germany. General Dibrovna proclaimed a state of emergency. Armoured units of the Red Army patrolled the streets of East Berlin: Russian troops restored order.

Chapter Twelve

I

THERE WAS TO BE A SECOND CONFERENCE on the Rightist crisis in Bonn in a month's time. By then I was supposed to have a comprehensive report on the current activities of Klaus von Rummelsberg and the refugee movement. Sir Peter Dodd made it clear before I left Bonn that he himself would be satisfied by my personal assessment of the man and his following and that he would back my judgment. His only wish was that I myself should be sure.

I relied upon Klaus's brother Helmuth to help me. After all, in spite of what had happened, I could still count on Helmuth as a friend. I telephoned him at his night-club as soon as I got back to Berlin but was told that he was away in the Far East. I asked after his niece and was told that she no longer lodged with him.

Stone was also back in Berlin and asked me to lunch. I suspected that he wanted to find out what line of inquiry I was going to pursue but he told me at once that he wanted the lunch to be in his house, with his family. And again, as I came in the door, he said: 'I want this to be friendly. No business, no discussion. It's not a good idea to meet on business, is it? Especially when people have different points of view.'

I had met Stone's family before. His wife was about his size but in better proportion—a quiet woman who had also been born in Germany though they had met and married in America. His elder daughter, Rachel, was like her mother. I had never known her open her mouth except when forced to by a direct question. She was the kind of girl who at first sight elicits sympathy because she seems a shy child. However she was twenty-five and shy with deliberate purpose, like the city of Dubrovnik which built enormous and ingenious ramparts for its defence and took great civic pride in them: but the city was never attacked because within the ramparts there was nothing worth the siege except the defenders' view of the magnificent ramparts. Rachel did not sit down to meals; she preferred to eat hamburgers with mayonnaise from the PX store at odd times of the day.

Stone's younger daughter, Rosie, was also there; I had not met her before. She was quite different from her sister and from her parents—having grown out of the physical proportions of an expatriate Rhineland Jew into those of an all-American girl. She towered above her parents and sister and had none of their control or reticence. Her hair was long and black, her skin light-brown, her eyes dark-brown, but she seemed as completely American as the other three were squarely Jewish.

Rosie had just spent two years in the Peace Corps in Thailand and was visiting her parents on her way back round the world to America.

Now the all-American girl has an irresistible charm to the man who would style himself accomplished and European. The significance of experience is that it is knowledge to be imparted to innocence: and innocence is the negative and supine, eagerly but helplessly awaiting the indentation of what is hard and positive. This is the way things have been arranged: it is no great truth. There is often more to be learnt from innocence; the innocent have often been through more. But the experienced, even if their experience is as flat as mine, have narrow eyes and impart, whilst the innocent have wide eyes and receive. She (Rosie) was to me innocent and I was to myself experienced. I would never claim to be positive except in that one semi-sexual respect that I have automatically positive parts that influence the brain.

I doubt whether I was experienced to Rosie. Americans do not see Europeans as Europeans see themselves. To her I suppose I was a nice guy and she needed one at the time. So she came to the opera with me and talked to me all the time, during the interval and afterwards while we had dinner.

'This Peace Corps—God—do you know what it is? Of course you do. You've got the VSO in Britain, haven't you? There was a VSO boy in a village up country. But I guess it's not quite like the Peace Corps. You see, all the guys and girls walk into it back in the States full of ideals—you know. Then they send you to Hawaii and I did a crash course in Thai. Enough to get around, anyway. Then they dump you, they just dump you, in a God-forsaken village with one other volunteer and leave you. Christ. And those Thais. They don't want you there. Christ, they're as corrupt as hell, those generals and they don't care if you sit there if that's the way they get American dollars. And the villagers, they're just scared to death. So your ideals last you a month. I was lucky, though. I could get to Bangkok every once in a while—there's a Peace Corps hostel there. And the other volunteer in my village—he was a nice guy. But

Christ, he had a bad time, you know. These Thais—do you know the Thais?—they're little guys who are always smiling and, you know, if you don't smile right on back they stick one of their pretty ornamental knives in your spine—anyway they were scared as hell of me because I was a big white American and I taught at the convent—but this other guy—Jameson—he was a negro and the Thais may be scared of Americans—but they think negroes are dirt whether they're American or not. I mean, they think the Laos are low and the Maos lower than that, but negroes are way, way down below. As to learning crop cultivation from a negro—boy oh boy. He didn't get to talk to anyone in that village except me, I can tell you. And he hadn't had too good a time in the states before that . . .

'I had a bicycle but those Thais could hardly believe it— an American girl on a bicycle . . .

'Christ—I ate that food of theirs but they aren't famous cooks, you know, and certainly not in that dump of a village. You'd either cook your own or go to the market and get a bowl of something. But then—God—I had the trots almost the whole time I was there. Two years. Can you imagine it? Christ, it's depressing, that.

'We'd go into Bangkok, Jameson—that's the negro boy— he'd spend most of his time there. I guess he liked the girls there. You know, they didn't care, as long as his dollars were dollars. But then there was that business—did you read about that—some guy—I guess he was Commie or something—took a photo of a Peace Corps jeep parked outside a brothel. So they just walked, I guess.'

At dinner. 'Bangkok . . . hell, it's not a bad place—as far as bars and things are concerned, anyway. There was a Peace Corps hostel there—I told you that, didn't I?—well, it used to be full up every damned weekend. The boys—I can tell you—they wanted just one thing and they could get it easy as anything. The girls wanted it too, mostly, but it wasn't so damn easy. Christ—most girls thought they'd find some Thai boys but—Christ—Thai boys'd rather die than be seen with a white girl—I mean an American girl—a British girl too, I guess. So the girls—God—they got a bit frustrated. One girl—she came up every weekend and'd go down to the Regina hotel and just walk up to any GIs who happened to be there. Christ—she just wanted it.'

'What about you?' I asked.

'Me? Yes, I did. God, it got depressing just stuffing tampons up there all the time. There was this guy at Berkely when I was there and so I was kind of used to it. You know, God I got fed up. Wouldn't you? Men are meant to need it more than girls. I don't know if they do.'

'So what did you do?' I asked.

'Well . . . I went with this girl, sometimes, you know—the one I told you about—to the Regina and there was this volunteer—we'd meet in Bangkok. But he'd talk about the Great Society—you know—seriously; anyway they'd think —hell, they could have American girls any time in their life so they went after the Thai girls. At the end—you know— just a few months before the end—Jameson and I—you know—we got to like each other. God. When I think of those months in the same dump and nothing happening . . . but it's so difficult with negroes. Oh, I guess you don't have them in Britain. But, you know, they're so jumpy and that makes you so scared of making them more jumpy. In the end it worked out—I guess we both just got tired of going ten hours in a bus to Bangkok to get it. But that's the trouble . . .' she paused.

'What trouble?' I asked.

'You know. The usual.'

'What . . . er . . . some sort of disease?'

'Clap? God, no. I had that enough. If it were only that. No . . . Christ . . . I'm pregnant.'

While she had been recalling her experiences in Thailand her eyes had been in the air, on the lamp, on the table, following the waiter (as she spoke) or on her knives and fork. Now she looked straight at me, with the full force of her dark irises and black pupils.

'What are you going to do?' I asked.

'I don't know. Get rid of it somehow, I guess.'

'Why don't you have it?'

'A negro baby?' She laughed—a pretty, not a bitter, laugh. 'I'd sure like to see my father's face when I walked in with a negro baby.'

'Wouldn't you and Jameson get married?'

She laughed again. 'It'd still be a negro baby . . . and a negro husband . . . boy . . . that'd be worse.'

'But surely they wouldn't mind if you were married.'

'Boy oh boy. You don't know much about Chicago. Where we live in Chicago, it's Jewish, Jewish, Jewish. There's no negroes and there's no Catholics, Baptists, Irish, Italians or even plain Americans. My pa'd just be finished there if I married a negro. I think he'd rather I married a Red. I don't know, though. It'd be a near thing.' She smiled at her thought.

'That's not very . . . tolerant.'

'Wouldn't your parents mind if you married a negro?'

I paused but did not think because I knew. 'Yes. I suppose they would.'

'Pa's a heel, all right,' Rosie went on. 'Everyone in the

service thinks he's great. You know ... people come up to me and say, "Rosie, you must be proud to have a father like that—coming over as a refugee and ending up so high in the State Department." I say, yes, yes ... but I know he's a heel all right.'

'And he wouldn't let you marry a negro.'

'He couldn't stop me if I really wanted. Thanks very much but no thanks. Jameson in a bum Thai village is one thing. But a neurotic negro husband in America these days, always getting at you for being white? No thanks.'

'Then why don't you have the baby without him?'

'No. God. I couldn't. It'd kill Pa and the whole family. I can see why, too. He came to America as a refugee without anything. His parents and his sister were killed in the concentration camps, you know. He got his citizenship and his job and a nice house in a respectable Jewish district. He goes to the synagogue. He thinks he's got his kids fixed for the best life the world's ever had to offer. Well, it'd dish everything for all of us if I popped out a black baby: he's a heel, but I couldn't do that to him.'

'So you'll have an abortion?'

'I guess so. Out here, if I can.'

'How many months?'

'This is the third, I guess.'

I arranged the abortion for her. I gave her the money for it. I even, during the ten days there was to wait for the free bed, gave her what she liked and was used to, what I liked and was used to—my eager homunculuses shooting uselessly up for a limpet's place already occupied by those of a buck nigger.

*

269

My secretary telephoned the night-club from time to time to see if Helmuth had returned. The people there were not sure when it would be, but about ten days after my return Helmuth was back in Berlin and I met him for a drink at the Steinplatz hotel.

He was looking tired and old and did not seem particularly pleased to see me. I thought it must be the effects of his journey.

'I was told that you never went abroad,' I said to him.

'I don't like to, that's true. Did Suzi tell you that?'

'Yes. It must have been Suzi.'

'I don't like travelling, least of all to the other side of the world. I did it once, during the war, and that was enough. Of course it's much easier now with these jets but they seem to tire you as much.'

'Then why did you go?'

'Why indeed? It was a personal thing. I had several friends there, one in particular called Shosuke Ienaga. I suddenly felt I wanted to see him again before I died.'

'And did you see him?' I asked.

'Yes. I found him. I hadn't heard from him since the war but I found him through their Foreign Ministry. You see, he was a diplomat, too.'

'And was it worth it?'

'Seeing him? Seeing Japan? The man and the country— they've been through a similar experience to ours, you know. I was able to talk to him. He helped me make up my mind on some issues I had been thinking over. I told you I only thought about women? I only wish I did. Sometimes one is forced to make decisions about other things.'

'Was . . . your friend still in the Foreign Service?'

'No. He left it after the war, like me. His father had been

270

in the war cabinet so the family was discredited. Blame and prejudice often passes on to the second generation, you know. It's human nature.'

I looked up at him, wondering whether this remark was a gibe at me. But Helmuth was not looking at me—he seemed to be thinking of someone else. Anyway, my prejudice was my secret.

'Let us hope it won't be passed on to the third,' I said.

'To the third,' he replied. 'That's it. That is what was so terrible. Do you know the Japanese? Shosuke, you see, was a noble, philosophical man and above all, he was detached. He practised the exercises of Zen. I was never converted to Buddhism but I admired Shosuke very much. He was the only friend I think I have ever had. There had been a bad patch in my life before I went to Japan and from Shosuke I learnt a certain detachment myself. I was very influenced by him: he was so noble and fine.'

'And isn't he still?' I asked.

'Yes, he is,' Helmuth said slowly. 'He is noble and philosophical; but he is less detached. You see, he would accept the effects of Japan's defeat and the American occupation on himself and on the nation as a whole. The tragedy was what happened to his son. They'd sent him out of Tokyo during the war to avoid the bombing raids. I know, because we went down to visit the boy just before I was recalled. I remember that quite well—he was an enchanting child. Shosuke loved him very much—the Japanese seem to love their children more than we do. The place they sent him to —the home of some relations—was in a suburb of Hiroshima. The child didn't die but he's been in the hospital they have there ever since. I don't know exactly what happened to him—they didn't say—but it has changed Shosuke.'

271

'He must be very bitter,' I said.

'That's what you'd expect, isn't it? But he isn't bitter. It is just that he is driven out of his detachment. He is less philosophical—more practical. He has taken to business—built up an enormous concern—one of those great paternalistic empires they have out there. It is difficult for you to imagine what it would be like to lose a child if you haven't got one. This lingering death for Shosuke's son was particularly cruel. Think what it must be—to grow up in a hospital just to die there. I don't think Shosuke will ever forgive the Americans. That's where he has lost his detachment. He's a capitalist tycoon but all his influence is squarely on the other side. It's strange, isn't it? I can't see that happening on this side of the globe.'

He finished his glass of schnapps. I finished mine and ordered some more.

'I visited your brother Klaus in Bonn,' I said.

'Klaus? Did you? How was he?'

'Very well.'

'Yes. And did you meet his wife, Katerina?'

'Yes. Briefly.'

'When I was a boy . . . no, a young man, I was very much in love with her, you know. She was my first love.'

'Yet she married Klaus?'

'Yes, she married Klaus. Or rather, she ended up with him. They were only married ten years ago.'

'What happened between?'

'Between? That is a strange story. She lived for a long time with my younger brother Edward, in the East. She always seems to end up with a von Rummelsberg.'

'She is Suzi's mother,' I said.

'Yes,' Helmuth said, 'she is Suzi's mother. Now you know.'

272

'Why would you never tell me?'

'Oh, it was that silly Suzi. She was afraid that if you knew about her parents, you would be put off her. She didn't want to risk it. I told her that it was ridiculous but she made me promise.'

'Not to tell me about Strepper?'

'Exactly. She is so loyal to that man, just because he is her father. He may be, but if you won't tell Suzi—no, of course you don't see her any more—I can tell you it is even possible that I am her father. Her mother—well, most German women at that time—just at the end of the war—were not very particular. Suzi was born prematurely so who knows when she was conceived. Katerina was still married to Strepper, so Suzi got Strepper's name, but it is unlikely she's his daughter. They had no children before. Perhaps she's Edward's but I doubt that. Do you know, I don't think he has ever slept with a woman. Of course, one cannot carry on this sort of guessing game with Suzi, poor girl. She thinks Günter Strepper is her father—Katerina is such a respectable West German these days that she'd never deny it— and so Suzi'll stick by him through thick and thin though she's never set eyes on him and it makes her very unhappy at times.'

'Suzi has never met her father?'

'Strepper? No, not up till the time she lived with me. But don't call him her father. As far as I am concerned, I am her father. I persuaded her to use my name—a title too—when she lived with me here. I care about her more than anything else.'

I felt hot. My skin prickled and my clothes rubbed uncomfortably against my skin. 'The reason I went to see Klaus,' I said, 'was official.'

'You were investigating him, I know.'

'How did you know?'

'Klaus knew about it and told me. In fact he asked me to find out what you were after.'

'Did Suzi know?'

'Oh yes. She tried to find out what you were up to. I hope you don't mind. It was my idea. But she wasn't very good at espionage. She said she had discovered that you were working on trade figures.'

'Is that why she . . . befriended me?' I asked.

Helmuth smiled. 'Was she a little Mata Hari, you mean? No. I'm afraid not. It was the very truest of true love.'

'I didn't realize that you and Klaus were . . . so close,' I said quickly.

'We kept in touch . . . as a family. You may not realize it, but we Pomeranians are almost as much foreigners as you are in West Germany and expatriates always keep close together.'

'Are you part of the refugee movement?'

Helmuth looked abstracted. 'I have never been part of any movement or any party in my life,' he said. 'That was always the role of my brothers. I was detached . . . from the beginning . . . interested in other things, you know, than politics. But, I can assure you, you have no need to worry about Klaus and his refugees. They're a sad lot—lunatics who amuse themselves by frightening us all with their loud gibbering. But they're harmless.'

'Is Klaus a lunatic?'

'Klaus? No. He has the qualities of . . . well . . . saintliness which might be mistaken for lunacy but in fact he's one of the few real statesmen in the country. He was always the one of us who felt responsible for other people. I admire

274

him very much. He made a great mistake over National Socialism—and so did most of us—but that didn't destroy his sense of responsibility. He came back and took up the cause of the real unfortunates—all those people who had not just lost their homes but their homeland too. He shares their madness just enough to be able to lead them into a society and a way of life they hate and he despises. And then he married Katerina. I don't think he ever wanted to do that. He knew her too well. But he could never have deserted her.'

'Stone,' I said, 'do you know Gerry Stone? He thinks Klaus is a nationalist of the old school; that he would compromise with the Communists for the sake of reuniting Germany.'

Helmuth looked seriously at me. 'Stone said that? Strange, coming from him . . . Since he helped Klaus back into public life. Of course he may be right. It may come to that. There are decisions that have to be made for Germany. We have drifted in the current now for too long.'

When we talked about Klaus and politics, the heat subsided in my body. My profession was a cool retreat from the thoughts that affected my blood, my pulse. Helmuth looked at his watch. I knew that he would soon leave for his club.

'How is Suzi?' I asked.

He looked sideways at me, quickly, to see the expression on my face. I felt that I had as little control over that as over my tone of voice so I blushed.

'I am not really sure,' he said slowly.

'Isn't she staying with you?' I asked.

'No. You see, she went to Baden-Baden and then stayed with her mother.'

'Yes, she was ill, wasn't she? What was wrong with her?'
I asked.

'There was nothing exactly ... wrong with her,' he answered. 'She was expecting a baby. I suppose you didn't know. How could you have? She would never have told you. It was rather a nasty business because it was well on its way. I think at one time she was going to have it but then, suddenly, she conceived a terrible hatred for it. She had even thought of a name for it—Harry, she was going to call it. I would hear her in her room, talking to it. Then she decided to abort it and her mother arranged for the operation in Baden-Baden. She was very depressed after it and when she came through here she was still very grey in the face—and serious.'

'Where did she go?'

'She went to the East. I don't know why. She said that she wanted to continue her studies there. We aren't so worried, you know, because my brother Edward is over there. He's quite high up in the Communist Party so he can look after her. She lived with him for the first eight years of her life; and she is staying with him now. You should go and see her if you can get over there.'

II

I drove Rosie to the clinic in Dahlem next day. She had a small room to herself (as Suzi must have done). There were two white sheets, one blanket and a cased pillow on the bed. She was, naturally, less ebullient than usual. She had liked lying to her father about where she was going but here her liking ended. It was three in the afternoon. I remained in the room while she changed from the clothes she had been wearing into her nightdress. She had been dressed respectably—for travelling. The clothes, as she put them on the chair (I stood) were useless—a useless skirt on the arm of the chair, cold as her feet must have been cold, as the body is always cold when it is uncovered before night.

My kind cheerfulness was quite broken by the sadness of these garments—the pathos of the flowers printed on her blouse. Her breasts, as I saw them, flopped uselessly away from her arm moving vigorously to take off her petticoat. She put on the nightdress provided by the clinic and bent to take off what was left under it—the underclothes that held up her stockings and the covering with its frills of the entrance to her womb. She threw that small piece of synthetic cloth on the top of the heap of cold clothes but its dingy decorations and faint stains could be seen clearly in the daylight so she tucked it under the jersey she had worn with her skirt.

Rosie got into the bed. She said her feet were cold.

(Suzi got into the bed. Her feet were cold.)

I sat on the bed and held Rosie's hand. I kissed Rosie on the cheek, asking Rosie if this was really what she wanted to happen to her and the child. Rosie said she hated it, that she was frightened but that it was the only possible thing to do.

A doctor came in, shook hands with me. 'It is a sad business, isn't it?' he said to Rosie. 'We don't like taking life.'

Rosie nodded. I looked out of the window onto the dusty grass between the building and the road.

I left the hospital but I knew quite well what was happening (what had happened).

277

A nurse comes into Rosie's room. The blanket and sheet are pulled back, her nightdress is pushed up to her breast. A rubber blanket and a rubber cushion are placed under her buttocks and her legs are splayed apart. With soap, water and a razor the nurse shaves her groin. The blade rasps at the hard black hair: it is cut off in clumps, some dropping onto the rubber sheet. The firm thumb of another woman holds back the thighs which jerk as the nerves, thin under the smooth inside, twitch at the sensation of the razor's blade. Soon the experienced hands leave the groin, black stubs on the white and brown skin above and around the entrance to the womb. The rubber blanket and cushion are recovered. The nightdress is pulled down, the sheet and blanket again cover the girl's body. The thighs close together.

A man in a white coat, a doctor, comes into the room. He pricks the skin of her arm with a needle and injects an anaesthetic liquid into her veins. She becomes unconscious.

Rosie (Suzi) is lifted onto a trolley, wheeled from her room along corridors into a lift and from the lift on another floor to the operating theatre. She, this girl's body, is lifted onto the table. The hospital smock is again lifted above her thighs. The legs of the body with an oblivious mind are laid apart on a metal apparatus that reveals the space between her legs to the surgeon's lamp, to his eyes and his instruments. One of these instruments passes the commonly known parts of the woman—the clitoris, the opening to the urethra —through the entrance to the vagina, up the vagina, through the cervical canal and into the uterus where its hard edge scrapes the sides to dislodge the growing embryo embedded in the endometrium. The spot is found. The creature squirms under the point. The soft skin breaks. The child is

278

burst. Its blood, its mother's blood, hers, flows into the flowing water that had protected it and the blood and water sweep out the embryo.

The child is dead. The child that had hardly lived is dead. It has been successfully scraped off the mother before it was black or white (or English or German); it is only inches long but the doctors and nurses can see what was its head, what was its body. Was there brain enough in the head, I wonder, to feel security in that womb? And is there a Christian burial, I wonder, or a burial at all? What do they do with the slime they scoop out between the woman's legs? Drop it in a bin first of all, I imagine, something in plastic or enamel. Then they put a lid on it or cover it with a cloth. It is put on the lower shelf of a trolley and wheeled out, but wheeled out where? Is there a grave, is it washed into the sewer, or is it boiled and burnt? Do they then keep an urn of the ashes, sending it to the mother? That must be thought cruel. I know nothing is sent to the father. The father wanders about knowing or not knowing what has become of his seed, of his child or of what is not considered one nor the other. He has probably been throwing his hundreds of millions up several spouts. How can he keep an eye on them all? God is the one who watches over sparrows. He sees one drop from a hedge; so he may be the one to see a spermatozoon latch onto the ovum. Doubtless he sees, if he adds a soul to that. Or does the soul come later—after eight weeks, perhaps, when the embryo is termed a foetus? Or when he hears the scissors snap on the umbilical cord? If it is at the moment of conception, the moment of creation, what is done with the soul (the soul) so quickly returned? The soul of that slop in the bucket? But then there are many people who believe that the slop has no soul and many more believe that no one has a soul, neither you nor I nor the scraped-out foetus.

Rosie came to my house for a few days after she left the clinic. She was very gay, relaxed, seemingly not hysterical; but she kept suggesting that we make love when she knew quite well that, if only because of her physical condition, it was quite out of the question. At the end of the week she returned to her parents' home and a week after that to America.

Chapter Thirteen

I

ALREADY MY FLESH was settling on its frame. My muscles were weakening so that the openings to my body on their sagging mounts did not seal in the odd liquids that oozed in globules from the inner patches of decay. Alien secretions of unknown and insignificant bacteria thriving in tubes and crevices of my insides dropped haphazardly on the carpet or my clothes. My eyes were red and itched from the activities of small creatures nesting in their sockets. Viruses burrowed into my skin and clung there to their home. My life was already running down to its end, however long it had to go, and it stood for nothing. I was and had been a nullity... but now the weak compulsion to fulfilment, to significance, that I had always had and every man has, suddenly, finally was alive and its first demand was Suzi.

The realization that I still loved Suzi settled in my inflamed mind after days of unspecific anguish. The thoughts and feelings in my head that had been so moderate and comfortable for most of my life began to grow extreme and distraught. I felt as if I had caught a disease which, like Denghi or Malaria, had lain dormant in my blood and now re-emerged more virulent than before and immune to my resistance. I tried, first with my memory, then with my imagination, to reconjure the abhorrence I had felt towards her and towards that hypothetical child of the two of us that I now knew had been conceived. But the reasons for leaving her that the revulsion had pushed into my conscious mind —her rough ways and nationalistic ideas—would not, when thrown back at the less concrete thoughts and feelings in my head and stomach, revive that basic revulsion. It would not even twitch, and the attempt only provoked another violent feeling—the fear that she had recovered enough from the harm I had done to her to smile at someone else— a normal German boy who shared her views, her past. Each day might be the one when they finally took hands and her fondness or bitterness towards me finally went out of her mind.

Breaking the regulations governing diplomats attached to the armed forces in West Berlin, I crossed at the Fried-richstrasse checkpoint using my own car and my civilian passport. To the left and right of me there was the wall with its great propaganda hoardings. I ducked under them, my errand being private. It was autumn and more than a year now since I had first met Suzi—almost two years since I had first seen her at Café Zuntz. There was a pale sun which illuminated the faint colours of the plaster, the sign-posts, the cars. It was enough to warm my skin—the air was cold enough for me to keep wearing my coat—my old check coat with the Pomeranian collar. Helmuth had given me his brother's address, which was no longer that of the flat in Berlin-Mitte. I drove along the Friedrichstrasse, turned right at Unter den Linden, passed the Opera House, St Hedwig's Church, Marx-Engels platz, the Red Town Hall and came to the Alexanderplatz. There I turned right and then continued along the side of the Spree towards Köpenick. There were rough streets past large factories and barge depots on the riverside: facing the factories were brick blocks of flats. At one point there was a cluster of empty pleasure steamers and later stretches of park were to be seen on the other side of the Spree.

I drove into Köpenick and turned left at the centre. Then I drove through the pine trees of the forest of Köpenick, then along the side of Grosser Müggelsee to Rahnsdorf.

It was about five when I reached Rahnsdorf. I could find the street—Peitzerweg—quite easily and the house in the street. This must have been built sometime between the two wars by a civil servant or a prosperous member of Berlin's middle class. It was solid, with large windows and a view of the lake. A line of trees veiled it on both sides from the other houses in the street. I parked my car, climbed the steps to the door, rang the bell. The door was opened by an old woman whom I took to be a housekeeper. I asked if I could see Fräulein Strepper. I was told that she was out. Then I asked for Herr von Rummelsberg. The woman asked me for my name, left me in the dark hall, came back a few moments later and showed me into a room leading off the hall. This was a front room overlooking the lake. Its walls were lined with books on roughly made shelves. There was a desk covered with more books and piles of paper. The man who stood up from the desk and came to meet me was, I remembered, the one who had spoken to Suzi in the Theater am Schiffbaudamm.

'Yes,' he said, holding out his hand, 'I think we have seen each other before but we have never met.'

'Yes,' I replied, shaking his hand, 'and I have heard a lot about you.'

'Suzi is not back yet,' he said, this Edward von Rummelsberg, beckoning me to sit down, fetching a bottle of schnapps and two glasses from a small cupboard set in the book shelves. 'She is studying in Berlin, you know, and comes back every evening on the S-Bahn. She will be here soon.'

'How is she?' I asked.

'I think she's quite well,' he said gruffly, 'but she is silent. This is not a very lively household, you know. I am not used to social life but it is very nice for me to have her here.'

'I hope you don't mind my coming here without any kind of invitation,' I said.

'Of course not,' he smiled like his brothers.

'I am a friend of your brother,' I said.

'Which brother?' he asked.

'I have met Klaus, professionally, you know. But Helmuth is the one I know best.'

'Ah, Helmuth. And now you know all three of us. And our Suzanne.'

Edward was, I knew, the younger brother but he seemed the eldest. His face had deeper lines in it—though it was undoubtedly the face of a von Rummelsberg. But while the general expression on Klaus's face was that slightly stolid look of leadership or responsibility, on Helmuth's that of irony and cynicism; on Edward's face it was of suffering. He did not have the dumb, plaintive look of a miserable wretch, an unfortunate, but the hard and gentle eyes of an ascetic, the man whose suffering was self-inflicted, like that of the doctor who catches a disease to test its cure.

I had once been in the room of a Catholic priest in Lille (an English Jesuit, a cousin of my mother, who was teaching there) and this room of Edward von Rummelsberg's smelt the same as that. As with my cousin, I was afraid that Edward's smile would suddenly freeze at something I said. I knew that this man was a Communist, not a Catholic; but I also knew that in him the one mingled weirdly with the other.

'Tell me,' I asked him, 'why did Suzi come to East Berlin?'

'You must ask her,' he answered. Then he smiled and said: 'Is it inconceivable to you that anyone should come and live here? After all, it is Germany.'

I blushed. 'I suppose a few . . . ?'

'I know some young people like Suzi who have come East: not very many, of course, but of a certain quality. After all, they have come from idealism and—well—our Democratic Republic is a great test for ideals.'

'I know nothing about ideals,' I said.

'You know nothing about ideals? Then you should study my brothers and me.'

'Are you an idealist?'

'Of course. I am a Communist.'

'All Communists are not idealists.'

Edward von Rummelsberg turned down the ends of his mouth—an expression I could not interpret. 'We are not a race,' he said, 'so what are we if not men with the same ideals? Of course we come to them for different reasons.'

'Why did you?' I asked.

'I was an army officer, you know. I saw some of the . . . unreasonable . . . cruel things that were done in the war. I was enough of a Christian to believe that we should love others. After all, there is no *a priori* reason for believing that men are equal, is there? No one could say that men are self-evidently equal. It is a matter of faith. I looked around then, I still do now, for men who demonstrate that they love

285

other men, that they consider them equal. It is hard to do that.'

He did not look as gloomy when he said this as his words suggest. The words he used were spoken as if they were algebraic symbols in an equation.

'I saw then,' he said, 'and I see now, one group of people whose harsh idea of charity and equality was total, indiscriminate and effective. These were and still are the Communists.'

'Don't we all believe in a general prosperity and justice?' I asked.

'Do you think so?' he said sharply. It was the priest questioning the casual truism. 'If we do believe it, we evidently don't believe it strongly enough: for in your world the rich countries become richer and the poor countries become poorer.'

I shrugged my shoulders.

'You think our republic drab, don't you?' he said. 'You would rather live anywhere else? Yet, you see, we are an exception to that rule. We were left with the poorest part of Germany. Yet in spite of that we have a higher standard of living than any other country in the East. Our optical products and machine-tools compete with any produced in Western Europe.'

'I can quite believe it,' I said.

'And all this achieved under a totally new social system that one day ... one day will give an extra dimension to our concepts of justice.'

He finished this piece of rhetoric, the answer to the equation, which he spoke in the clipped, intense way one would expect of a Communist. I knew the facts of the East German economy probably as well as he did. Through the

286

arrangements I undertook for British businessmen at the Leipzig Trade Fair I knew how much truth there was in what he said about economics.

'One day,' I said.

'Yes, one day. You see, we all need to believe in some better future, to fight for it, and to feel a sense of adversity . . .'

'Is it just for the game, then?' I asked. 'Don't you believe that capitalists are wicked men . . . as such . . . as capitalists?'

He smiled. 'Well, I was once a capitalist myself . . .' He stopped, and said more seriously, 'But they are wicked . . . the rich. The Jews—they are the scapegoats for the rich. There is some science to our politics: but the Nazis . . . they never had any . . . they were so stupid.'

It was getting dark. I expected Suzi to come into the room at any time. I barely grasped what Edward von Rummelsberg, this Communist, was saying: but I answered flatly—'It is against human nature to expect continual idealism. It is impractical.'

'No, no.' Edward stood up and faced the window, looking out over the lake. 'That is how it seems: that is how it seemed to a lot of people before the war. But it was a great mistake, wasn't it? The capacity for a faith, an ideology— that is what is natural . . . animal.'

'People of my generation in the West,' I said, 'have no faith at all. They are non-political and religiously agnostic. I don't think we will ever believe in anything any more— neither the English, nor the French, nor the Germans.'

'Couldn't I have said that about Germany in 1918?'

'Was it then natural to be a National Socialist?' I asked.

'Yes. It was natural. It was false and ridiculous but it fulfilled a natural capacity.'

'How do you judge that that was a false ideology and that Communism is a true one? They seem very alike to me.'

'By the actions of the men who believe in them. By what the dream contributes to reality. Nazism had its own... imaginative integrity but its contact with the tangible aspects of life were self-evidently wrong. The wars, the concentration camps.'

'And our belief in Liberty and Democracy in the West?'

'It is the same thing, isn't it? Plausible as a belief. But the result of its application—exploitation and liquidation all over the world.'

'The Communists have their crimes to answer for.'

Edward shrugged his shoulders. 'It is the direction that matters. We will forever be making a better world... you, not at all.'

I had been expecting to hear the sound of the front door opening and I did, as I told Edward von Rummelsberg, his back still half-turned to me, how sceptical I was of any ideals embodied in any ideology taking hold of the minds of the young in Western Europe. He turned and his pained face smiled again. 'We'll see,' he said and then: 'That must be Suzi.'

He went to the door of the room, opened it and said: 'Suzi, there is someone who has come over to see you.' He came back into the room. I got up off my chair and turned. Suzi stood at the door of the room, her coat on, her hand holding a scarf she was unravelling from her neck. She looked, certainly, as if she had never expected to see me again.

'Yes ... hello,' she said.

She was much paler than I had remembered her. Her cheeks were mottled now from the cold of the air and the warmth of her blood from walking. Her coat was blue and long—reaching half-way down between her knees and ankles.

'Wait a minute,' she said, 'I'll take off my coat.' So she turned away from me.

Edward's face was expressionless. 'Then come in here and have some schnapps,' he said to Suzi. He walked to the shelves and filled my glass. 'It takes forty minutes from Berlin to Rahnsdorf on the S-Bahn,' he said.

Suzi came in. My eyes could not focus on her body, nor really on the eyes in her head and their transference of her thoughts or feelings. Her shoes seemed oddly plain.

'I saw a car outside,' she said, 'but I didn't think it could be yours because it wasn't official.'

'No,' I said. 'I disobeyed the rules.'

'I am sure you shouldn't do that.'

It was difficult to talk to her in the presence of Edward von Rummelsberg: 'Would you like to stay and have some supper?' he asked me.

I said I would and he went to tell the housekeeper. I thought he might leave us alone but he came back into the room before Suzi and I had exchanged a word. Through supper—a simple one of sausage, cheese and black bread—the conversation was general. We talked about Suzi's course in physiotherapy, about the excellent climate of Berlin and about the Berliner Ensemble—how we had seen each other there.

When we had finished, Suzi said to Edward: 'We'll leave you to do your work now.'

'Where will you go?' he asked. 'You needn't worry about me if you want to stay here.'

'No. We'll go into Rahnsdorf and have a drink somewhere. I won't be back late.'

289

In the car she said: 'He's never been married, you see. I don't think he realizes that men and women have private conversations.'

'How have you been?' I asked.

She looked at me. 'I wasn't very well,' she said.

'I know. I heard about it.'

'Who told you. Did my mother?'

'No. Helmuth.'

'I didn't want you to know. It was my business.'

'Wasn't it my business too?'

'A bit, I suppose,' she smiled.

We stopped at a beer house in Rahnsdorf, a small place, nearly empty, with the usual scrubbed tables.

'I am very sorry . . . that it did happen,' I said.

'You don't need to be.'

'I would like it to be alive.'

'Now?'

'Yes.'

'You didn't want him then, did you?'

'I didn't know . . .'

'Yes. But you wouldn't have wanted him.'

'No.'

'I could sense it. That's why I didn't tell you. Then you left me anyway. I was going to have him but . . . in the end I thought that if you didn't want him . . . I didn't either.'

She moved her finger round and round on the scrubbed table and watched it. Her hair then covered her eyes a little and I could look at her closely. The finger which moved had again the same perfection I had seen in her ankles that first time. She wore a soft cardigan and I watched her shoulders —I would have touched them if I had dared. The sight of her shoulders and her fingers so filled my mind with anguish

290

that it closed itself once again to any contemplation of her shape, the expression in her eyes, her tone of voice. As if I had a letter to read or listened on a telephone, her words were all I had to judge her by.

'But I am glad to see you again,' she said.

'I wanted to see you some time ago,' I said, 'but I didn't know where you were. Helmuth was in Japan.'

'Yes. Did he like it, do you know?'

'He seemed a little depressed.'

'You used to think we were lovers. Do you remember?'

'Yes.'

'And now, I suppose, you think uncle Edward is my lover?' She laughed, looking me in the eyes quite easily. I smiled.

'Why did you want to see me?' she asked—firmly.

'Have you fallen in love with anyone else?' I asked her.

'No,' she replied in a straight tone of voice. 'And you?'

'I love you again,' I said.

She bent her fingers into the palms of her hands and looked at the nails. 'Of course I still love you,' she said without looking at me. I took one of her hands. It was limp and cold again so I let it go. I did not know what to say and nor, it seemed, did she. The ease with which she had treated me before had gone; neither of us looked at each other directly, both merely glancing when we felt the other was not.

'It's difficult to talk about it,' I said. She did not answer. Of the times she had cried, this might have been one of them but it was not.

'Do you think we could go on?' I said.

'I have changed a little; haven't you?' Suzi asked me.

'If people change . . . I suppose I have,' I said. 'There was

291

a time when I hated the idea of your father...so...I couldn't help myself.'

'Yes. It was my fault for arguing with you about that... so stupidly.'

'It doesn't matter about it now,' I said. 'I don't mind what you think or anything about your father.'

'But that does matter, my dear.' She looked at me sadly.

'What do you mean?' (I would very much like to have said 'my dear' but could not quite manage it.)

'I am a Communist.'

I gibbered on about that not mattering either and took hold of her hand again but as I spoke I realized that it did matter, that it did change everything.

'Do you really believe in all that stuff?' I asked her.

'Yes, I do.'

'Did Edward convince you?'

'It was I who came to him and I had made up my mind before that. It was the reason for my coming East.'

'Why? Can't you tell me why?'

'It was Klaus more than anyone else who ..'

'Klaus?'

'Oh, he didn't mean to do it. It was when I stayed with them after being in Baden-Baden. I was very depressed. Because of the child and because of you. There was a man who was pestering me. You didn't know about him. I kept that secret too. He was before you—the only one. He was a businessman from Cologne but I met him in Munich. He kept a flat there for his girls—it had dark red carpets and a fridge that was always full of German champagne and artificial caviare. I had a key and we'd meet there. He was loathsome. I don't know why I did it. My girl-friends all had boy-friends of that type—middle-aged businessmen. Klaus

and my mother never knew him then. Anyway, he pestered
me. He was the only man I knew but I wouldn't see him but
we kept running into him. Klaus met him and loathed him
—he loathes that type—you know, the Rhineland businessman. But Klaus kept saying that he was typical, typical . . .
So I asked him what there was so precious about West
Germany if this man was the typical citizen, without morals,
without values. He said that there was nothing precious
about West Germany; that the religion of a man like that
could do with some persecution. Then he said that the only
set of values that would convince a future generation of
Germans was a kind of Communism. So I asked him if
people who could believe in Communism should live in the
East. He said yes. He said he was in the West to die in
peace but that the East was the only hope for Germany. He
gets depressed you know, and he was in a depressed mood
when he said all this. And then I think he is influenced by
Edward. They write to each other, you know, all three of
them do. Edward was the only one who did anything about
the Nazis. He didn't do much but he did do something.
Klaus and Helmuth did nothing, so I think they are rather
impressed with Edward . . . since he turned out to be right
about that. Anyway, I believed what Uncle Klaus said. I
suppose I needed to believe in something. It is dreadful over
there if you notice it. There is no reason to do anything
for anyone else. No one cares for anyone else. No one tells
people like me what is right or wrong so we never know
and just drift miserably through our lives . . . I have seen it
happen to my friends. They get depressed with their flats,
husbands and cars. Only a new coat, now and then . . .'

There is a choking in the chest as a man begins to cry. I
choked and tears brimmed out of my eyes. I could not

understand her—I could not understand any of them. I could not believe that the man I had always suspected there might have been was not a fellow student or another show-jumper, but a Cologne businessman with a vulgar love nest. Then I had always believed that Communism was crooked and wrong and decent people could not believe in it. Edward I had taken to be eccentric because he was religious too, but that Suzi should believe it shattered me. I would have argued with her but I had no thought, no belief, no feeling, but that I wanted her. I was humiliated at crying but only hoped she would comfort me.

'You mustn't be upset,' she said, and took my hand. 'I love you just as before. I will always be a Communist because it's the only way I could live now, but it may still be possible to live with you.'

'But I'd have to leave the Foreign Office,' I said.

She bit her lip. 'We'd find some way,' she said, 'but you must think about it—whether you still want me—because I'm not the same person . . . being a Communist.' She leant across the table and easily touched my mouth with her mouth.

I drove her back to Edward von Rummelsberg's house. It was after midnight before I passed through the Berlin wall. If Suzi no longer loved me I might not have crossed this way but dashed to the wall itself and dangled from a concrete block for a bullet in my back. As it was I completed the formalities and drove into the brighter lights of West Berlin feeling very happy to know that Suzi might soon come with me out of that sober area of the town—and I damned the cost to my life and my career.

I imagined her now that I was away from her, quite freely. She came towards me, smiling. She came towards me in the rain, the collar of her coat turned up. She came towards me, undoing the top button of her blouse. She came towards me on the pavement, on the carpet, on the grass. She came towards me holding the soap and scrubbed my back in the bath.

I imagined the slight plumpness of her cheeks as she brushed her hair; the nylon clinging to her ankles and her thighs as she walked; her hanging from the branch of a tree and kicking her feet in the air; her pretending to be asleep in the morning, her eyes clenched, when it was past time to get up; her mixing a salad dressing; her trying to persuade me to buy her a coat; her coming deftly to kiss me—to kiss me.

I imagined her waiting, for me to take her up, the only sensation in her body the weight in one foot and a general longing. I imagined her opening but closing again when I smiled; her hand coming round my neck; her hand down my side; her hand smoothing my brow—her hand.

And then I imagined her through our life, older and sweeter, laughing at me for my pedantry, advising me, showing me how I seemed to others. I imagined her stomach with a child in it. I imagined her rising, urinating and putting on the kettle to make coffee. I imagined her scraping out a pan in which she had made fish pie. I imagined her washing the ears of our son with her delicate fingers. In my mind I saw her kiss another man at a street corner. I saw her take the thermometer out of my mouth and read it. I saw her smooth out my shirts. I saw her talking to my sister. And then I felt her dispassionate warmth beside me in bed: I felt her naked across my knees like a see-saw. I felt her hair caught under my elbow. I felt her bosom in the palm of my hand.

I could imagine her looking bored. I could imagine her sharpening a pencil. I could imagine her getting slightly drunk. I could imagine her trying to paint a door with a brush that had already gone hard. I could imagine her wanting to leave a party when I wanted to stay. I could imagine her arguing stubbornly when she knew she was wrong. I could imagine her glancing jealously at another woman to whom I was talking. I could imagine her pretending to respond when I made love to her. I could imagine her best slippers and her worn ones—the pink and the blue. I could imagine her resentment. I could imagine her forgiveness and smile. I could imagine her throwing talcum powder on her body after a bath. I could imagine the blue veins showing on her leg.

There is what one knows and what one does not know—between the two, what one imagines. I imagined her dying. I imagined her at my side as I died.

Chapter Fourteen

I

It was clear that I was being followed, probably by a private agency hired by Gerry Stone. I realized that they must know that I had been into the East, but was not sure if they knew where I had been once on the other side of the sector border.

I wanted to see Armand, and thought it best that Stone should not know about it. My secretary arranged for us to meet in the Hansa quarter the next afternoon at four. I used a simple expedient to shake off whoever was following me. Assuming that he was someone who was unable to go East (agents who can cross over are there most of the time) I took the S-Bahn from the Zoo station to the Friedrichstrasse on the other side. There I went down as if to the passport control, waited for some minutes in the lavatory, then crossed to the other platform and took the next train back to the West, getting off at the second station, Bellevue. There, under the railway, was the café where I had arranged to meet Armand.

He was already there, sitting in his open overcoat drinking coffee. He seemed particularly shaggy—much more like a poet than a diplomat. In this respect, as in many others,

297

the English and the French are like each other and unlike the Germans—the most professional disguises himself as the amateur.

'My dear friend,' he said. 'I haven't seen you for such a long time, but I have heard so many stories . . .'

I hung up my coat—the check one—and sat next to him. 'What stories?' I asked.

'That you went East . . . unofficially.'

'How did you know that?'

'One of our men at the checkpoint raised his eyebrow at this recognition of the German Democratic Republic.' He smiled.

'Luckily they didn't recognize me,' I said, 'or else I'd be in trouble. I'm in trouble enough as it is.'

'Yes. I hear stories about that too. Frantic consultations among the Anglo-Saxons without a word to France.'

'It is more personal than that—but it's all mixed up together. You know Suzi?'

'Of course I know Suzi.'

'Well—I told you—I ditched her just before I went on leave. I found out about her father . . .'

'That really made so much difference?'

'In fact . . . yes, well, I thought it did: and I thought she was a little Nazi herself.'

Armand smiled at me. I felt awkward but went on. 'I can't say that I've been particularly happy without her. In fact I still loved her so I thought I'd try . . . well . . . to see her again, to get her back.'

'Good.'

'But she'd gone. Helmuth had disappeared too.'

'He was in Japan.'

'Yes. And she'd gone to her uncle in the East.'

'Edward.'

'Yes. Helmuth came back and told me where I could find her. I went East, as you know, and saw her again. We more or less patched things up but now there's another complication . . . she's . . . she's become a Communist.'

Armand leant back and laughed. 'It's an easy step from a Nazi to a Communist in this country,' he said. 'The same uniform, the goose-stepping, the torch-light processions.'

'You may find it funny,' I said, 'but it lands me in a terrible mess. For one thing—I shouldn't be telling you this, but still—I am meant to be finding out whether Klaus von Rummelsberg and his friends constitute a danger to Allied interests—and to be in love with his Communist stepdaughter at the same time . . .'

'Is she really a Communist?' Armand asked, more seriously.

'Yes. She's joined the Party. What can I do about that? She's so stubborn . . . she won't give it up.'

Armand sat back and shrugged his shoulders.

'Mind you, it was largely my fault. There was a baby, you know, and she had to get rid of it. The shock—well—it gave her some kind of revulsion against . . . I don't know . . . life over here . . . our values . . . so she simply went East. And as far as I can make out, Klaus more or less encouraged her to do so.'

Armand leant forward. He was about to light a cigarette but his hands hesitated. 'Do tell me about that . . . it interests me.'

'I don't know, I can't make it out: but from what Suzi says, he is really . . . resigned to Communism. He seemed an old-fashioned nationalist to me, when I saw him. And

Helmuth . . . whom I'd always thought quite unpolitical, he gave me a left-wing lecture on Japan.'

'Klaus,' said Armand, 'Klaus didn't take this attitude six months ago.'

'How do you know?' I asked.

'Oh, we have our von Rummelsberg file too. They are of interest to us because of Klaus. He has great influence among West Germans, you know, not only among the refugees . . .'

'And there are his warm feelings for France,' I said, smiling.

'More his feelings for a Europe of Fatherlands. He fits in with the Gaullist wing of the Christian Democrats—but until now, you see, he has always resisted our persuasion towards a compromise in the east.'

'That is what I am meant to find out. If he won't agree to a settlement in the east, then perhaps he is working up to a march back to Pomerania.'

'Oh no,' said Armand, 'it isn't that. He's no fool. He knows quite well that Russian power creates a permanent imbalance in Europe. Russia will always be able to snuff Germany out in ten minutes—Germany, even with nuclear weapons, would never be able to obliterate a country as immense as the Soviet Union. Klaus can see that.'

'Then what were his objections to a settlement in the east?'

'Quite valid ones. He thought it was too soon. He insists that people's dreams are as much a political reality as their economic potential. In his opinion a premature recognition of the Oder-Neisse line would have dangerous psychological consequences in the minds of many Germans.'

'But you think he'll come round to it?'

'His political aim, I think, is to prevent his generation of Germans doing any further damage so that the next generation are able to be dispassionate about a settlement in Europe.'

'And what kind of settlement does he think that will be?'

'Well, Klaus clearly has different ideas about that from, say, Edward—and Helmuth's pig in the middle. But they try to come together . . .'

'And what role do they see for the Americans?'

Armand lit his cigarette and puffed at it. Every now and then he looked straight into my eyes; I expected him to speak but he did not, so I repeated, 'And the Americans?'

'Don't you know what I think about the Americans?' Armand asked me. 'I told you once how rare it was for me, a diplomat, to find myself in agreement with my government.'

'Yes.'

'This "way-of-life" of theirs—it is rather different to ours, don't you think?'

'Well,' I replied, 'it seems almost . . . German.'

We laughed.

'When I was a student,' Armand said, 'I was a great internationalist—the idea of being a citizen of anything less than the world meant nothing to me. But now . . . I think the cohesion of communities is an observable fact.'

'Well . . . yes . . . people do live in . . .'

'No. I mean observable in the minds of individuals. If patriotism is an artificial emotion, as I used to believe, stimulated by politicians for their own ends, how is it that it is so universal?'

'No,' I said, 'it is organic.'

'But in Europe it has been so mixed up with the worst

kind of nationalism. Now what the von Rummelsbergs would like to do is believe, and have others believe, in something between chauvinism and national self-immolation.'

'And what does that mean for the Americans?'

'A country is not a country if it is occupied. If it depends for its security on another. Defence is sovereignty.'

'Evicting the Americans from Europe won't give European countries the self-respect they have lost ... our two wars and ...' I stopped.

'All European countries,' said Armand, 'have compromised their self-respect, their patriotism, through imperialism, or fascism. The former imperial powers will recover from their malaise easily enough because imperialism, well, it was just a losing stage of history: a natural, rather peaceable method of aggression. Swindling rather than killing. Of the fascist powers, Germany is the one we must worry about because their past was not just a losing stage of history but something murderous and criminal which affected almost every family on this continent. The problem is not so much that the sufferers bear a grudge but, for our purposes as Europeans, that the criminal nation is paralysed by its complexes of both guilt and self-justification. For other countries to establish their identities within Europe is only a matter of time—for Germany it is a problematic recuperation and here we come to what, from the point of a united Europe, is the greatest danger: the Americans, in the last war, only came across the Germans as fighting men. The civilian population in America had no experience of either bombing or atrocity. The Germans, now, sense that the Americans can forget the past in a way that is impossible for Europeans.'

'Of course,' I said, 'Germany, not Britain, may turn out to be the Trojan horse.'

'Exactly.'

'I don't see what can be done about it.'

'The Americans must not be allowed to use this advantage: they must not be allowed to know what is going on.'

'How can we stop them?'

'Well, we are lucky in that at the moment the Americans are not interested in Europe. The government is totally preoccupied with Asia. As long as their attention is not drawn to what we are doing, the chances are they won't realize it until it is too late. Now there is only one man who might expose us. Stone. He is a clever man. He was brought up in Germany: he understands the Germans, and from the point of view of the interests of his adopted country, he is quite correct in his suspicions. My government has been in touch with Klaus von Rummelsberg, and other West Germans. Klaus has been in touch with the Communists—with his brother, anyway. A general settlement in Europe now seems possible. Klaus and others are coming round to the belief that the price we might eventually have to pay for a united Europe and a united Germany is worth paying ...'

'What price?' I repeated.

'What price would you expect to pay?'

'For what? For a united Europe?'

'From the Atlantic to the Urals.'

'I would expect ... I don't know ...'

'Would you expect the Communist countries to return to capitalism?'

'No.'

'Well, then?'

'Communism of some sort? Is that it?'

'Yes. In my opinion anyway. The patriotism wouldn't be enough.'

'No.'

Silence.

'What can I do in all this?' I asked.

Armand looked at me. 'I don't even know if you are with us or not.'

'Armand ... I ... I'm with you, yes, but I have to admit it's because of the girl ... because of Suzi. The rest ... I don't know.'

Armand smiled. 'We can be quite sure of you if it's because of a girl.'

'But are you a Communist?' I asked him.

'Not yet.'

I shrugged my shoulders. 'What is it, then?'

'You must convince your government and the American government that Stone is wrong about Klaus. Otherwise everything would be ... more difficult.'

I returned to Bonn for the Ambassador's meeting. As before I stayed the night at the Embassy. Sir Peter Dodd called me into his study after dinner.

'Well, my dear boy. Have you got what we want?' he asked.

'Yes sir,' I replied. 'I know as much as there is to know about Klaus von Rummelsberg. He is safe ... quite safe from our point of view. I can tell you ...'

'No. You don't need to go into it with me. I have complete confidence in you. If I can't trust you, who can I trust? I knew your father, I knew your housemaster and you were at my college at Cambridge. You have your say at the

meeting tomorrow and I'll give you all the backing you
need.'

Was I a traitor—now that I had decided to hold back
what I knew about Klaus?—now that I was working with
the French and the Communists? I expected my external
appearances to change (my eyes to narrow or sink deeper
in my face) but the Ambassador had still patted me on the
shoulder and trusted me implicitly; my voice must have
sounded the same.

Would the fields of Suffolk steam now when I walked on
them? Had I brought the day nearer when monkey-faced
foreigners would peer into the dark pew-filled greystone
church on a Sunday morning and abduct Mary-Rose Cul-
lingham to the requisitioned rectory?

Was I an agent of the enemy? If so, say who the enemies
are. Were they the French twenty miles away who eat five-
course lunches for a pound? Their wine is certainly as cheap
as our beer. Or the type-cast Germans? But they are divided
amongst themselves, so half must be on the same side. The
Americans who speak English and were once, nominally,
Englishmen? They have never been our enemies since we
burnt the Capitol. They are open and straightforward—
they warm to simple kindness and withdraw from bitterness.
Of course, there are schemers there as there are everywhere.
If only the Chinese or the Japanese were as likely enemies
as we want them to be.

I wondered, that night, if I was a traitor, and concluded
that there was nothing I could betray. Great Britain, or
some of its citizens, have a few economic interests here and
there, left over from the nineteenth century on different
continents: but it was no longer possible for them to lose

what they had gained because they had gained it many times over in generations of fat living, and could only lose it once. The other citizens who had not shared the plunder were now without even those little loyalties to the coloured flag and white sun helmets which had tricked them. I could see, though they might not, that their interest was to be eased into the next phase as quickly as possible.

I did not consider myself a traitor to my country—I considered myself its representative, as Armand was the representative of France, in the first real community of Europeans. If the von Rummelsbergs could sort out their country, we should answer for ours.

We met next day at the American Embassy. The same people were there as before—Perkins, Sir Peter, his first secretary; the American opposite numbers, including Gerry Stone who shook my hand in a friendly way.

The meeting was short. The atmosphere of crisis over the summer elections had been dispelled by their lack of consequence. Most of the diplomats seemed embarrassed that we should still be discussing it. I was asked what I had found out about Klaus von Rummelsberg and, considering that the best lies are always part of the truth, I began.

'The first factor which confuses this issue is the unreliability of the public pronouncements of Klaus von Rummelsberg or any other person in the refugee movement. These people live on their dreams but their dreams bear no relation to reality. I spoke to Klaus von Rummelsberg and after I had promised that what he said would be treated in confidence, he made this point to me. He was amused that anyone should take his statement to the refugees seriously. A policy of return would be impossible, he said, because most of the refugees had done so well in West Germany they would never be persuaded to go back to their homelands even if it were practicable. It was just that they wanted to go on shouting. I asked him, then, if he had any political objectives. He said he had none beyond the restoration of a certain sense of patriotism in the refugees and other Germans.'

'That is vague, isn't it?' Stone said sharply.

'Yes, it is vague. He was vague.'

'And is that all the evidence you have on him?'

'No,' I said. 'It happens, as you know, Mr Stone, that I am acquainted with Klaus von Rummelsberg's brother, Helmuth, who lives in West Berlin. This man was in the German Foreign Service until the end of the war—and has always been politically detached. I asked him, quite casually, about his brother. He said that his brother had always felt a great sense of responsibility towards Germany, that the mistake he had made in joining the Nazis had increased rather than destroyed this, since most of his fellow countrymen had made the same mistake. He said Klaus saw his function now as helping his fellow refugees to accept their exile.'

'Do you say you trust this brother?' asked the American Ambassador, who must have noticed my truthful manner.

'Yes sir, I do. He knows I am a British diplomat but it is very unlikely that he has any reason to lie to me about his brother.'

'Is this all the evidence?' asked Stone.

'As I have said, there cannot, by the nature of Klaus von Rummelsberg's position, be documentary evidence of his personal convictions. The politics of the refugee movement are so much a science of cant that it cannot be expected that there should be.'

'It would be hard enough,' Perkins said, 'to show what the politicians in either of our two countries think or believe.'

'Nevertheless,' said Stone, 'I am not sure that your assessment is enough to convince me.'

'My dear Mr Stone,' said Sir Peter Dodd, 'we have here one of our very best men. I have complete confidence in his judgment and I see no reason why you should not.'

'Yes, Mr Stone,' said the American Ambassador, 'what else do you expect?'

The large head of Gerry Stone, as well as his eyes, moved quickly from side to side. 'I expect my judgment to be considered,' he said. 'I know the von Rummelsbergs. I have known them since before the war. They are extremists. They will stop at nothing to make Germany a united country with its own atomic weapons and land us all in another war.'

'I doubt that,' I said.

'You doubt that?' he asked, raising his voice. 'I should think you do doubt it since you are in so thick with them.'

'What do you mean?' asked the American Ambassador in an impatient tone of voice.

'Isn't it true,' Stone said, looking at me, 'that you crossed into the Soviet sector of Berlin last week? Do you deny that you met Edward von Rummelsberg, member of the People's Chamber, minister in the government of the so-called German Democratic Republic? Aren't you chasing the girl who lives with him?'

I kept my head still and answered him with more of the truth: 'Your observation of my movement is quite accurate, Mr Stone, but your innuendo is erroneous. I did see Edward

308

von Rummelsberg and I did see Suzanne Strepper. She is the step-daughter of Klaus von Rummelsberg and had formerly, while living in West Berlin, been a very close friend of mine. I did not tell her what I wanted to know but inadvertently she told me. She had gone into the Russian sector and joined the Communist Party. When she told her step-father that this was what she was going to do, he shrugged his shoulders and said that at her age she could do as she liked; that he was only waiting, with the other refugees, to die in as agreeable circumstances as possible. Now I ask you, Mr Stone, is it likely that Suzanne Strepper made up this anecdote? If so, for what reason? To confuse me in an investigation she could not possibly have known about? And if the anecdote is true, as I believe it is, does it sound to you like the sentiments of an unrepentant nationalist who is about to build an atom-bomb or sell his country to the Russians?'

'Why, may I ask, didn't you tell us about this trip to the East?' Stone asked.

'Because I did not think it was necessary. It was an irregular step taken through private channels to double-check on the impressions I had formed.'

'It was irregular,' said Sir Peter, 'but I think it paid off. Don't you, Ambassador? The girl's evidence backs up what we've heard.'

'Yes,' said the American Ambassador. 'I guess it does.'

The others at the meeting nodded and tapped their pencils on the blotting paper.

'It doesn't back it up at all,' said Stone in a voice still higher and louder. 'Can't you see, Ambassador, that he's in with them? He's in love with the girl. It's turned his head. You don't know these people. I do. I've lived with them.

They killed my sister—I know. They're hiding that girl's father, Günter Strepper, somewhere. You don't know them. They'll trick you all, like Hitler. They're just the same as before. It's beginning again.

'But Gerry,' I said, 'who was responsible for Klaus von Rummelsberg's denazification? Wasn't it you?'

Stone paused; he hesitated, he thought, he reflected—but there was very little he could say. 'I . . . yes . . . I . . . it was a mistake . . . clearly . . . I . . .'

'Shut up, Stone,' the American Ambassador said in a very heavy drawl that made the remark drag out over several seconds. Stone said nothing more but rolled his yellow eyes in his big head on his small body.

After this we had to be careful not to prove Stone right about my feelings for Suzi: but it became easier when Stone himself was posted back to the United States. I was no longer liable to be followed. Armand and others wanted me to remain a semi-spy in my present position for as long as possible; but my feelings for our hypothetical country—Europe—were not as strong as my feelings for Suzi. I went into East Berlin to fetch her. She still had her West German passport so there was no difficulty about getting her out. She had by then agreed to marry me.

We were married in a church near Munich—in a church because Suzi said she would not trust me to keep my vows if it was only a state wedding; in Bavaria because Klaus and Katerina had a nice house there which looked over a lake and had a view of the Alps. In the small baroque church there were only Armand and the von Rummelsbergs and Suzi's embarrassed face behind a white veil: but at the reception afterwards in this house overlooking the lake

310

there were quite a number of people. From my side there was only my sister and her husband who had flown out from England at the last minute: both had brave expressions on their faces. Otherwise the guests were Germans, old friends of the von Rummelsbergs, many from their Pomeranian days. There were several names out of German history —mostly attached to dowagers of the line, many of them mothers of sons who had died raggedly after 20 July 1944. A Gräfin von Y. said to me: 'We are so glad that Suzanne is marrying an English gentleman. There are so very few gentlemen in Germany nowadays.' Helmuth overheard this remark and kept repeating it to Suzi which made her very angry.

The food and drink were lavish by German standards and Katerina, my mother-in-law, kept saying that it was like the old days. 'But what a pity we don't have tail-coats and top-hats as you do in England.' Somehow these words did not sound convincing—she was playing a part. I did revise my opinion of her because behind the actress playing a West German wife there was her tall figure, her narrow nostrils, and something baffled and wild which made her unusual. I tried to imagine what she and Klaus said to each other when they were alone—when she was filing her nails which were so well filed: but Klaus came up to fill my glass with champagne. Probably they did not say much: Klaus kept silent at the reception, moving around filling glasses.

There was a von Treblitz cousin who directed an art gallery in Pretoria and happened to be in Europe that year. He had his twelve-year-old daughter with him who said she hated Germany because it was so cold.

A girl of eighteen or so was introduced to me as Betta Trübner's daughter. She explained that she was training to be an actress and asked me if actresses in England were expected to kiss actors 'really' on stage. I said I did not know—I thought not. Then this girl took me across the room to meet her mother, Betta Trübner who had been imprisoned and tortured in the Nazi period and whose name, like those of the dowagers, was famous in the history of resistance against Hitler. She spoke to me with a kind smile about the social reform that was being undertaken by the Catholic Church in Brazil.

From her I went on to talk to a second cousin of the von Rummelsbergs who was a professor of Mathematics at the University of California in Los Angeles: and then I stood aside for a moment, watching the whole picture.

Katerina had fussed over her daughter and this wedding: and it was undeniable that a white wedding dress made my Communist bride seem more beautiful than ever. The white. The vows. The spectators. She was my wife.

There was an old man I thought I might have seen before, perhaps in Berlin, who wore a blue jacket and grey trousers—not a suit like all the other men. I went up to talk to him but for some reason he would not talk. He gave me a smile and a punch in the chest and wheezed off into a corner where he sat alone.

'The man in the corner,' I said to Helmuth. 'He seems to have lost his voice.'

'Yes,' said Helmuth, 'Cancer of the throat. We don't expect him to be around much longer.'

It seemed (to me) a callous remark to make almost within hearing of the man: and Helmuth was normally so kind. Of the brothers, I decided, Helmuth was the one that I liked best, perhaps because he was the one who had suffered the understandable sorrows of unrequited love, not the unwholesome horrors of recent history. Also there was something comforting in his preference for the texture of life over its meaning. It was the knowledge of his part in the informal conspiracy around Armand and the von Rummelsbergs, the French government and the German Right, that persuaded me to join it—even if other factors prepared me to do so. And Helmuth, at least, enjoyed the wedding reception and became slightly drunk. 'We are all glad you are marrying Suzi,' he said to me. 'She's had enough of Germany. Germany has had enough of herself.' Later on he said I was very wise to marry a physiotherapist because at his age a good massage was more important than anything else.

The daughter of the cousin from South Africa sang a German song. An old countess gave a reading from *Bérénice* in croaky French. Then someone put on a gramophone record but only Helmuth and the little girl danced at all and she soon became too shy.

At about six, Suzi and I decided to leave for Italy. We had booked a hotel room in Garmisch for that night and I did not want to arrive there too late. I kissed Katerina and said goodbye to the Prussian dowagers. My last impression was of the man in the blue jacket sitting in the corner and the two smiling faces of the brothers, the two Germans, and Armand's friendly expression—there, I knew, were three men of great integrity, who, with the brother in the East, had the finest feelings towards me and my wife: and that the five of us were five of the same kind, five friends, five Europeans.

Suzi and I said nothing for a long time. She stroked the hair on the back of my neck with two fingers of her left

313

hand. When we were on the Olympiastrasse I said to her: 'Who was the man in the blue jacket, the one who couldn't speak? Was he your father?'

'Yes,' she said after a short silence. Then, after another pause, she said: 'I wanted him to be there.'

'It's just that I thought he was in Argentina.'

'He came back. He's in a clinic on the Starnbergersee.'

I tried, with my tongue, to get a piece of chicken out from between my teeth.

'I'd never seen him before,' Suzi said. 'I didn't think he looked very nice, did you?' She screwed up her nose and smiled at me.

'I don't know,' I said and I smiled too but kept my eyes on the road.